To Kimberley

MAVERICK WILD

Stacey Kayne

So great to visit 2RW!
with you at the   *the*
wishing
best with y *Faith.*
Keep the *Best, Stacey*
Kayne

⊚™ MILLS & BOON®
Pure reading pleasure™

First published in Great Britain 2009
Harlequin Mills & Boon Limited,
Eton House, 18-24 Paradise Road, Richmond, Surrey TW9 1SR

© Stacey Kayne 2008

ISBN: 978 0 263 86761 9

Set in Times Roman 10½ on 12½ pt.
04-0109-75143

Printed and bound in Spain
by Litografia Rosés S.A., Barcelona

Stacey Kayne has always been a daydreamer. If the comments on her elementary school report cards are any indication, it's a craft she mastered early on. Having a passion for history and a flair for storytelling, she strives to weave fact and fiction into a wild ride that can capture the heart. Stacey lives on a ranch near the Sierra Nevada, with her high-school sweetheart turned husband of eighteen years and their two sons. Visit her website at www.staceykayne.com

A recent novel by the same author:

MUSTANG WILD

Special thanks to:

Kimberly Duffy for her 'Wild' title inspiration.

Carla, Kathy, Marlene and Sheila for their tireless critiquing and for believing in this story.

My family for their wonderful support.

My readers.
I've been truly touched by all the letters and emails—thank you for the wonderful welcome into a genre I love.

Prologue

❧❧❧

Virginia, 1862

"If we don't ride out, she'll have us whipped to the bone before the old man comes back."

Chance didn't spare the breath or energy to agree with his brother, the urge to ride fast and hard burning stronger in his gut than the welts flaming across his back. Their father's short visit meant his camp was close, freedom was within reach.

The darkness in the stable didn't impede his deft movements as he tossed his saddle over the blanket and reached for the cinch. They couldn't risk lighting a lantern.

"How could he leave us here to deal with his raving-mad wife?" Tucker ranted in a low whisper. "She ran him off like she always does with her screaming and bawling. Did you see how he rode out this evening and didn't even look back?"

"I saw."

"I don't know why he doesn't ever stand up to her. If she were my wife—"

"We won't be fool enough to marry," Chance cut in.

"*Amen.*"

"Before the old man rode out, I told him we'd be on his heels in a day."

His twin spun around, his pale-yellow hair flashing in streaks of moonlight seeping through the barn windows. "What'd he say?"

"That a rebel camp ain't no place for young boys."

"Can't be worse than living with Winifred. We'll be thirteen come the spring—nearly grown men!"

Chance gave a nod of agreement as he secured his bedroll behind his saddle.

"He should'a taken us with him," said Tucker. "We're old enough to fight for our home."

The way Chance saw it they'd lost that battle two years ago when their father had taken a wife. Seemed like foolish business to him and Tucker. They'd gotten on just fine for ten years without a woman in their lives, but they hadn't had any say in the matter. The old man had come home from a business trip up north hollering loud enough to raise the dead about the underhanded shenanigans of starched-up fancy women. The next thing Chance knew, he and Tucker were standing beside their father in their Sunday trousers and stiff collars as he married Winifred Tindale.

A slender woman with a mess of blond curls tumbling about her head, a blushing smile and fluttering blue eyes, she'd seemed harmless enough. But it hadn't taken much to crumble that gentle mask. At their slightest fidget, all that pretty contorted into a glare fierce enough to scare bark off a tree. He'd known right there in the church that their days of doing as they pleased were over. True enough, she'd made the past two years a living hell.

While their father had been off at Virginia state meetings, his witch of a wife had turned their house upside down, changing everything from the wallpaper to the staff. She'd fired the people who'd raised him and Tuck, taking away everything familiar to them. She'd brought in her own staff, strangers who didn't give two wits if their mistress gave an order to whip the dog or her stepsons.

Chance shoved his winter coat into his saddlebag, knowing there'd be no coming back. He took Star by the reins and led the black mare toward the moonlight streaming through the open doors. A chilling breeze helped to soothe his aching shoulders. His breath uncurled like a cloud into the crisp fall air.

Across the yard shaded by a giant hickory tree, the moon lit up the white two-story house he'd grown up in, a home he no longer recognized. His gaze locked on the center second-story window. Their stepsister hadn't escaped the witch's tirade unscathed. Winifred didn't have her daughter dragged outside for public floggings, but on occasion Chance had spotted bruises hidden by ruffles and lace, and too often watched Cora Mae flinch at her mother's callous words.

His fingers fisted around the reins in his hand as hatred welled up inside him. He and Tuck used to feel cheated, their own mama having died the day they were born. He'd since realized they'd been the lucky ones. The first day he'd met Cora Mae, she'd brought an ache into his chest he'd never felt before.

After returning from the chapel, the old man had been shocked to discover a seven-year-old daughter among his new wife's possessions. Chance had never seen anything like her, not a single orange ringlet out of place and skin so white it glowed.

Perched on a settee amid stacks of trunks and other parcels in the grand foyer, she'd reminded him of the fancy porcelain dolls on the high shelves at the general store. All frilly and fragile—something he wasn't allowed to play with. Just like those delicate dolls, Cora Mae's pink lips didn't smile or frown, just stayed frozen in place as though painted on. He and Tuck had fixed that.

Despite his stepmother's efforts to keep her daughter locked away from the world, that ol' hickory got more use than the staircase during their frequent moonlight rides and walks to the creek. He'd become real partial to Cora Mae's smiles and wild giggles. If he'd had his way, she'd be riding out with them.

"I know what you're thinking," Tucker said from beside him.

"Doesn't feel right, leaving her here," Chance admitted.

"Nine years old is too young. And she's a *girl*. We'll be lucky if they don't chase us off."

Star tugged at his hold on the reins, anxious for the ride her saddle promised.

"Besides," said Tucker, "she belongs to Winifred."

"I don't belong to anyone," a soft voice whispered from the shadows. Cora Mae stepped into the moonlight, her orange hair flaring up in the pale light like a wick touched by a flame. Two thick braids draped over a pair of their old denim overalls—her usual sneak-out attire. Her dark eyes went from Tucker, to him, to their horses and back again.

"Where are you going?"

Chance couldn't seem to find his voice.

"We're meeting up with our father's unit," Tucker informed her.

Her wide gaze locked with his. "*Chance?*"

He liked how she did that, recognized him from his brother with nothing but a glance. His own father couldn't tell him from his twin and was never home long enough to have reason to. He was going to miss her something awful. Knowing there'd be no one to check on her after one of her mother's temper tantrums felt like a kick in the gut.

"Are you all right?" he asked.

"I was until now," she said, her voice escalating. *"You can't leave me!"*

"Shhh!" he and Tuck said together.

"Do you want us to get whooped again?" Tucker ground out. "We're already torn up."

Cora Mae clamped her lips tight, but that didn't keep her lower lip from trembling. "You can't go without me."

Chance stared in horror as fat tears rolled from her eyes and leaked down her pale cheeks. He'd never seen Cora Mae cry—though she often had reason. He dropped his gaze to his boots, not wanting to see it now.

"Damnation," Tucker muttered. "I can't handle no more crying females. You're the one who's always yammering on with her through all hours of the night." He nudged Chance's arm. "You explain it to her." He mounted his horse and started toward the woods.

It was just like Tucker to stick him with the hard stuff!

"Chance." Cora Mae took a step toward him. *"Please.* Don't leave me here."

"If we were going anywhere else, I'd—"

"I'm not afraid to go."

He knew she wasn't. When she was away from her mother, Cora Mae had a fearlessness to be marveled at. They hadn't accepted having a girl along for their late-night adventures without putting her through her paces.

Cora Mae didn't back down from a dare and had tackled every challenge he and Tuck had put before her. She'd turned out to be more fun to have around than a new puppy. But this was different. They were going to war.

"We're not taking a ride down to the creek, Cora Mae. The soldiers would never let you stay."

Sniffling, she wiped at her damp cheeks. "What am I to do without you?"

He hated this. What was he supposed to tell her? That it would be all right? He wouldn't wish her mother on a Yank! He wanted to do more, to be able to protect her. But he *couldn't*. Leastways, not yet. "We'll come for you," he said at last. "When the fighting's over."

Sullen brown eyes held his gaze. She tilted her head, the way she did when she was trying to make up her mind. "Promise?"

"Soon as we can," he said with a nod.

Tucker whistled softly, and Chance took a step back.

"I got to go."

"Wait." She grabbed his sleeve as he lifted his boot to the stirrup. "Take this." She pulled a ribbon from one of her braids, setting free a mass of orange ripples. Shoving the wide strip of satin through a buttonhole on his shirt pocket, she began working it into a pink bow that would have Tucker laughing clear to the next county.

"Cora Mae, I can't—"

"So you won't forget," she said, the catch in her voice stopping his protest.

Heck, even if she weren't his stepsister, he couldn't forget a girl with bright orange hair and the biggest brown eyes he'd ever seen. "That's not likely."

She stepped back and drew a jagged breath. Her eyes

shimmered with unshed tears he could tell she was trying hard to hold back. "Be careful."

"You, too." He swung into the saddle and started toward the thicket of trees before she had him covered in ribbons.

Not about to let Tucker catch him with a pink bow on his chest, Chance tugged the thing from his shirt. He rubbed the silken fabric between his fingers then shoved it deep into his pant pocket. Feeling Cora Mae's gaze on him as surely as the cold breeze whispering across the back of his neck, he spurred Star into a gallop.

No wonder his father never looked back—he didn't have to.

As Chance rode into the darkness of the woods, all he could see was the image of Cora Mae standing in moonlight, her somber brown eyes silently pleading for him to take her with him.

Chapter One

Wyoming Territory, 1883

One hand clutching her valise, the other flattened atop her ivory bonnet to prevent the biting wind from snatching it away, Cora Mae Tindale charged through the dusty, pitted road of Slippery Gulch. Horses and wagons clamored through the small strip separating the parallel rows of buildings. She leaped onto the crowded boardwalk. Folks swarmed like bees as the stagecoach driver continued to toss parcels and crates down from the stagecoach that had brought her this far.

Only twenty more miles.

Cora drew her carpetbag of dusty traveling clothes against her aching ribs and forged her way through. Her corset pinched beneath the straining fabric of the yellow gown her mother had starved her into just one agonizing month ago. Lord, what she'd give for a full breath. She hadn't inherited her mother's petite build, but the raving woman wouldn't relent.

There was nothing to be done for it now. This was the nicest dress she'd managed to stuff into her trunk. She couldn't arrive at the Morgan Ranch appearing a vagabond in need of charity.

Keeping her gaze on the livery just a few shops down, she quickened her pace. Beyond the noise and bustle of the crowded strip, tiny canvas-topped homes spotted the uneven grasses. Miles of rolling hills rippled into the distance like great green waves. Farther out, snowcapped mountains spiked up into the clear blue.

Cora's heart constricted painfully. The imposing view made it all too clear that this settlement was nothing but a tiny speck in a vast expanse of hills and sky. She'd heard Wyoming Territory was largely unsettled, but hadn't imagined Tucker and Chance would have built their ranch so far out into sheer wilderness.

She wouldn't be discouraged. She'd waited so long to see them again, though these were not the circumstances she had envisioned.

An instant burn of tears stung her eyes at the thought. The eight years she had spent at the textile mill had truly been a kindness. She'd been such a fool to believe her mother had summoned her home because she had missed her. Had she even suspected—

"Miss Tindale?"

Alarmed by the foul scent of bourbon on the breath so close to her ear, Cora swung around.

A tall cowboy shifted his hat over curly black hair. "Name's Wyatt McNealy. I hear you're headed to the Morgan Ranch and are, uh, *in need of my services.*"

Cora took one look at Wyatt McNealy's smug grin and winking eye and knew she'd crawl the twenty miles to the

Morgan Ranch before she'd travel in the company of a man carrying the stench of alcohol.

"You are mistaken, Mr. McNealy. I am not in need of any services."

"Spud tells me you're headed out to the Morgan place. I happen to be traveling in that direction. No sense in you having to struggle with a cart across such rugged ground."

Cora squared her shoulders. "I appreciate your concern, but I'm quite capable of handling a horse and cart. After traveling for weeks without altercation, I'm sure I can manage another twenty miles." She attempted to move past him. "Good day."

He sidestepped, blocking her way.

Fear nettled beneath her skin. Her fingers tightened around the handle of her carpetbag, preparing to knock him out of her way. Her other hand curled into a fist, just as her stepbrothers had taught her.

"You kin to the Morgans?"

"We're a kin of sorts," she said, hoping Chance and Tucker still thought of her as such.

"Well then." His fingers closed around her elbow. "I know they'd want me to make sure you reached their homestead safe and sound."

Cora wrenched her arm from his grasp.

"*Wyatt!*" boomed a voice from behind them. "You black-hearted son of a bitch!" The cracking of knuckles against Wyatt's jawbone punctuated the hard-spoken words. Wyatt dropped to the boardwalk. The crowd around them dispersed like a clutch of spooked chickens. Cora swallowed a shriek and backed against the building as Wyatt's attacker brushed past her.

The dark figure seemed a giant, well over six feet and

covered in dried mud. He turned toward his companion standing in the road. Wyatt started to rise. The giant tossed something at him, knocking him back down with a loud clunk.

A dead foal caked in mud pinned him to the boardwalk. Cora clamped her hand over her gaping mouth.

Wyatt groaned and shoved against the weight.

"I'll be sending you a bill for that foal and any others should they die from the stress you put them through. You better pray they make it, Wyatt."

Wyatt shifted. Cora saw his hand going for the hilt of his gun. Before she could shout a warning, a younger man stepped forward and pointed his rifle at Wyatt's head.

"The kid's known to have an itchy trigger finger," said the muddy rogue. "I'd hold real still if I were you."

Her pulse thundering in her ears, Cora glanced beyond the giant pillar of dirt and his young accomplice, toward the spectators gathered at a safe distance. Most watched with mild interest, while others continued on about their business.

Where was the sheriff?

The beastly rogue moved closer. Cora pressed her back against the rough wood of the building, holding her breath as his filthy trousers brushed across her yellow skirt.

He knelt beside Wyatt. "You got anything to say for what you did?"

"I didn't do—" Wyatt's whimpered words ended in a squeal as the man grabbed his boot and wrenched it up.

"Sure looks like the dainty boot prints we saw in that riverbed, don't it, Garret? A notch in the left heel."

The younger man spared a glance, his hazel eyes taking in the notched heel. "Sure does. Matches perfectly."

"You so much as kick a pebble into that river to divert water from my land again, and I'll be gunning for you, Wyatt. That's a promise."

"You're the one bent on using that devil wire!"

"Got tired of waiting for you boys on the Lazy J to learn your alphabet. Our brands are distinctly different. I've been patient with your boss, but if you don't catch on, I'll have no choice but to believe you're rustlers. Stupidity's forgivable, Wyatt. Stealing isn't." He lifted Wyatt's gun from its holster and tucked it into his own grimy waistband. "Just a precaution to keep you from filling my back with lead." He straightened and turned away, stepping out into the street.

Cora released a hard sigh of relief but found herself stuck between the building and Wyatt's sprawled legs, the rest of him still struggling with the muddy carcass.

"We didn't mean to startle you so," the younger man said, his gun now lowered at his side. "Let's get you out of harm's way." He flashed a gentle smile and offered his arm.

Cora nodded and allowed him to lead her around Wyatt.

"I sure hate that you were caught in the midst of our quarrel." Reaching the road, the young man stepped away from her and removed his hat, revealing short cotton-white hair. The dirt on his trousers didn't go past his knees. "I hope you'll accept my apologies."

"Of course," she said, forcing a tight smile.

"Garret!"

Cora jumped at the harsh shout and spotted the other man standing on the boardwalk across the road.

"I's just apologizing to the lady for scaring her half to death," Garret shouted back.

The beastly man tugged off his hat. His matted hair was

just as dirt-filled as the rest of him. He batted the hat against his thigh, scattering dust and chunks of dried mud. "If she's looking for formal socials and tea parties, she bes' get back on the stage. There's nothing but backstabbers and mudskippers around these parts."

He was obviously a mudskipper, Cora thought, watching him shove his hat back onto his crusted hair. His sharp green eyes burned with irritation before he turned and walked into the general store.

"Don't mind him," said Garret. "He's just havin' a real bad day. You be careful, now." He tipped his hat to Cora, then turned and darted across the busy road.

Cora didn't waste a moment. She hurried to the livery at the end of the road. Rounding the corner, she was pleased to find a large bay mare hitched to a cart just outside the open double doors. Her trunk had been secured to the back. She tossed her bag onto the seat, then stepped into the shadows of the large stable.

"Mr. Spud?" she called out.

"Miss Tindale." Mr. Spud stepped from a stall. His stringy gray hair poked out in all directions from beneath his battered brown hat. A grin pushed high into his whiskery face. "Don't you look pretty as a spring daisy," he said, brushing his hands across the front of his striped shirt as he walked toward her.

"You're too kind," she said, certain the old man's eyesight must be failing. "May I assume my cart is ready?"

Mr. Spud's bushy gray eyebrows pinched. "Didn't Wyatt find you?"

"Yes. He's been detained. As I said earlier, I'm quite capable of handling a cart."

"I can't send you out into those hills by your lonesome. The Morgans won't—"

"You've given me explicit directions. I can assure you—"

"Hey, Spud! You in there?"

Cora tensed, recognizing that strident voice. *Not again.*

"Well, speak of the devil," Mr. Spud said as he peered toward the open double doors, "and he's bound to surface."

Coated with dirt, the man did look as though he'd crawled up out of the earth. Garret walked in behind him. When he spotted her his young face beamed with a smile.

"What in thunder happened to you?" asked Mr. Spud.

"Had to pull a few colts from a muddy riverbed. I was told you've got the feed stocked up in here. I paid for six bags."

"Sure do. Right inside the door there. Help yourself. Now that you're here, I won't have to worry about finding the lady an escort."

"That's quite all right," Cora quickly cut in. "I don't need an escort."

Cold green eyes raked across the length of her. "If you're headed in our direction—"

"*No.* Thank you. I really do not require an escort."

His broad shoulders shifted, creating tiny avalanches of dust and dirt. "Your choice."

"But that don't make no sense," said Mr. Spud. "Not when—"

"I can manage," Cora insisted. "Thank you, Mr. Spud. I'll be on my way."

"You heard the lady. Let's get these loaded, kid." He turned away and hoisted four large sacks of feed.

"Nice seeing you again," Garret said, smiling brightly as he backed toward the open doors carrying the other two bags. "See you next month, Spud."

"Uh, Miss Tindale?" Mr. Spud poked his fingers under

his hat and scratched at his hair as he squinted at her. "Ain't you headed to the Morgan place?"

"I am," she said, walking toward the cart.

"Then you ought to change your mind about the escort, seein' as that there's one of the Morgans."

Cora's gaze whipped toward the hitching rails outside the stable. *"No."* She looked from the nice young man who couldn't be more than sixteen to his broad-shouldered companion securing bags of feed to the back of a horse. "Are you certain?"

"Yes, ma'am. He's either the married one or he ain't. 'Bout the only time I can tell 'em apart is when Tuck brings his wife along."

She thought of the man's piercing green eyes, and her heart skipped a beat.

Oh, my goodness. Struck between horror and disbelief, she slowly made her way outside.

Garret laughed as the Morgan man dunked his head into a trough. He whipped back, spraying water across the sky and revealing golden blond hair. Drops of water trickled down handsome features to his sharp jaw. His head tilted back as he raked his fingers through his hair, and she spotted a tiny scar hidden beneath his chin. A scar she'd given him accidentally.

Chance.

Smoothing her hands across the front of her skirt, she continued toward him. She had so wanted to make a good first impression. She stopped a few feet away. Tears stung her eyes, constricting her throat when she would have offered a greeting. She had waited so long.

"You're gonna get mighty cold by the time we reach the ranch," Garret said through his laughter.

Chance Morgan welcomed a chill, but he doubted it would help. "Trust me, kid, I won't be cold."

"She caught your eye, too, huh?"

"My eye didn't catch anything," he countered, still irritated that he'd been attracted to a pile of fluff and lace. Not his style. It was just as well *Her Highness* had opted to decline their escort.

"All that mud must be clogging your vision," said Garret.

Not likely. He'd made out all those curvy features with crystal clarity. He had enough trouble without adding fancy women into the mix. Five minutes in the general store and mothers were nudging their frightened daughters toward him. What was wrong with townfolk? Why would anyone assume that because he had a ranch, he'd be suitable marriage material? Or that he *wanted* a wife?

"Mud wouldn't have kept me from noticing that little lady was prettier than a buttercup," said Garret. "A buttercup bloomin' in the, uh…um…"

Pressing his hat over his wet hair, Chance glanced at Garret's beet-red face. He followed the kid's wide-eyed gaze to the "buttercup" standing a foot to his right, and grinned. That'll teach the kid to go spouting off at the mouth.

"You again?" He allowed his gaze to slide across her alluring figure. "Did you change your mind about the escort?"

She stared up at him through watery eyes and appeared to be choking.

"Miss, are you okay?"

"Chance," she said, sounding breathless.

Shock rippled through him. Being one of the prettiest women he'd ever seen, he knew damn well he'd never laid eyes on her until today. But she sure as hell seemed to know him.

"Have we met?"

"Oh, yes," she said in a rush. "I've been waiting forever to see you again." Her pink lips formed a bright smile. A smile that sparkled in eyes the shade of cinnamon.

His gaze honed in on the light dusting of freckles across her small nose. Spotting a spiral of bright-auburn hair poking out from beneath her wide fancy hat, Chance was hit by the flashing memory of big doe eyes, long orange braids and the mischievous grin of a little girl he hadn't seen since he was twelve. He looked deeper into brown eyes flecked with bits of gold and amber.

Holy hell.

Chance took a cautious step back. "Cora Mae?"

She gave an excited shriek. Her body seemed to vibrate before she leaped at him, her arms banding around his waist.

"Goodness, how I've missed you!" she exclaimed, damn near squeezing the life out of him.

Chance patted her back as she smiled up at him, hoping the light touch would release him from her tight embrace.

"You're so tall," she said, squeezing him tighter still. "And handsome! I've missed you so much. And Tucker. How is Tucker? You can't imagine…"

As she continued to jiggle and talk, Chance didn't know what made him dizzier. The woman's rapid-fire sentences or the soft, supple curves pressed flush against him. The discomforting stir of his body answered his quandary, while bringing about a stark realization.

He may have lived under the same roof as a red-headed tomboy during two years of his childhood, but he didn't know this shapely woman from Eve. Certainly not well enough to have her rubbing herself all over him, her pretty face gazing up at him as though the sun rose and set in his eyes.

"You've heard of Lowell's Textile?"

Chance nodded and gently pried her arms from his waist and set her away from him. The abrupt shift didn't slow her excited chatter.

"—but I was so certain I'd find you. And here you are. My goodness gracious, so strong and tall."

He smiled, her jubilation seeming somewhat contagious as he tried to keep up with her rapid-fire sentences.

"—ornery dickens that you were as a boy, and twice as cunning. Mother was sure you'd perished in the war, but…"

Her rush of words shattered into meaningless fragments at the mention of a name that never failed to put ice in his veins.

Mother.

Her mother, to be precise. The pristine witch who'd made life a living hell before he and Tucker had left home to follow their father into war. He and Tuck hadn't been the only ones anxious to get away from their vicious stepmother. Their father couldn't have beaten a trail off that ranch fast enough and had spent countless hours around a Rebel campfire warning the boys about the guiles of fancy women.

"Cora Mae," he blurted out when she finally paused for breath. *"What the hell are you doing here?"*

She flinched at his hard-spoken words. Her smile dimmed.

Damn. "I didn't mean to sound harsh. I just…can't imagine what would bring you all this way."

"I tired of waiting."

He'd never been one to guess at the mysteries of a woman's mind. "Waiting for what?"

"For *what?*" she repeated, planting her fists against sweetly rounded hips. She sure hadn't turned out anything like her starchy, whip-thin mother. He couldn't keep his gaze from roving the tight yellow bodice hugging full breasts. The gentle dip at her waist and prominent flare of her hips left no doubt that a man would find a soft, warm landing in her arms.

Lord, have mercy. He was sure he shouldn't be noticing such things about a woman who used to be his stepsister, once upon a time.

"For you to make good on your promise," she said, bringing his attention back to where it belonged: on her pretty face.

"My promise?"

"Yes," she said, her eyes growing misty. *"To come back for me."*

Old guilt rushed across his conscience, along with a wave of unwanted memories. He recalled Cora Mae's big brown eyes filled with tears, her frantic plea for him not to leave her behind. He *had* promised to go back for her. And at the time, he'd meant it. He'd also been twelve years old and hadn't known war from a Sunday picnic. It was a guilt he'd gotten over a long time ago.

"You promised to go back for her and never did?" Garret asked, sounding outraged.

Chance's gaze snapped toward the kid. He'd plain forgotten Garret was standing beside him. "I was twelve!"

"I waited," Cora Mae said, her sad eyes twisting the pain in his gut.

"We couldn't go back." He shook his head, trying to

shrug off the meaningless memories he'd spent too many years trying to forget. "You might recall there was a war going on. Tucker and I happened to be in the middle of it. Until we managed to get ourselves thrown into a Yankee prison camp."

"Oh, Chance." The warmth of her hand closed over his forearm, the light touch burning into his flesh like a fiery brand.

"It was a long time ago," he said, brushing her hand from his skin. "We survived." *Barely.*

Lily-white hands pressed against her full bosom. "I never imagined."

Of course she hadn't. She'd been busy with art classes and piano lessons. "You never answered my question," he said, wondering again what Cora Mae Tindale was doing in Slippery Gulch, fawning all over him.

"What question was that?" she asked, smiling so sweetly, it set his gut on fire.

"What are you doing here?"

"Once I heard of your ranch, I had to come. Surely you're aware that your ranch is broadly known?"

Damn right it was. He and Tuck had worked their asses off to make their ranch a success. The last thing they needed was Winifred sending her daughter in to sniff things out.

"Hearing that twin brothers by the name of Morgan were the owners, I had to find out if it was really you and Tucker."

"You could have sent a letter."

Her eyes widened, hurt registering in those rich brown depths.

"Chance," Garret said, stepping in between them, "what's gotten into you? She just finished telling us how she traveled all the way from Massachusetts to see you."

But Chance hadn't heard much beyond the roar of his blood as he stared down at the woman resurrecting demons from the past he'd long since put to rest. If Winifred thought she'd worm her way into their business by sending her daughter, she'd be disappointed. He was no longer a little boy who could be hauled out to the woodshed and whipped for the sheer delight of hearing him scream.

"That's quite all right." Cora Mae's jaw stiffened in a way Chance remembered it could. "I know there's no blood shared between us. If I'm not welcome—"

"Of course you're welcome," Garret insisted. "Isn't she, Chance?"

Chance regarded her for a long moment, certain he wouldn't have to see her fancy yellow-clad body again if he suggested she wasn't welcome. He had to remind himself it was never Cora Mae he'd hated. He'd once been as close to her as he had to his twin brother. In some ways, closer. That fact didn't help to slake his unease.

"Sure you are," he said, though his tone didn't carry a note of Garret's enthusiasm. "It's just a little hard to believe you'd travel clear across the States all by your lonesome just to see me."

"And Tucker, of course. How is Tucker?"

"Just fine. How's *your mother?*" he asked, forcing the words through clenched teeth.

Her bright expression blanched. He couldn't blame her for that. Thoughts of Winifred made him downright ill.

"I…I haven't seen her in years. Not since I went to work at the mill."

Cora Mae had been a lousy liar at the age of nine. It seemed some things hadn't changed. The tightness in her delicate features told Chance she was lying through her pearly white teeth. "Cora Mae, if Winifred sent you here—"

"Oh, no. She didn't. She's…*dead.*"

His eyebrows kicked up. He wasn't sure he'd heard her right. Over the years he'd envisioned Winifred Morgan choking on her own meanness and dying a very slow and painful death.

"Dead?" he repeated, trying not to sound hopeful.

Her ivory hat bobbled with her vigorous nod, but Cora Mae's wide eyes didn't reveal the certainty he wanted to see there. As if sensing he could read her doubt, she lowered her gaze to her clasped hands.

Some things were just too good to be true. "How'd she die?"

"Well I…I don't know," she said, her voice a tad too high. "I only received a note telling me of her passing. Since I was no longer obligated to send my wages to Mother, I chose to come west."

"She took your wages?"

She bristled at that, her brow pinching in annoyance, the starch in her spine making the most of her five feet. "Of course she took my wages," she spat. "Had I not been of some use to her, she'd have abandoned me years ago. My mother held no fondness for me. Surely you haven't forgotten."

He'd tried, and had been doing a fair job of blocking out the bad memories, stupid mistakes and unkept promises made by a boy too young to understand his limitations.

"Don't think I've come looking for free room and board."

He had a notion she'd come seeking a lot more than room and board. Cora Mae might have been fun as a kid, but she'd since been groomed by a woman who had a nose for money and a penchant for lying.

"I'm fully capable of finding work for myself," she insisted. "Though…" Her gaze skated briefly toward the landscape stretched out behind him. "I hadn't planned on you living quite so far removed from any kind of township."

"We've got plenty of room on the ranch," said Garret. "Tuck's been trying to talk my stubborn sister into hiring help for around the house. With the babies coming and all, this sounds like a perfect solution."

Cora Mae kept her wary gaze on Chance. "I don't want to intrude."

A little late for that.

"Chance," said Garret, his tone low with warning. He nodded to his left. Chance spotted the four riders coming in from the hills. Even at a distance, he recognized the rowdy ranch hands from the Lazy J. "We should get movin'," said Garret.

The kid had a point. Once those boys found Wyatt, travel would become somewhat more hazardous than usual. "Line the horses." He took Cora Mae by the elbow and ushered her toward the livery. "I'll drive the cart."

"More trouble?" asked Cora Mae, her neck craned to see what had captured their attention.

Chance smiled at the pretty patch of trouble he was about to take home. "I seem to be blessed that way." He checked to make sure her trunk had been roped down, then held a hand out to help her up onto the seat. "After you, Cora Mae."

She shrugged off his touch and stepped onto the cart without his assistance. "It's just *Cora*."

"I beg your pardon?"

"My name," she said, smoothing down the full yellow

skirt that had swallowed the entire seat. "I shortened it when I began working at the mill. I prefer to be called Cora."

"That sure is a pretty name," said Garret, already mounted on his pinto with Chance's horse and the pack horse lined up behind.

The kid had a lot to learn about women. *Pretty* didn't mean trustworthy. There was no denying the truth he'd seen in her eyes. Cora Mae was hiding something. He was in no mood to play a charlatan's game.

"Better secure your hatpin, *Cora Mae*. It's going to be a bumpy ride."

Chapter Two

Cora clutched the seat, her feet braced wide on the buck-board as Chance drove her cart across another green valley as though he were leading the last wagon train out of hell. A biting wind flattened the tall grass before them.

Chance's strong frame seemed to follow every shift of the seat while she shook until her teeth rattled. So focused was he on the uneven terrain, he'd likely not notice if she toppled out. Perhaps he *intended* to send her careening to the ground. What on earth had she been thinking, travel-ing into the middle of the Wyoming wilderness to find two boys from her childhood?

The wagon slowed as they reached the crest of another rise. Chance reined the horse to a halt. A valley stretched out before her, covered by swaying grasses bursting with wildflowers and spotted with boulders and trees.

She uncurled her fingers from the seat and ran them briskly over her arms, trying to rub some of the chill from her skin. She glanced beside her and found Chance's gaze intent on hers. His striking features could have been carved in granite, the sparkling green of his eyes cold and clear as a gemstone.

"Sorry about your dress."

She glanced down at the dark smudges on her yellow skirt. Knowing more were on the dress front hidden beneath her crossed arms, an instant heat flared in her cheeks.

"It's nothing," she said, certain the dress had fared far better than her pride. Had she actually hugged him? She must have been blinded by images of the boy who'd long since outgrown her memory of him. What a spectacle she must have made.

How could she not have expected the full-grown man beside her to be a stranger? *A frightening one at that.* Chance's reception had fallen drastically short of her expectations.

Seemingly out of things to say, he gazed across the windswept grasses. She took the opportunity to secure her hat before the wind snatched it away completely. After a few minutes of listening to the jingle of horse harnesses and watching the wind chase leaves and grass, she couldn't stand it. Unfriendly as he may be, it was still Chance Morgan who sat beside her. The closest friend she'd ever had.

"Did you never wonder about me?"

His jaw flexed as though the question annoyed him. "Sure we did."

"Are your memories of me so terrible?"

He eased back against the seat and released a long sigh before he finally met her gaze. His expression softened, revealing a sadness Cora felt to the bottom of her soul.

"You know I didn't want to leave you behind."

She'd clung to that hope for two decades.

"Tuck and I, we spent countless nights plotting all kinds of scenarios for going back for you."

"You did?" Warmth blossomed inside her.

"But we were kids, Cora Mae. And you were Winifred's daughter."

And just that quickly the spark died, stamped out by the hatred buried in those last two words. *Winifred's daughter.* "Has it been so long that you've confused me with my mother?"

"No. But apparently you believe enough time has passed between us that you can lie to me and get away with it."

Cora froze, stunned by his candid accusation.

Her mother's manipulation may have driven her here, but Cora wouldn't allow Winifred's influence to ruin her chance to know her stepbrothers again.

"I've not lied," she insisted.

"Cora Mae." His voice was barely a rumble above the wind.

The sudden warmth in his green eyes stole her breath. His lips tipped into a slight smile, and Cora was struck by the urge to…certainly *not* hug him.

"I think you forget how well I know you," he said.

She hadn't forgotten. She'd never stopped praying for the day he would come back into her life. Winifred wouldn't steal this from her. She wouldn't allow it.

"You knew a child. The man sitting before me is proof that people change over time. You're hardly the sweet boy I once knew."

"Sweet boy? I recall doing my best to set off a certain prissy tomboy's spitfire temper and landing her in a mess of trouble on several occasions."

He'd been the best adventure of her life. "You were worth the trouble."

He arched a golden eyebrow and Cora averted her gaze, suddenly uncomfortable with the intimacy of sitting so close to him and speaking of such personal matters. "You were my very best friend," she clarified. "It's one of the few childhood memories I hold dear."

"All clear!"

Cora jumped at the sound of Garret's voice. She glanced back to see him approaching on his horse with Chance's horse and a packhorse trailing behind him, realizing only then that she hadn't seen him since they'd left Slippery Gulch some time ago.

"Have you been right behind us all along?" she asked as he reined in beside them.

"No, ma'am." He dismounted and began changing the lineup of the three horses. "I stayed a short ways back, making sure Wyatt didn't send any of his men after us."

"After us?"

"You don't need to fret none." Garret met her gaze with a grin. "I didn't spot any riders." He mounted the other saddled horse now standing at the front of the line. "Which pass are we taking?" he said to Chance.

"Northeast is the shortest."

Garret gave a sharp nod.

"Mr. Spud mentioned a distinct trail to your ranch," she said, certain this was not the direction he'd described. "I haven't noted one."

"We're using a stock trail," said Chance. "Not the smoothest ride, but it shaves nearly an hour off travel. We'll make it home in time for Skylar's supper."

"Tucker's wife?"

"Yeah."

At thirty-three, she had truly expected them both to be wed by now. "You've not married?"

Chance gave a short, humorless laugh. "Marriage is not for me. Not in this lifetime."

She found an odd sense of comfort in that response and rather agreed with his outlook.

"Miss Cora," Garret said, reining in beside her. He leaned over and dropped a large coat over her shoulders, enveloping her in a warm lamb's wool lining. "No sense in you shivering all the way to the ranch."

"Thank you." She pulled the thick coat tight and breathed in a musky, masculine scent.

"Chance can't use it. You might as well stay warm."

Chance noticed the sudden stiffness of her spine. She paused in the midst of securing the top button at her throat. After blindsiding him with all that sentimental talk about being her *best friend*, he didn't see why she should be repulsed by wearing his coat.

"Do you mind?" she asked, meeting his gaze with clear reluctance.

"Why should I?" he said, unsure of how he felt about anything at the moment. He only wished he'd thought of it sooner. The heavy brown leather enveloped her from her chin to her knees. Keeping her covered up was a definite improvement.

"I have a layer of mud to keep me warm. Your lips are practically blue."

"See you at the ranch," Garret said as he set off ahead of them.

The wagon lurched forward. Cora resumed her hold on

the seat as her exhausted muscles prepared for another jarring ride.

"Sure hope you got more sensible clothing in that trunk."

"I have." Indeed, there was nothing but sensible clothing in her trunk. Not that it mattered. Chance's reception had made it painfully obviously she would not have been well received, no matter what she'd worn. Thankfully she'd ignored her mother's order to throw out her *maid attire*.

She owed her mother nothing. Her life was her own.

Descending the hillside at hair-raising speed, she sucked in a deep breath of crisp Wyoming air, and tasted freedom.

Hours later the warm hues of sunset streaked the sky as they rode into a green valley with a horse ranch at its center. Snow-capped mountains rose up on either side. Cora gazed out in amazement at all Chance and Tucker had accomplished. A maze of fencing and outbuildings surrounded a massive two-story house. Horses milled about in the various pens and dotted the distant pastures.

As they neared the house, they captured the attention of men on horseback and others inside fences. Garret stood in the yard near a large barn. He held a little boy with the same pale shade of white-blond hair.

The moment they stopped, Cora shrugged Chance's coat from her shoulders and jumped from the cart, ready to have her feet on the blessed unmoving ground.

"Unco 'ance!" The little boy, no older than two, ran toward them.

"Hey, Joshua." Chance stepped beside Cora and crouched down to catch the child at midleap into his arms. He lifted him high, initiating wild giggles before he set him down on his little booted feet. It was the wide smile on Chance's face that stole Cora's attention, the pure joy that lit his eyes as he looked at Joshua. "You been good for your mama?"

Cotton-white curls flipped in the wind as he bobbled his head enthusiastically.

"Go tell Uncle Garret to give you your treat."

Joshua glanced past his uncle, his big blue eyes taking Cora in before he turned and ran back to Garret.

Chance stepped around her, not bothering to introduce her to his nephew.

"Chance Morgan!" shouted a woman's hostile voice.

He looked toward the house, his broad shoulders blocking Cora's view. "Don't worry. I plan to go around back and clean up before stepping foot in the house."

"I should hope so!"

Cora eased around her rude host to see the tall woman standing on the porch. Her loose blond hair and blue dress whipped in the wind, the midsection of her dress strapped tight over her protruding belly. She appeared dreadfully overdue for giving birth. Her brilliant blue eyes surged wide as she spotted Cora.

"Oh! I didn't realize we had company."

Chance put his hand on Cora's lower back and ushered her forward. "Skylar, this is Miss Cora Mae Tindale, my, uh…stepsister."

Skylar gaped at her from the top of the stairs. "Truly?"

Cora struggled to smile as she shuffled up the steps. "I am sorry to arrive unannounced."

"*Nonsense.* Tucker will be so excited. He's mentioned you on several occasions. Isn't this wonderful, Chance?"

He stood at the base of the steps, stiff as a stone statue, her carpetbag in one hand. "It is."

"Where have you traveled from?" asked Skylar.

"Del-uhum, Massachusetts," she corrected, catching her slip and the sudden scrutiny in Chance's gaze. He knew full well her mother's family resided in Delaware.

"Del—um, Massachusetts." He held up her valise. "Can't say I've heard of it."

She snatched her luggage. "Yes, well, it's…small." Goodness gracious. This was going to be a very short visit.

"You came all that way alone?"

Cora turned to Skylar, anxious to escape the intensity of Chance's green eyes, unnerved by the flutters in her belly. "I was able to travel by rail for much of the journey. The past week on the stage was a bit unsettling at times."

"I can imagine. The stage line—" Skylar's words broke off, her startled gaze looking past Cora. "Joshua, what's in your mouth?"

Clutching his uncle's big hand, he smiled a red toothy grin. "Canny."

Skylar sighed before casting a disapproving glance at Chance. "You're going to rot his teeth."

Chance grinned as he ruffled the child's white hair. "Baby teeth fall out anyhow, don't they, cowboy?" He turned away, his nephew in tow. "I'll bring the trunk in after I finish with the horses and wash up."

"No more candy," Skylar called after them.

"Fine."

Skylar took Cora by the arm. "Let's get out of this wind. You must be chilled to the bone."

Cora stepped into a great room lined with honey-colored polished pine from the floor to the high ceiling. Instantly enveloped by heat, it felt like walking into pure sunshine. A fire crackled in the massive stone fireplace to her left. Across the room, a banister staircase led to an open second story. She was quite taken aback by the grandeur of it all, yet everything in the room spoke of simplicity.

Four oversize chairs covered in cowhide, a single rocking chair and a few wooden footstools were spaced around the fireplace and what appeared to be a sheepskin rug. To her left, in the immediate parlor area, a tapestry sofa and wing back chair complemented a bare coffee table.

"What a beautiful home."

Skylar beamed. "Thank you. The kitchen is straight back." She led her through the formal dining room. Oil lamps glowed from a circular chandelier above a long table already set with at least a dozen place settings. "I'm just finishing up with supper preparations."

The scent of fresh bread wafted from the kitchen—another tidy room polished to a shine from floor to ceiling.

"Please, sit." Skylar motioned to one of the six chairs.

"Thank you." Cora set her bag beside the table and removed her pin and hat. Skylar eased onto a chair, folding her hands over her round stomach. Despite her smile, the woman appeared thoroughly exhausted.

"I hope you don't think me too rude for asking but are you carrying twins?" Cora was fearful she already knew the answer.

"There'd better be two in there," Skylar said, patting the rounded rise. "I wasn't half this big at the end with Joshua."

Cora forced a smile, knowing Chance and Tucker's mother had died shortly after their birth.

"There's coffee on the stove, and hot water if you'd prefer tea."

"Tea sounds wonderful. Please, allow me to get it,"

Cora said as Skylar began to rise. "I've been sitting for days on end and find I'm quite restless."

The hiss of a pot boiling over drew their attention to the stove before she could retrieve a cup from the open cupboard. "I've got it," she said, quickly grabbing a dish-towel and lifting the lid from the sputtering pot.

"Thank you."

"My pleasure. I ran a boardinghouse for four years in Massachusetts. You can't imagine how I've missed my kitchen." She missed it all, being in charge of her house, her girls, *her life*.

The back door opened, letting in a gust of wind and a clean version of Chance, yet there was something distinctly different about his presence, the ease in his expression, the smooth slide of his smile as he looked at Skylar.

Tucker.

He slammed the door and dropped to his knees in front of his wife. "How are my little kickers?" he asked, pressing his cheek to Skylar's protruding belly. It was one of the sweetest displays of affection Cora had ever seen.

"Um, Tuck." A pink hue rose into Skylar's cheeks. "You have company."

Tucker glanced over his shoulder. "Oh," he said, and quickly stood. "I beg your pardon."

Cora could only grin.

"This is Miss Tindale," said Skylar. "Your stepsister."

Tucker's green eyes surged wide. *"Cora Mae?"*

"Hello, Tucker."

He gave a shout. In an instant she was wrenched off her feet in a tight hug before he set her back down. "Look at you!" He took a step back, a grin pushing high into his cheeks as he shook his head. "My God. All grown up."

"Twenty years away will do that to a person."

His laughter initiated her own. What a switch. Tears burned in her eyes as joy swept through her. This was the reception she'd hoped for.

"Well, let's have it," he said. "What are you doing here? How did you get out here?"

"By rail and stage," she said, batting away her tears. "I'd heard about some fine horses coming from the Morgan Ranch in Wyoming Territory, and I had to see for myself."

His grin widened. "I'll be damned. Who brought you out?"

"Chance. I ran into him while leaving the Slippery Gulch depot."

Tucker's smile fell. His gaze paused on her dirty dress as his brow knitted in a look of concern. "How'd that go?"

"He didn't throw me in the dirt, if that's what you're wondering." She smiled at the blatant relief on Tucker's face. "But he didn't seem pleased to see me, either."

"Thoughts of your mama can sure put ice up the spine."

"Yes, I know. And I'm sorry. You may recall she was no fonder of me, her own flesh and blood."

"I do recall."

"She's passed on, and I've been on my own for quite some time now. I wanted to see the brothers I'd missed so dearly. I promise not to wear out my welcome."

"You're welcome to stay as long as you like, Cora Mae. With the babies due any day, some extra help around here would be really appreciated. Right, honey?"

"I won't complain," Skylar said, her hands folded over her belly as she watched them with a wide smile. "I usually have help from our foreman's wife, Margarete, but since Zeke's been hurt she's had her hands full. Tucker, why don't you help Cora get settled in a room upstairs so she can freshen up before supper?"

"Be happy to." His arm closed around her shoulders and Cora was overcome by a sense of relief.

She'd made it.

The moon was well up in the night sky by the time Chance put out the lamps in the barn and headed to the house. He'd opted to clean up in the bunkhouse while the others had their supper. After the long ride to the ranch and fighting an attraction he had no business feeling, he wasn't up to sitting across the table from Cora Mae.

He tugged up the collar of his jacket as a cold wind swirled around him on his way to the back porch. Cursing the misfortune of his day, he tugged off his boots and left them on the step before slipping inside.

Tucker glanced up from the small kitchen table. One of their account books lay open beneath the lamplight. "Wondered when you'd show up."

"What are you doing to my ledgers?" The last time Tuck had offered to help with the books it had taken Chance a week to get everything back in proper order.

"Just checking our numbers, making sure we're on schedule for filling our contracts."

His brother's frown wasn't reassuring. "How's it look?"

"Tight. All the trouble with the Lazy J is costing us time. We'll be lucky to bring in our band of wilds and have them broke in time for the first drive. The number of mavericks increases every time our fencing goes down, some of our best horses. We don't have time to chase them to hell and back before the first drive to the stockyards."

Chance gave a nod of agreement. "We'll start rounding

up the mustangs tomorrow and get a solid count. If need be, we'll pay a visit to the Lazy J, see if they're being neighborly again by rounding up our strays."

Tucker's lips tipped in a wry grin. "More likely they've driven them out to the badlands just for spite. Where've you been all evening?"

"Catching up on chores."

Tucker's smile widened. "And here I thought you were avoiding Cora Mae."

Chance thought the reason they'd settled at the back end of nowhere was so they wouldn't have to avoid anyone, but decided to leave that unsaid as he opened the breadbox on the counter. He found half a loaf of Skylar's bread and took it to the table.

"She mentioned you weren't too happy to see her," Tucker added, closing the ledger as Chance sat across from him.

He shrugged and bit into the bread. "I brought her out here, didn't I?"

"All in one piece. I am impressed."

"I was polite."

"Must be why she frowns at the mention of your name."

He tore off another bite of bread, annoyed by the notion that he'd somehow behaved inappropriately. "Have you forgotten who we're talking about? Winifred's daughter shows up unannounced and I'm supposed to just welcome her with open arms?"

"There was a time when you'd have crossed two enemy lines to do just that."

"That was a lifetime ago. A lifetime she's spent under the influence of a witch. What's more, I think she's lying about Winifred."

"You have a suspicious mind, Chance."

He grunted. "I'm blessed that way."

"Why would she lie?"

"Why do most women lie? To get something. What do you want to bet Winifred's finally squandered all she stole from our family and is looking for a new source of pay dirt?"

Tucker shook his head. "Cora's nothing like her mama, and you know it."

"You could tell that in one evening?"

"I could tell that when I met her at age seven. She's already proven to be helpful in the kitchen, and Skylar happens to think she's a pure delight."

"I'm glad it's all worked out, then."

Tucker stared at him for a moment before releasing a sigh and looking away, obviously not seeing the sincere joy he'd hoped to find on Chance's face.

How the hell was he supposed to react to Cora Mae turning up in Slippery Gulch?

"How'd it go down at the miners' camp?"

"Just dandy. I gave Wyatt his colt and told him I'd be sending a bill for it and any others that died because of his ignorance."

"Why am I thinkin' there's more to that account than what you're telling?"

Chance shrugged and ate the last of the bread. "Might have tossed in a punch before giving him Starlet. No less than he deserved."

"I sure wish you'd told me before you lit off into that valley."

Chance wished he had, too. Then Tuck could have endured Cora Mae's bright smiles and excited jiggles. The memory of how quickly he'd squelched that excitement tugged at his conscience.

Noticing some breadcrumbs on the table, he brushed them into his hand.

"Wyatt could have had others with him."

"I had the kid along." Chance stood and emptied his palm into the sink basin. "We took care of it."

"Did Wyatt admit to damming the river?"

"He didn't have to." Chance leaned back against the countertop. "We knew it was him."

"What makes you so certain he wasn't following orders?"

"What's that supposed to mean?"

"He works for Widow Jameson."

"Wyatt's the one who controls her crew. What cause would Salina have to dam the river? She told me she didn't have a problem with our use of wire fencing."

"Yeah, but what a woman says and how a woman feels are two different things. Especially when you become *personally involved* with her."

Chance groaned. "We're not personally involved."

His brother arched an eyebrow. "Not the way I heard it."

"That was nearly two months back, and I didn't do anything!" She had latched on to him in front of half their crew before he'd known what had hit him. For a tiny slip of a thing, she had the grip of a grizzly and the kiss of a skilled temptress.

"One kiss does not make us 'personally involved.'"

"I can hardly ride out without finding her and her black buggy pulled up right beside you."

"She won't leave me alone," he argued, frustrated and downright peeved by the amount of gossip she'd created. "I have more sense than to sow my wild oats in my own backyard." Since they'd put down stakes, his oats hadn't been getting sown at all! An inconvenience he hadn't foreseen before settling in this valley. It was one thing to spend a few hours with a willing woman when he was just passing through—quite another to bed a woman close enough to start conjuring expectations.

"We were having trouble with the crew from the Lazy J long before Salina mauled me—that's *why* we took to using the wire."

"Nothing like the trouble we've been having in the past two months. Zeke took some heavy hits by whoever jumped him out on the north pasture last week. I wasn't sure he was gonna make it. If he hadn't—"

"There'd have been a hanging," Chance finished for him. He would have been the first one on the Lazy J. If Skylar and Zeke's wife hadn't barred the stable holding shotguns, he and a few others would have ridden to the Lazy J and beat the identity of the coward who'd attacked Zeke out of their whole crew of worthless cowpokes.

Damn women. Always interfering!

"The old man can still barely walk," Tucker continued. "Our boys are getting sick of fixing cut wire and having to look over their shoulder the whole time. You sure Wyatt isn't her latest bed warmer?"

"How the hell should I know? So what if he is? I've never proclaimed an interest in Salina. I don't know why she's suddenly stuck on me!"

"Clearly you're the victor," Tuck said in a droll tone.

"Well I forfeit!"

"Good luck with that. In the meantime, her crew's creating a powerful hostility among the men. We're a stone's throw away from an all-out range war."

"Why do you think I rode down into that valley?"

"I just hope you targeted the right source." Tuck picked up the ledger and stood.

"Are you saying I should have ridden to the Lazy J and punched out Salina?"

Tuck chuckled and turned away. "I'm going to bed. We can talk more tomorrow. By the way, I put Cora Mae two doors down from you."

Chance beat him to the doorway and blocked his path. "Why is she on my side of the house?"

"Why do you think? Skylar could go into labor any day now. Our only spare room is between Josh and the nursery. Garret has the only room down here. You better be nice to her," Tuck said, wagging a finger at him. "It won't kill you to show a little politeness."

"I don't trust her."

Tucker's laughter tightened the anger twisting inside him. "You don't trust anyone. I'm not asking you to like her. Just *be nice*." Tucker moved past him, heading for the stairs in the front room.

Chance glanced at the stairwell at the end of the kitchen leading to his section of the house. As if it wasn't bad enough that she was in Wyoming. Grumbling to himself, he put out the lamp and climbed the stairs. His footsteps slowed as he reached the light spilling out from beneath her door.

He remembered a time when they'd snuck into each other's rooms on a regular basis and would talk for hours or climb out of the window for a late-night venture to the river. They'd also been caught on occasion and, though Cora Mae hadn't gotten off unscathed, it was him and Tuck who'd lost strips off their hide.

Rage tightened over Chance's body as old hatred welled up inside him. He couldn't separate the good memories from the bad, and preferred not to think about the past at all.

Be nice.

He walked into his room thinking he was well beyond the age when niceness got him anywhere. He was tired of tripping over marriage-minded women and sick to death of being celibate! Unless a woman was interested in getting naked and getting lost, she could get the hell out of his way.

Did he go around shouting such things? No! He was *polite,* damn it! And hadn't it been his idea to knock on Cora Mae's window and invite her along that first time. Tucker had griped for days about a girl tagging along with them. Who was Tucker to tell him to be *nice?*

He found the matches on his night table and lit the lamp, spilling light across his room and the wooden box beside the glass kerosene globe. Slumping onto his bed, he flipped the lid up and took a small leather pouch from the clutter of coins, cuff links and pocket watches. Dipping his fingers inside, he pulled out the thin silken fabric.

Faded by time, the only color left in the frayed thing were smudges of dirt and dried blood. *Just a stupid ribbon…*that had brought him the slightest comfort in times when he'd desperately needed to believe there was more than pain and violence in this world. He'd think of Cora Mae, her smiles, her sweetness, her *resilience.*

He wasn't sure why he still kept it. It had been too many years since they'd been informed that Winifred had sold their birthright and taken her daughter to Delaware to live in luxury at Tindale Manor.

He glanced at the lamp's flame, so tempted to lower the ribbon into the bright light and be done with it.

What the hell good will it do now?

She was here, her big dark eyes full of sadness and shadows, tying him up in knots, just as they always had.

And he was supposed to be nice?

Chapter Three

If a woman wanted something done right, she had to do it herself!

Salina Jameson snapped the reins, picking up speed as the Morgan house came into view. Her buggy wasn't moving nearly fast enough. She knew it was close to suppertime, and their household was likely busy. *Didn't matter*.

She wasn't about to risk her claim on the man she'd been trying to seduce into her bed for the past year. Elusive devil he may be, but Chance Morgan was hers. The sooner he realized marrying her would end his troubles with the Lazy J, the sooner everything would work out best for all of them.

She'd listened to Wyatt's account of Chance's retaliation as he'd moaned about his bruised ribs for over an hour, all before he'd casually mentioned the woman.

Pretty young woman, he'd called her. *Miss Tindale*, he'd called her.

Seething with rage, she snapped the reins again. How could Wyatt not see this woman's arrival as a threat to their plans? Perhaps she was becoming too relaxed with him. She'd clearly have to set her affair with Wyatt aside for now. She had to keep her eyes on the real prize. Merging with the Morgan Ranch.

The highwaymen calling themselves a cattle association were robbing her blind. By joining with the Morgans she would more than meet the land requirements to avoid their penalties. She'd save her ranch from ruin and gain a man worth having in a marriage bed. The mere thought sent a surge of arousal through her body as she guided her buggy into the yard. She paid no notice to the men stopping to glance at her from various corrals. She only wanted one man in her bed, *for now*.

As she reined in near the house, Skylar's younger brother rode toward her. *Not too young*, she thought, admiring the strong build of the young man as he reined in beside her. A sixteen-year-old was fine for passing some time, but not what was required in a husband. She needed a man who could intimidate those overlording cattlemen. There wasn't a man who didn't step aside when the Morgan brothers moved through the railhead stockyard.

She needed Chance Morgan.

"Afternoon, Mrs. Jameson," Garret said, the spark in his eyes and kick of his smile assuring her she'd chosen the right gown. Black didn't have to be basic.

"Mr. Daines," she said, giving him a coy smile. "Is your sister home?"

"Yes, ma'am. I'd take you in, but Tuck's waiting on me. Skylar will answer the door." His horse sidestepped away. "Good day to you."

Not so far. She set the brake, stepped down from her buggy and strolled toward the two-story ranch house.

Quite grand, she thought, crossing the wide porch to the double polished-oak doors. Surely Chance would want his own home, away from his brother's family? Her home wasn't nearly as large, but it was quaint and she was settled. She rapped her knuckles three times against the wood. Tugging off her gloves, she decided she was very anxious for a visit with her future sister-in-law, and her guest.

The door opened and her gaze locked on an impossibly large belly.

"Salina. What a surprise."

The poor dear! "Hello, Skylar. Aren't you…"

"Huge," Skylar supplied, patting her round stomach.

She couldn't argue. She'd never seen a woman so heavy with child.

"Twins," Skylar said.

Salina had always counted her inability to produce a child as a blessing—and was now twice as thankful.

"What can I do for you, Salina?"

"I heard there was another woman in the area, and I thought I'd pay a social call."

Her neighbor stared down at her in clear surprise.

Salina couldn't deny that she'd never been one to pay social calls in the past, at least not to women. But that was before they'd brought in a rival.

"We're in the midst of preparing supper."

"Oh, thank you, but I can't stay to eat." She stepped between the small gap of the door frame and Skylar's belly and slipped into the house. "I just wanted to say hello and give a proper greeting." She glanced around the large yet frightfully simple home. The bare tables and clunky furniture reminded her of a bunkhouse. The woman of the house clearly had no sense of fashion or style.

Movement beyond the dining hall caught her attention. A rather plain woman with reddish hair walked toward them, wiping her hands on a white apron tied at her waist.

This is my competition? Wyatt hadn't mentioned the splash of freckles on the woman's face or her sturdy build. *Pleasantly plump,* thought Salina. The woman's drab gray smock and black dress were similar to that of Salina's housekeeper's.

"You must be Miss Tindale." She hoped.

"Yes."

Salina glanced back at Skylar and awaited her introduction.

"Cora, this is our neighbor, Mrs. Salina Jameson, owner of the Lazy J ranch, just beyond the east end of our valley."

Salina flashed her best smile. "Charmed."

"Likewise," Cora replied.

"Cora is such a lovely name."

"Thank you. My condolences on your loss," she said, glancing at her diamond wedding ring.

"It was a shame," she said, releasing a mournful sigh. Catching his wife at the peak of passion with a ranch hand had been too much for her late husband's elderly heart. Had she realized such a scene would divest her of him so efficiently, she wouldn't have waited four years before seducing Wyatt in the parlor.

"Shall we sit?" Salina asked, making her way toward the furniture.

Cora glanced at Skylar's perplexed expression as Salina Jameson made herself at home. The young widow flounced onto one of the chairs. Light chiffon ruffles fluttered around her, the black mass emphasizing her tiny waist. The dress could hardly be referred to as widow's weeds, the stiff bodice barely covered the ivory mounds being pressed toward the woman's dainty chin. A black bonnet secured a bundle of cascading brown curls.

Cora followed Skylar to the adjacent sofa and offered her arm for support as Skylar leaned back. She felt a twinge of caution as she seated herself across from the woman watching her with calculating brown eyes. Salina sat on the edge of her chair, her hands folded in her lap, her posture impeccably straight, as though she might spring up at any moment.

"So," Salina said, her voice dripping with sweetness, "how do you know the Morgans?"

"My mother was married to their father for a short time during our childhood."

"Oh, so you're related?"

"No blood relation, of course. Two years after our parents wed, their father perished in the war. Chance and Tucker have stayed dear to my heart."

"And now you've come to Wyoming to settle close to your brothers—how lovely. I think you'll find your chances of finding a husband greatly improved. Men around these parts aren't so choosy."

Cora looked into Salina's perfect smiling face and felt as though she were back in her mother's house. Skylar leaned forward in a rush, clearly picking up on the barb, but Cora knew this game all too well. "How reassuring," she said, patting Skylar's arm as she returned Salina's fake smile.

"Indeed. And don't feel as if you have to settle. I feel quite fortunate to be courted by Chance."

"*Courted?*" Skylar repeated. "I wasn't aware."

"Yes, well. Chance is not much of a talker. Lately I've not seen as much of him as I would like."

"I think that's wonderful," Cora said, certain this announcement was for her benefit. "I was just telling Skylar today that I'd never had a sister. The prospect of having two is thrilling."

"I'll anticipate seeing more of you, then," said Skylar. "Seems a shame that in the three years we've been neighbors, this is your first formal visit."

"Truly," Salina said, beaming. "I would love nothing more."

A side glance from Skylar told Cora she had her doubts.

Boot steps pounded against the porch just before the front door burst open. Tucker stormed in as though he intended to foil a robbery. Chance walked in behind him. Both men stopped short as their gazes collided with Salina.

"Salina," said Tucker. "Is everything okay on your ranch?"

Her gaze moved a bit frantically between the two, as though trying to distinguish one brother from the other, which Cora found rather amusing. "Yes. Thank you."

The seething chill in Chance's eyes must have given him away. "Hello, Chance."

"Evening."

The temperature in the room seemed to drop a few degrees. It appeared she wasn't the only one subjected to Chance's less-than-welcoming reactions. For a reason she couldn't explain, her spirits lifted.

Salina sprang up in a flutter of black chiffon. "I really must be going. Skylar, Cora, it has been lovely." She stepped between the two brothers and slid her arm beneath Chance's. "Chance," she said, not seeming to notice the narrowed eyes that had never left her. "See me out, won't you?" Chance stared down at Salina's smiling face, then glanced at her arm hooked around his.

What the hell's going on?

He didn't wait to find out in front of his family. He turned and guided Salina toward the front door as quickly as he could.

The moment Garret had told him Widow Jameson was at the house, he and Tucker had hightailed it home. If Tucker was right and he had roughed up Salina's current lover, he didn't want his sister-in-law bearing the brunt of her anger. Judging by the eerie pleasantries he'd just witnessed, that didn't seem to be the case.

Salina nestled against his side as he led her onto the porch and closed the door behind them.

"I've missed you," she said, tightening her hold on his arm.

"Lately, I seem to be blessed that way." Being *missed* by women was becoming a true hazard.

Once in the yard, he slipped his arm from her grasp.

"Chance," she said, puckering her lower lip. "If I didn't know any better, I'd think you weren't happy to see me."

"Well…" He rubbed a hand against the tension in the back of his neck. "I suppose that all depends. Did Wyatt give you my message?"

"Are you referring to the news of your guest, Miss Tindale?" she asked, batting her thick eyelashes.

"I'm referring to Wyatt blocking one of our rivers. I lost one of my best colts yesterday as a result."

"My gracious. That is truly terrible. I had no idea our pond construction would have such a diverse effect on your land."

"Pond construction?"

"Yes."

"Nearly eight miles from your house?"

"Yes." Her eyes fluttered as she flashed a smile.

"And you didn't realize diverting water from my land would turn the riverbed into a mud bog?"

"Why, I suppose I just didn't think it through. I must admit, having you to help oversee such business decisions would clear up this kind of confusion."

The woman was talking in riddles. "Oversee your business decisions?"

"After you put a ring on my finger, of course."

He'd definitely missed a big part of this conversation. *"A ring?"*

She batted those long lashes. "Well, I've tried being subtle."

"Salina, you're about as subtle as a thunderstorm."

She beamed a smile. "Then you must have realized that I fancy you."

The way he heard it, she'd fancied quite a few men even before she'd been widowed, but he wasn't one for re-peating gossip. It wasn't his business and she wasn't the first to marry for material comfort.

"You see, I've decided it's time to start thinking about the future, and I want that future to include you."

"Why?" The question shot from his mouth as if by its own accord, surprising him—and Salina.

"Well…" she said, seeming to search for an answer. "You're the first real gentleman I've come across in a long while."

"You'd be the first to label me as such," he said, amused by the title. Just because he hadn't tossed her to the grass and taken what she'd repeatedly offered didn't mean he was a gentleman. He'd been tempted. He enjoyed a roll in the hay as much as the next man, but not at the risk of gaining a wife he hadn't sought. For now, reason outweighed his lust.

"Surely you can see the advantages of seeking my hand," she persisted. "You'd gain my land and the profit of my stock."

"That's a hell of a proposal, Salina."

Anger firmed her delicate features. "I wasn't proposing! I was merely suggesting the good that could come from merging our land."

"Only, I don't have the need for a cattle outfit. My business is horses. The cattle we range are for training and our own consumption. The ones your men don't steal, that is."

"By merging our ranches, there'd be nothing to steal."

Now he was getting somewhere. "So you admit your awareness of the problem?"

"You're straying from the topic of conversation."

"Which is?"

"Marriage."

This just wasn't his week. "Then let me be blunt. *I don't want a wife.* And we're getting real tired of dealing with the thieves and thugs you call a cattle crew."

She sashayed toward him in a way meant to gain a man's attention. "I think I can change your mind," she said, placing her hands against his chest, slowly sliding them up to his shoulders. He wasn't immune to her touch. He'd gone too long without the physical gratification of a woman. "Perhaps you're not comprehending the finer points of marriage?"

He comprehended just fine.

He let his hands fall against her tiny waist, noting she smelled of rose petals. Not one of his favorite scents, he decided.

"Salina," he said, leaning his head toward hers.

"Yes?"

"If your men don't learn to behave themselves, someone's gonna get killed."

She shoved him with a huff and planted her fists on her narrow hips. "You're a difficult man, Chance Morgan."

"I'm a businessman, Salina. And you are an independent, business-minded woman."

She beamed as though he'd given her a compliment. "Exactly. We're well suited."

She certainly matched him in persistence. "Perhaps," he conceded. He glanced past her toward the darkening sky. His men had already headed around back to clean up for supper. "It's getting late."

Her lips puckered in a pretty pout. "Will you think about what I said?"

Being hog-tied into marriage? He'd more than think about it—he'd surely have nightmares. But that wasn't the answer that would get her off his land.

"I will," he said, forcing a slight smile.

Her face lit up like the electric lights he'd seen down in Cheyenne. She stepped up into her buggy, seeming quite pleased. "Very well. I do hope you'll pay me a visit soon."

"I'll keep that in mind. You have a safe ride home."

Chance watched her until she disappeared over the distant rise before he started toward the house.

Holy hell. Stolen stock was one thing. Being railroaded into marriage sounded like a punishment worse than death.

Inside the house a rumble of voices echoed across the high ceiling of the dining room. A succulent aroma filled the air, something he'd missed his first time through the door. His mind hadn't gotten past the fact that Salina had been sitting in his living room. Hunger replaced the cold ache in his belly as he walked to the dining room.

He found everyone seated at the long table. Tucker at the far end with Skylar to his right, his son between them in his high chair already chewing on a crust of bread. Garret and the eight ranch hands filled in the sides of the long table. Their supper steamed from large bowls spaced across the polished surface.

Chance pulled out the chair on his end and glanced again at his crew of horse wranglers sitting at attention, every one of them so spruced up he had to wonder if it was Sunday. Seemed every man had found time to slick his hair back, or at least dunk his head in a trough.

"We invite the old preacher over for supper?" he asked as he sat down.

Tucker laughed. "I don't recall John ever getting this kind of reception."

Cora Mae. He'd been so preoccupied by Salina, he hadn't noticed her absence.

"Can't blame a man for wanting to spiff up a bit before sitting down to supper," Duce said, sitting two chairs away from Chance on his right, his shaggy, sun-dried orange hair now slicked back against his scalp.

"Spiffed up?" Mitch said from beside him. "Looks like you dumped a pint of grease on your head." The sharp edges of Mitch's thick brown mustache were clearly defined against smooth tawny skin. Seemed his horse trainer had found time to shave before supper.

"You and Salina have a nice chat?" asked Tucker.

"No." Chance glanced at the empty chair on the right. "Where's Cora Mae?"

"Finishing up with the ham," said Skylar.

"All done," Cora Mae called from the kitchen. She appeared in the doorway holding a platter laden with sliced ham.

The sudden tension in Chance's chest told him he'd missed more than the scent of food the first time he'd entered the house. With only a swath of her hair pinned up on each side, her auburn mane flowed across her shoulders and stood out against a dark-gray pinafore. He tried to convince himself she couldn't have gotten prettier in the day he'd been away from her.

There wasn't anything fancy about her drab dress, but her plain attire only drew attention to the shapely woman beneath. He couldn't pull his gaze away from the subtle sway of her hips.

Sweet mercy.

She stepped up to the empty spot beside him and leaned over to place the platter on the white tablecloth. The red, gold and copper of her hair glimmered against the lamp-light from above. What had once been carrot-orange hair had become a burst of fall colors. He didn't dare allow his gaze to drift below those lovely locks to all the curvy changes he'd rather not notice.

"Allow me, Miss Cora," Garret said, jumping up to shift the chair that was already directly behind her.

"Thank you, Garret."

The doe-eyed kid beamed as he retook his seat. The flush in Cora Mae's cheeks stole Chance's attention. She looked his way, her lips tipping with a nervous smile before she averted her gaze. Even her long lashes had an amber tinge against her pale skin.

Peaches and cream, he thought noting the light dusting of freckles across her small nose.

She's Cora Mae, he curtly reminded himself, disturbed by the sudden stir of his body. The reminder didn't do a damn thing to dampen the hard rush of attraction.

Just because she doesn't look a thing like her mama doesn't mean she hasn't been soured by her. He'd be a fool to believe she was still all sunshine and sweetness.

"Chance?"

He blinked and realized Cora Mae was holding up the platter of ham. Apparently he'd missed his brother saying grace.

"I swear I didn't poison it."

"*You* cooked supper?" he asked, taking the platter.

Her lips thinned in clear annoyance. "You needn't sound so shocked. I'm used to feeding thirty girls three times a day, as well as tending to the laundry and other household needs."

In truth, he *was* shocked. The idea of a Tindale woman actually working hadn't yet registered in his mind. "I'm surprised Skylar gave up control of her kitchen," he said as he forked a few slabs of ham onto his plate and passed it on.

"If you'd joined us for breakfast or dinner," said Skylar, "you'd know I haven't cooked a lick since Cora arrived."

Chance glanced from Cora Mae to the spread currently working its way around the table. *I'll be damned.*

"I'm glad to help out," she said. "After a month of travel, I've missed cooking."

"Running a boardinghouse with so many girls must have kept you busy," said Tucker.

"It did. Having worked in the mill for a few years, I understood how much an organized household could help with the strain of living on factory time. A twelve-hour workday is long enough without having to worry about walking home on a thirty-minute break only to discover supper wouldn't be ready before you had to walk back to the mill. The time clock didn't care if you'd eaten or slept on filthy sheets or had clean clothes in your wardrobe. But I cared. I made sure my girls were taken care of."

"Sounds like you enjoyed your job," Chance said, taking a bowl of fresh greens from her.

She smiled. Sheer pride lit her eyes. "I loved it."

The sincerity in her voice intrigued him. "So, why'd you leave?"

"Well…" Her smile collapsed, taking the spark from her eyes. "I guess…I was ready for some change."

"We're sure glad you're here," said Garret.

"We certainly are," Skylar put in. "I'm grateful for all your help. If these babies don't make an appearance soon, I may become permanently lazy."

Suddenly overwhelmed by a staggering sense of loss, Cora couldn't muster a smile. She lowered her gaze to her plate as her mind flooded with the image of Mr. Grissom's cold expression and callous gaze. Standing on the front porch of the boardinghouse, her mother's mercenary had announced his intention to take her home. It hadn't been a request. She'd been packed up and carted off—no explanation, no time to give notice or goodbyes. And for what?

To be starved into satin bonds and handed to a drunken laird as though she were nothing more than a bargaining chip in her mother's reserves.

Anger twisted through her at the memory of a closet full of beautiful gowns, all fashioned for a woman a third her size. *A welcome home gift,* her mother had called them. A gift laced with the usual ridicule and insult. A reminder of why she'd been sent away, considered unworthy of a place in society. Lord knew all her cousins fit perfectly into the Tindale debutant mold.

"Miss Cora?"

Garret smiled brightly and passed her a basket of bread. She took it but realized she'd lost her appetite as swiftly as she'd lost control of her life. She passed the bread on, telling herself she didn't need the hassle of letting out her dress seams, but it was her mother's voice she heard.

What have you done to yourself, Cora Mae? Honestly, Cora Mae, it's no wonder you are nearly thirty and unwed.

She hated the sound of her full name, knowing insults never trailed far behind it. Not that changing her name had done anything to improve her appearance.

Salina Jameson's sweetly spoken remarks resurfaced, this time grating over sensitive wounds.

What does it matter? She'd rather die a spinster than find herself at the mercy of another man.

Chance took the basket being offered to him and wondered if anyone else had noticed her hesitation to answer his question or the sadness still darkening her eyes as she stared blindly at her plate.

"You won't have time to be lazy when those girls get here," Garret was saying to Skylar.

"Why do you keep calling them girls?" demanded Tucker.

Garret shrugged while swallowing a bite of food. "Margarete is predicting girls. She said Josh'd be a boy. And he was."

"How's Zeke?" Chance asked, determined to get his focus off Cora Mae. The mention of their foreman's wife reminded him he'd forgotten to stop and check on him.

"Better," said Skylar. "Cora and I took them some

supper. Margarete has her hands full enough trying to keep Zeke in bed and off a horse."

Well into his sixties, Zeke was as tough as they came. The beating he'd endured would have taken the starch out of any man.

"It was good to see him sitting on his porch this morning," said Duce.

"He's still favoring his left leg," Garret added.

Duce shook his head and jabbed his fork into a piece of ham. "Not one of those cowards on the Lazy J poked a head out while we tore down that dam."

Not surprising. Serving himself a helping of potatoes, Chance caught a glimpse of Cora Mae's plate. The circle of porcelain was dabbed with hardly enough food to fill a sparrow. He glanced again at her downcast gaze and pale complexion.

"Are you not feeling well?" he asked in a hushed voice, leaning toward her, not wanting to draw attention from the others.

She looked up in surprise. "I feel fine," she whispered back.

"Then why aren't you eating?"

Her eyes widened. Red splotched her cheeks. "I am."

Chance glanced again at the spot of green and sliver of ham. "Cora Mae, you don't have to starve yourself to be polite. A body can't survive on a few bites of food."

"Mine can," she said, her voice barely audible.

The sad bow of her mouth sent a lash of anger through him. Every dip and curve of her sweetly shaped body was enough to drive him to distraction. He heaped a spoonful of potatoes onto her plate. *"Bullshit,"* he said, knowing her mother had likely planted such thoughts in her mind. "A few more pounds won't make you any less attractive."

A sudden silence fell over the dining room and Chance realized he hadn't kept his voice as low as he should have.

"What?" He shoved the bowl into Mitch's hands, annoyed by the shock on everyone's faces and the wave of heat rising up from his collar. "Am I out of line for stating the truth?"

"You'd have to be blind not to notice," Garret piped in.

"I've been meaning to ask," said Mitch. "Are you spoken for?"

Chance stopped short of taking a bite of greens. Cora Mae visibly stiffened.

"You're bound to have suitors," said Tucker. "Single women don't last long around these parts. If you've a mind to marry—"

"Certainly not," Cora Mae answered with a speed and sternness that put instant frowns on the men, and nearly had Chance smiling.

"I have no interest in marriage," she said, "so there's no provocation for suitors. Or courtship. Of any sort," she added, hammering a final nail into the courtship coffin.

That settled that.

"Do you have reason to leave soon?" asked Skylar.

"Well…no. But I don't intend to wear out my welcome."

"So," said Duce, "if you was to take a shine—"

"I won't marry."

Chance admired the firmness in her tone, and had to refrain from kicking his temporary foreman.

"I don't intend any insult," she said, clearly noting the glum expressions around the table, "I just…"

"She's not interested," Chance interjected. "And we

won't tolerate any pestering." His gaze pinned every man at the table. "Duce, did you finish bringing in the mustangs on the north side?"

"Not by half. We spent our morning tearing down the last of the Lazy J dam."

The rest of the conversation was a hum in Cora's ears as Chance's protective words played over in her mind. He'd been her strength for so long. Even as children, he'd taken the sting out of her mother's endless insults.

Your mama's stupid. I like your orange hair.

She stole another glance at him. Perhaps he hadn't changed so much. The blond hair reaching his collar and flipping up around his ears was darker than she remembered, his strong masculine features far more handsome than she could have imagined. Could the Chance she'd known as a child be buried somewhere beneath that rugged exterior?

His gaze caught hers. Flutters erupted low in her belly.

His brow furrowed as he looked away. Anger darkened his eyes. "Salina said *what?*"

Cora glanced at the shocked expressions around the table and realized there'd been a drastic shift in the conversation.

"That you're courting her," said Skylar. "Her words. And she was rude to Cora while making her announcement."

Chance's questioning gaze whipped toward her.

"It was nothing," Cora quickly put in. "She was obviously staking her claim on you, which is none of my business or my concern."

"Bu-shit!" Joshua slapped the tray of his high chair, capturing everyone's attention. He shoved a soggy crust of bread back into his mouth and continued to babble incoherently.

Skylar glared across the table at Chance.

"Thanks a lot, partner," he said to his nephew. "Mumble everything but the swear word."

"Much like his uncle," said Skylar.

Cora laughed into her napkin.

"You know," said Mitch, "courting Widow Jameson ain't a bad idea. You take over the Lazy J and maybe we can actually get some work done around here instead of just repairing the fencing."

"I think I'd rather take my chances with Mad Mag," said Duce, initiating a roar of laughter.

Cora leaned close to Garret. "Who's Mad Mag?"

His hazel eye winked at her. "Crazy trapper woman who lives up on the mountain."

Chance's chair scuffed across the floor as he shoved away from the table. "Excuse me," he said, tossing his napkin onto his plate. "I've lost my appetite."

Cora couldn't blame him. The thought of suffering through a forced marriage turned her stomach as well. At least Chance was aware of his situation and had his brute strength to fight off such unwanted advances.

She'd had neither the warning nor the strength.

Chapter Four

The floors swept, the chopping block oiled and every other surface polished to a shine, Cora had run out of reasons to avoid heading upstairs. Skylar had bidden her good night some time ago. Tucker and Garret had also retired for the night. She set the dishcloth beside a sparkling sink basin and started toward the darkened stairwell.

Sheer exhaustion had afforded her some sleep last night. She doubted she'd be so fortunate tonight. A sense of dread washed through her as she climbed the stairs. Since the night she'd left her mother's house, she couldn't lie in a bed without remembering the foul scent of bourbon hot on her face, waking to darkness and a great weight upon her.

We won't tolerate any pestering.

The steel in Chance's voice rang clear in her mind, easing the fear gripping her throat like a vice. She was glad to find the oil lamp already burning in her room, the warm glow spilling into the hall, as well as an odd scent. She stopped in the doorway, surprised by the large bouquet of bright flowers on the bureau.

Garret.

She couldn't fathom who else would have brought them up to her room. Shutting the door behind her, she approached the colorful cluster, unsure how to take the young man's attention. She leaned close to the tiny flowers in yellow, white, lavender and pink and breathed in their rather earthy, medicinal scent. A smile eased her tense expression.

No one had ever given her flowers. Garret had been nothing but sweet to her and couldn't be faulted for picking pretty weeds. They did brighten the room. She lifted the wildflowers from the water-filled jar and folded them into her apron. Once dried, they'd be a lovely decoration.

She knelt before her trunk at the foot of her bed, pushed it open and began sifting through her pride and joy— bundles of yarn and balls of thread in every color. When she'd fled, she'd simply shoved some dresses into her sewing trunk before lowering it out of the window. Her sole possession had given her the greatest comfort during her journey west, and had been her only escape during the month of imprisonment with her mother. Why couldn't Winifred have just left her alone?

She often wondered if her mother would have treated her differently had she not inherited her father's hair color and, presumably, his *sturdy* build. She'd never been given the name of her father, though she'd overheard enough whispers to surmise her existence was the result of her mother's failed attempt to secure a titled Scotsman.

She took some solace in knowing her father had had enough sense to outrun her mother. Just as Cora had more sense than to marry some drunken laird simply on her mother's say-so. She was finished being the martyr to her mother's past. She only wished she'd run sooner. She'd been such a fool to believe, *to hope,* her mother could feel sincere affection toward anyone. Winifred had shunned the Morgan name the moment it had been of no more use to her, just as she'd dumped her own daughter off at the textile mill, until she'd found use for her.

"It doesn't matter," she told herself, fighting the unwanted memories from her mind and the ache from her chest. She was here, making a new start. Wyoming could bring no worse a fate than her mother's betrayal.

She moved aside balls of yarn and stacks of small white flowers she'd crocheted during her travels. Once on the train west, she'd been thankful she'd shoved an armload of dresses into her sewing trunk before lowering it from her bedroom window.

Finding the lavender yarn, she quickly bound the stems. She left a long piece at the end and carried the bundle to the window where the colorful bouquet could dry in the sun.

The rod holding gingham fabric over the window was too high to reach, even on tiptoe. She pushed her sewing chest against the wall, climbed atop the curved lid, pushed back the curtains and stretched to tie the yarn around the wooden dowel. Outside, beyond the grassy lawn, the barns stood out like children's blocks against an onyx sky. A figure moved into the light of a single lantern at the end of a stable. He shut one of the wide doors.

Chance.

He wore the thick coat she'd borrowed yesterday. Tucking his hands into the deep pockets, he glanced at the house. His gaze slid up to her window as if sensing her presence. Their eyes met. White teeth flashed behind his smile.

Cora's heart bucked against her chest. Her fingers fumbled on the yarn.

Shaking his head, Chance looked away and blew out the barn lamp, cloaking himself in darkness.

Cora finished her bow and stepped down before she fell.

Good Gracious. It wasn't as though he'd caught her in the midst of a crime…so why was her heart racing?

Perhaps because he still had an alarming knack of seeing right through her. She hadn't really lied to him. In her mind, her mother was truly dead, buried with the memories of her deceit.

Too flustered to lie down, she pushed her sewing trunk back across the floor and opened the lid. She'd crocheted enough white blossoms to fill an apple orchard, figuring she could connect them later. Skylar's long dining room table came to mind. She likely had enough to make a tablecloth and a stack of doilies—perhaps some hot pads connected with green leaves.

She grabbed a stack and began spacing them across her bed, visualizing the stitching she'd use to connect them. Going back to her trunk, she found her needles and a bundle of white yarn and set to work. The scent of floral soap followed her into the room.

A murmur of voices woke Cora with a start. Still sitting up in bed, a half-finished tablecloth draped out before her, she glanced about the room in a moment's confusion.

"You take these to Margarete," Chance said from beyond her door. "I'll check the water on the stove."

The babies!

In a flash she was across the room and jerked open the door. Chance and Garret glanced over their shoulders. Garret wore striped pajamas and held a stack of white bedding. Chance's blue shirt was untucked, his feet bare.

"Are the babies coming?"

"Any minute," Chance said as he turned and hurried down the stairs.

"Sky's hurting something awful." Garret's eyes were dark with worry. "You should come. Margarete says she's close."

Cora didn't know anything about birthing babies but followed as he rushed down the hall leading to the bedrooms on the east side of the house. As she neared Skylar and Tucker's bedroom, she saw Margarete beyond the doorway, wearing a white robe, her black-and-gray hair pulled up in a thick bun at the crown of her head. She spoke in Spanish as she knelt before a settee draped in sheets at the foot of the bed where Skylar's feet were braced wide. Skylar's ragged breathing echoed from the room, and a rush of nerves nettled beneath Cora's skin.

She hesitated a moment, before stepping into the room behind Garret. Tucker sat on his knees in the middle of the big bed, helping to support his wife as she gasped for breath, her long hair and white gown drenched with sweat.

"Here's the clean linen." Garret dropped the stack on the floor beside Margarete. "Cora's here to help," he said before bolting from the room.

"Almost there," Margarete said, her focus on Skylar.

Skylar curled forward, groaning and gritting her teeth through the pain.

"Doin' good, angel," Tucker soothed, though his expression was tight with fear. She fell back against him and a shrill cry filled the room.

Cora stared in sheer fascination at the purple, glistening life in Margarete's steady hands.

"A girl," the woman said.

"A girl?" Tucker repeated.

Numb with shock, Cora glanced toward the bed. Still racked with the pain of childbirth, Skylar continued to breathe hard, her eyes pinched tight.

"*Rápido,* take the baby." Margarete looked directly at Cora. "*Vámonos!*"

Cora stared at the wailing infant and the knotted cord protruding from its tiny belly. A hard rush of fear kept her rooted in place.

"I've got her," Chance said, stepping in front of Cora. He knelt beside the old woman and wrapped the baby in a white blanket. "Sky, which color ribbon?"

"Green," Skylar said in a pant. She opened her eyes, a smile touching her lips as she looked at her daughter. "For Emily."

The name of Chance and Tucker's mother. Tears stung Cora's eyes.

"I'll have you bundled and warm in just a moment," Chance murmured to the squealing baby as he carried her past Cora to a chest of drawers. Water steamed from a bowl beside a stack of fresh cloths. Chance placed his niece on a bed of blankets and unwrapped her. Emily's bleating cry increased as he dunked a rag into the water and began to wash her face before bathing her thin little limbs.

Cora moved closer, watching Emily's skin flush to a soft pink beneath Chance's gentle strokes, his hands appearing so big on such a little infant. He shook out another cloth and swaddled her bottom in a diaper with amazing precision and finesse.

"You've done this before."

"I watched Margarete when Josh was born and caught on quick enough. I couldn't expect Skylar to go back to working with the horses if I wasn't willing to do my share of diapering."

The thought of Chance playing the role of nursemaid brought a smile to her lips. He worked Emily's little body into a gown with impossible ease. He pulled the soft white cotton down over her tiny pink feet and cinched the green ribbon threaded through the bottom. Finished, his big hand scooped up his tiny niece. The moment he cradled her close, Emily's cry subsided. She nuzzled into him and drew a shuddered breath.

"There, now," he said, smiling down at the wide contented blue eyes staring up at him. "Spread out that thick blanket," he said to Cora, nodding toward the folded stack at the end of the dresser.

Cora rushed forward and did as he asked.

A second baby squealed behind them.

"Pretty as her sister," said Margarete.

Chance stepped forward, rolling the bundled baby toward Cora's bosom, at the same time positioning her arms around Emily's tiny body.

"Got her?" he asked, his hands still holding her arms in place.

The most precious blue eyes blinked up at her. Cora swallowed her fear and nervousness and gave a firm nod.

A baby.

She didn't know why the sweet bundle in her arms came as such a shock. But it did. She'd never seen anything so perfect and sweet.

Chance walked by her with Emily's sister, saying, "Yellow for Grace."

Cora stood beside him as he repeated the bathing process. Grace didn't complain as her sister had, but watched her uncle with wide curious eyes as he rinsed her tiny blond curls and cleaned between all of her tiny fingers and toes.

"She likes her bath."

"She must take after her mama," Tucker said from behind them.

Cora turned to see Tucker stacking pillows against the headboard as he and Margarete helped Skylar into bed. Skylar leaned back, her usual tanned complexion frightfully pale against the mountain of white softness. "I want to see my girls," she said, looking at Cora.

Tucker sat beside her and looked expectantly at Cora.

Carefully walking to the bed, she passed Emily to her father. His hand supported her head, the rest of her fitting in his other large palm.

"She's so tiny," he said, easing back and leaning toward Skylar so she could see their daughter.

"Seven pounds," said Margarete. "Big for two." She picked up a tin pail filled with bloodied linens from the end of the bed and started for the door. "I will bring the linens back *por la mañana. Buenas noches.*"

"*Gracias,* Margarete," Tucker said, looking up from his daughter.

"Don't thank me. Was your wife who did all the work."

He slid closer to Skylar and placed their daughter in her arms. "You done good," he said, pressing his lips to Skylar's sweat-dampened hair.

"Come get me if she takes to a fever or starts feeling ill."

"Will do," Tucker said, his eyes on Grace as Chance tucked her into Skylar's arms beside Emily.

"How are you holding up, little brother?" Chance asked, glancing at his twin.

Tucker shook his head, his eyes bright with tears. "They sure are pretty."

"Everything okay?" Garret stood in the doorway.

"Want to see your nieces?" Skylar asked, her tired voice barely carrying across the room.

"Do I ever." He rushed over and crowded in beside Chance.

Cora stepped back and was instantly moved by the scene they created, a circle of family, the warmth and love shared between them nearly tangible. Emotion stole her breath. Tears stung her eyes. Not wanting to intrude on their moment, she slipped quietly from the room.

She hurried down the stairs to the great room, trying to stop the delayed rush of nerves. But it came nonetheless, in sharp gasps and scalding tears. She stopped in a patch of moonlight streaming through the front windows and clamped a trembling hand over her mouth.

"Cora Mae?" Chance's hand closed over her shoulder.

She tried to turn away from him, unable to stop the overwhelming wave of emotion.

"It's all right," he said, taking her into his arms. His embrace shocked her, but she didn't pull away, accepting his comfort, the heat of his body helping to calm her shivers. His chin touched the top of her head as he hugged her close. The feel of his breath against her ear steeled her spine. His strong arms pulled tighter, and suddenly his closeness was intolerable.

Chance seemed to sense the change in her and released his hold. He stepped back and stuffed his hands into his pant pockets, and her fear quelled as quickly as it had risen. Moonlight gilded his hair. His lips bore the hint of a smile, his expression revealing what she'd hoped to see in him since she'd arrived. Warmth.

"An incredible night, huh?"

She nodded and rubbed her hands over her damp cheeks. "I've never witnessed anything so wondrous, or *frightening*."

"I can't disagree with you." He pressed his hand to the small of her back and guided her to the kitchen.

Cora forced herself to relax at his touch.

"My breath didn't come easy until I saw both those babies tucked in their mama's arms," he said, pulling a chair out for her at the kitchen table.

"Really?"

He struck a match, his incredulous expression clear in the glow of the flame. "I guess you didn't notice me and Garret quaking in our boots?" He lit the table lamp, spreading the warm light across the room before he walked into the pantry.

She'd seen Garret's fear, and Tucker's, but Chance had seemed as calm as ever. He came back to the table with a corked bottle and two glasses. Cora tensed, certain the bottle contained some sort of liquor.

"Tension has been riding our spines since the moment we knew she was carrying two babies." He set a glass in front of each of them, then uncorked the bottle.

"I can imagine," Cora said, well aware that their mother had died giving birth to them, and wondering if such thoughts often drove Chance to drink. Fear and disappointment warred over the possible answer. "It must have been frightful."

"It was damn terrifying is what it was."

Chance rolled his shoulders against the tension still

pinching his spine. He hadn't just been afraid for his sister-in-law. Losing Skylar would have destroyed his brother, just as their mother's death had killed part of their father. It just wasn't safe to let a woman have such control over a man's life.

He reached out and poured a couple of inches of whiskey into each glass. "This will help to settle your nerves."

He nudged the second glass toward Cora Mae. She sat straight as a fence post, her wide gaze locked on the small glass.

"I don't drink spirits."

"Neither do I." He grimaced as he picked up the shot of whiskey. "A toast to the prettiest little girls to ever grace God's earth." He clicked his glass against the one sitting in front of Cora Mae, closed his mind to memories of the past, and sent the flaming liquid down his throat.

"I hate the stuff," he said, chasing the burn and bitter taste with a deep breath. "But my nerves need some fast soothing."

He slid Cora Mae's glass closer. "Your turn."

Eyes already the size of saucers drew even wider and he couldn't help but smile.

"Go on," he urged. "Give a toast and toss it back."

"It will help?"

"Would I lie to you?"

"Hmm?" She pinned him with a narrowed gaze. "Let me think… *'Just jump in, Cora Mae, it's only knee-deep.'*"

The image of orange braids and pink bows slipping beneath the surface of the pond flashed in Chance's mind. His laughter was instant. "We did teach you how to swim that summer."

"After you nearly drowned me!"

"You won't drown in that shot of whiskey."

"Whiskey?" Cora picked up the glass and took a strong sniff. The scent didn't seem entirely repugnant, in fact, it smelled strangely sweet.

"You were hoping for something else?"

Chance's teasing grin was far too charming. She laughed and shook her head. "I can assure you I've never consumed liquor of any sort. How fitting that the first time should be with you."

His smile widened. "Should I *dare* you, for old-time's sake?"

She laughed again, thinking his shot of whiskey must have worked. He certainly seemed relaxed, reclined in his chair, a smile on his lips.

"Oh, very well." She sighed and raised her glass.

"Don't forget to toast," he said, amusement shining in his eyes.

This was the side of him she had desperately missed, sweet yet utterly mischievous.

"To Grace and Emily," she said mockingly, certain drinking whiskey in the name of their infant nieces made it nonetheless improper. With a last uncertain look at the alarmingly pleasant man beside her, she swallowed the golden liquid, which burned its way down her throat like molten molasses.

"See? Not so bad."

"Not bad?" she wheezed, then coughed as tears rushed to her eyes.

"You always were gullible," he said with a chuckle.

"I was never gullible. I simply *trusted* you." She licked a coating of surprisingly sweet vapor from her lips.

"Want another?"

"Certainly not!"

"You catch on fast enough. And from what I recall, you got even with us on several occasions."

"I wouldn't have been much of a little sister if I couldn't best you some of the time."

Chance folded his arms on the table as his mind filled with memories of running through the woods, water splashing over moonlight, Cora Mae's wild giggles. "Sometimes I need reminding that the past wasn't all bad."

"You and Tucker were the brightest spot in my child-hood."

The sadness reflected in her eyes hinted of her life after he'd left, of a promise he'd failed to keep. He wanted to see a harmless little girl with orange braids when he looked at her. Instead he saw the loose auburn curls and cautious brown eyes of an attractive woman whose sweet smile made his mouth go dry.

"I must admit," she said, "you're a tad frightening as an adult."

"Am I?"

"You do like to intimidate."

He eased back in his chair and shrugged, not about to deny the fact. "If you don't push in this world, you get pushed."

"Quite right," she said softly. "Another lesson I could have learned from my stepbrothers."

Seemed to him she'd already mastered the technique. She pushed him on too many levels. He knew better than to trust her, he didn't want to like her, yet he was all too tempted to press his mouth to hers and find out if she tasted as sweet as she looked.

Footsteps coming from the dining room brought him back to his senses. They both looked up as Tucker walked into the kitchen.

"Everything okay?" asked Chance.

His brother's smile was so wide it appeared he might burst with pride at any moment. "Everything's great. Skylar's hungry."

"I'll fix her a plate." Cora Mae surged up, swayed and quickly grabbed the table to steady herself. She blinked hard before casting an accusing glare at him.

What? he silently mouthed, feigning a look of innocence. He hadn't told her there *wouldn't* be side effects. He chuckled silently, watching her take slow cautious steps toward the pantry.

"Since when do you drink whiskey?" asked Tucker, his twisted expression targeting the table.

"We gotta watch Cora Mae," he said in a loud whisper, "she likes to tip the bottle."

"I do not!" she called out from the shadows.

He and Tuck grinned at each other, and Chance recalled just how good it felt to tease her. "We were toasting our new nieces," he said. "Emily and Grace tucked in okay?"

"Snuggled up to their mama. They're beautiful, aren't they?"

"Prettiest little girls I've ever seen," Chance agreed. "That's quite a family you've got."

"Girls," Tuck said, shaking his head. "What am I going to do with two girls?"

"If they're anything like their mother, you and Josh had better rest up now. They'll be roping and riding circles around y'all in no time."

"I'm sure glad it's over and everybody's healthy."

Tucker sucked in a deep breath and slowly released it. "Skylar's amazing, isn't she?"

Chance smiled, fully enjoying his brother's elation. "She is. You'd better take her that food before she hauls those babies down here to get it herself."

Cora stepped beside him and held out a plate and a glass of water.

"Thanks," Tucker said. "For everything."

She smiled. "You're welcome."

"Good night."

Chance took the bottle back to the pantry and set their glasses in the sink. Cora waited for him at the base of the stairs.

"Feel better?" he asked.

"Yes. Thank you." She laid her hands against his chest and leaned up to kiss his cheek. "Good night, Chance."

Chance didn't answer. He couldn't. He stood motionless, listening to her rapid footsteps as she ascended the stairs and the sporadic beat of his pulse. Her sweet scent lingered in the air.

Her actions hadn't been flirtatious. He'd seen nothing but warmth and kindness in her gaze as she'd pressed her lips to his skin, the touch as light and fleeting as a butterfly's. So why had he been hit by the wild urge to capture her mouth with his?

He wasn't a man controlled by lust. He damn sure wasn't a man who could be manipulated by a Tindale.

Chapter Five

Chance woke to the pleasing scent of fresh biscuits and sizzling bacon; his body was fully aroused by the lingering image of soft warm curves, long auburn curls and a white nightdress falling to the floor.

Damnation.

He sat upright in a tangle of sheets, shifting his feet to the cold floor in the same motion.

He couldn't get away from her. Not even in his sleep!

Sunlight cast shadows across his room, telling him he'd overslept. The men in the bunkhouse would be through with morning chores and likely finished with breakfast by now. Shoving his covers aside, he stood and walked to his bureau. The cool morning air on his skin did little to douse the fire simmering in his blood. He lifted a pitcher of water, filled the basin and dunked his hands, washing away the feel of white cotton slipping from his fingers as he splashed his face.

What was his problem? It wasn't as if he'd even seen her in a nightdress! She'd been fully clothed last night. Which struck him as odd, now that he thought about it. At nearly two in the morning, everyone else had been in their nightclothes—except him. Surely she didn't sleep in the buff.

Drying his face, he pinched his eyes shut, fighting the image from his mind.

Just stop thinking about her!

Fifteen minutes later he was dressed and shaved. As he neared the base of the stairs, he paused, his gaze landing on five feet of curves and curls standing before the stove. Cora Mae hummed softly as she whisked the contents of a bowl nuzzled against her chest. Sunlight glittered like embers against the wild wisps of hair cascading down her back, the thick mass twisted into a knot at the nape of her neck.

A baby's sharp cry carried through the house from upstairs, along with the murmur of voices.

Realizing he was huddled on the stairwell, Chance bit back a curse and continued down. The strong scent of coffee beckoned him toward the stove. A plate of crispy bacon and a basket piled with warm biscuits sat on a table set for four. Joshua's highchair had been brought in from the dining room. She'd been busy.

The contents of her bowl met a hot skillet with a hiss. Focused on what she was doing, she didn't notice him as he reclined against the table behind her.

She wore another plain dress with puffy long sleeves—today's a charcoal gray. A white apron defined the curve of her waist, the strings tied in a perfect bow against the small of her back. Wide ruffles capped her shoulders. Everything about her was crisp and proper, just as she'd come to him in his dream, draped in white from her chin to her toes.

His body tensed. *She has to go.*

She wasn't just an attractive woman, she was Cora Mae.

Her big brown eyes still had a way of burrowing beneath his defenses, making him feel more than he wanted to, more than he should.

She turned and jumped, those cinnamon eyes flaring wide at the sight of him standing just a few feet behind her. "Goodness!" She pressed a hand to the generous swell of her bosom.

"Morning," he said, realizing he probably should have given a greeting long before now.

"How can someone as big as you creep about like a church mouse?"

"Boots are at the back door," he said, and watched her gaze drop to his stocking-covered feet. A smile eased her expression, and he found himself irritated all over again and wondering why she was here, in his kitchen, making him think about such foolish things as her sleeping attire.

"How long do you intend to be here?"

Her slender eyebrows shot up. "Ah…um, a couple of weeks perhaps?"

"So you have somewhere else to go."

Her back stiffened, her expression pinched as though he'd insulted her. It wasn't as if he'd told her to leave; he just wanted some reassurance that she would, eventually.

"I'm wondering what your plans are," he said. "You came west intending to stay, didn't you? Or is this just a holiday from your boardinghouse job back east."

"I intend to stay. I'll settle wherever I find work."

"I suppose you prefer the comforts of city life?"

"I prefer to live around people who appreciate me." She turned her attention back to the stove. "Should that be in the city, the country or the middle of nowhere, it matters not. I'm quite adaptable and hardly hapless."

"Yet you traveled clear across the country and seem to have forgotten to pack your nightclothes."

She whipped back around. "I beg your pardon?"

"A nightdress," he said, figuring it was too late to take back his observation. "It was nearly two in the morning when you popped out of your room, fully clothed."

Her fisted hands landed on her hips. "What about you?" she demanded.

"Me?"

"As you said, it was two in the morning and you weren't wearing pajamas."

"I don't own any."

A single amber eyebrow arched in clear challenge. "Well, neither do I."

Chance's mind instantly filled with the image of Cora Mae wearing nothing but bed linens, then nothing at all.

Good God.

He turned away from her and headed for the door. "Tell Tuck I'll be starting on the south side," he said, his voice sounding hoarse.

"Don't you want breakfast?" she called after him.

The slamming door was his only answer, sending a surge of disappointment resounding through Cora. She had hoped they'd made amends last night, but it seemed his good mood had been a temporary state.

She turned back to the stove and dug a spoon into the mixture of eggs bubbling in the skillet, struggling with a strange combination of frustration and flutters. The man could certainly fill a room. Crisp and clean shaven, he'd been a sight in his tousled hair and stocking feet. And a complete bully the moment he'd opened his mouth. What should he care if she slept in her day clothes?

She'd left her nightdress in a heap on the floor in her mother's house and didn't care if she ever wore another, for all the protection it had afforded her. She'd just as soon sleep in boots and men's britches. None of which was any of Chance's business!

"An' Cora! An' Cora!"

Joshua raced into the kitchen bouncing with energy. Cora's heart warmed at her new title. She'd never been an aunt before.

"Good morning, Joshua."

"I hold da babies!"

"You did?"

Tucker strode in behind his son, his smile wide. "He's a little excited about his sisters."

"How's Skylar?"

"Up and around," he said as he lifted Joshua into his high chair, "and trying to figure out how to handle two hungry babies at once. Emily has proven to be the impatient one. Garret will be down in a minute. He was keeping Grace occupied." He glanced at the set table. "I'm surprised Chance isn't down by now."

"He was. He said to tell you he's starting on the south side."

"Figures." Chuckling, he placed a biscuit on Joshua's tray. "Salina Jameson's place borders the northeast end of our valley."

The thought of Chance avoiding the seductive widow brought a smile to her lips. "Do you really own the whole valley?"

"Damn near. Jameson's land meshes with ours on the northeast side through a maze of canyons. They feed into some lowland meadows before opening up to the plains.

I'm hoping our missing stock is tucked into those canyons and not lost in that ocean of wide-open range."

Cora wrapped a dishtowel around the skillet handle and carried the scrambled eggs to the table. "Salina Jameson is stealing horses from you?"

"The crew of the Lazy J, to be sure. We didn't raise a stink when it was just a few mavericks here and there. Since old man Jameson died, rustling has become a real problem with horses and lately our steers. It makes no sense. We're not cattlemen. We don't keep a large herd, just enough for food and training the horses. Six months back we took to using barb wire, which caused a commotion all over the countryside. Not that it made much difference with the Lazy J, them being so skilled with wire cutters and all."

"Can't you just go take your stock back?"

"If we could find 'em. Those canyons have more twists and turns than a labyrinth. Right now we can't spare the time or the manpower. But once we fill the military's spring contract, we'll be looking to round up those mavericks for the rest of our outfitters."

"Aren't there sheriffs or marshals you could call upon to help enforce the law?"

"Not unless there's a body count."

Cora's eyes popped wide as she sat across from him. "Body count?"

"Out here, you either have the muscle to protect what's yours or you hire someone who does. For now, the rowdy bunch on the Lazy J is a serious annoyance. They're working their way to becoming a true hazard. One more stunt like stealing our water or jumping my men and they'll be finding themselves on the receiving end of our marshal law. That's a fact."

The glittering clarity in Tucker's green eyes didn't leave Cora with any doubt about his ability to protect what was his.

Garret walked into the kitchen with his jacket tucked under his arm. "Good morning, Miss Cora. You sure look pretty today."

"Thank you," she said, his compliment taking her by surprise, yet it was Garret's cheeks that flushed as he looked away, the bright tinge topping his ears.

He ruffled Joshua's white ringlets and sat beside him. "Chance down yet?"

Tucker reached across the table for the skillet of eggs. "He's already headed out to the south end. Guess he's in a hurry."

Garret's smile collapsed. He stood and shrugged on his jacket. "If he gets in a mood he won't be fit to work with." He grabbed a fistful of biscuits and snatched up some bacon. "See you at suppertime, Miss Cora," he said before rushing out the backdoor.

"Suppertime? Won't they be in at noon?" she said to Tucker.

"Not for the next few days." He spooned some eggs onto a plate for his son. Joshua grabbed a fluffy handful. "Mama likes you to use your fork."

Joshua shoved the fistful into his mouth, then obediently picked up his fork, grinning at his father as he chewed.

Tucker smiled and glanced back at Cora. "All but two hands will be riding out to drive in our free-range stock. It's too far out to make it back at noon. We'll be looking forward to supper all the more." He stood and moved around the table.

"Are you rushing off, as well?"

"I'm just getting the coffee." He picked up a towel and lifted the pot from the stove. "It'll take more than Chance's dark moods to keep me from having breakfast with my boy, ain't that right?" he said to Joshua.

Joshua held up his loaded fork. "Eggs, Papa!"

"We'll take some up to Mama when we're done." Tucker poured himself a cup of coffee and one for Cora, then dug in to his breakfast.

How strange, she thought while sipping her coffee. She had always pegged Chance as the considerate one.

He could be, she thought, thinking of his big hands handling his little niece with such gentleness, the same hands that had comforted her when she'd lost her composure last night. She hadn't seen a trace of that warmth this morning.

Push or be pushed.

She'd definitely been pushed.

Two-year-olds were a breed unto themselves, Cora decided after a day of keeping up with her young helper. A whirlwind of constant chatter and motion, Joshua had been by her side all day, counting out clothespins and berries and dishes in between running up and down the stairs to see his sisters. Though she couldn't always understand what he said, his animated expressions and wide smiles kept her laughing all afternoon.

By three o'clock the wash was put away, supper was simmering and pies were cooling. Cora had brought her sewing basket downstairs to finish the tablecloth for Skylar while Josh dumped out a box of blocks. One moment he'd been stacking wooden shapes and talking about barns, the next he was laid out on the rug, sound asleep with a block in each hand.

Finished with Skylar's tablecloth, Cora glanced at the little boy now curled up on the sofa beside her, his thumb tucked into his mouth. All in all, it had been a pleasant day.

She reached for the sewing basket on the floor and withdrew her knitting needles and a ball of blue yarn, which she perceived as one of Skylar's favorite colors judging by what she'd seen of her wardrobe. She placed the white tablecloth in the basket, then set her needles to work.

"I thought he must have passed out."

A deep-blue skirt swayed at the top of the staircase.

"*Skylar,*" she said, watching her slow descent. She was surprised to see her fully clothed. The fitted blue dress revealed Skylar's long, slender figure. Her blond hair hung over one shoulder in a thick, damp braid. A floral scent followed her into the room. Their home boasted some luxuries such as a room for bathing, both upstairs and down.

"What are you doing down here?"

"The house was far too quiet. I wanted to check on Josh. Now that I've had a bath and can finally see my feet again, I'm anxious to be up and about." She stepped up to the chair beside Cora and grimaced as she eased onto the cushion.

"Are you sure you should even be out of bed?"

"I'm not ready to leap into a saddle, but I'm tired of being cooped up in that room. I hope Joshua wasn't too much trouble today."

"Not at all. He keeps himself quite busy. He certainly loves to count."

Skylar smiled. "He gets that from Chance, I think."

"Really?"

"Chance can tally numbers in his head like nothing I've ever seen. Whether we're calculating poundage, shipping costs, feed conversion or a combination of all three, he can have the total in a blink. He's quite handy to have around. So are you. Do I smell berry pie?"

"Yes."

"I can't thank you enough. I was up and cooking the morning after Joshua was born, and back on a horse in a week. Having two babies is quite an adjustment."

Cora recalled Chance's comment about Skylar working with the horses. She couldn't imagine running such a large household and working the ranch as well. "You really do work outside with the men?"

"I help with training, but not so much anymore. With three little ones, they'll have to get on without me."

"Will Tucker expect you to continue?"

"With the horses, no. Chance will likely be disappointed," she said with a laugh. "Mitch was hired to take my place, but I start to miss my bullwhip at times. I don't mind going out once in a while to teach them all a new trick or two. Got to keep those men on their toes."

Cora gathered Skylar had no trouble in doing so.

"What are you doing?" Skylar asked, her gazed fixed on the knitting needles.

"Knitting some hot pads. I thought they'd be useful in the kitchen."

Surprise lit Skylar's face. "How nice." She glanced at the basket on the floor between them and leaned down to brush her fingers over the white tablecloth. "Did you make this, as well?"

"Yes. For you."

Skylar glanced up from the crocheted flowers. "For me?"

Cora lifted the cloth from the basket and held it out to her. "For you."

Skylar took it, draping the soft fabric over her skirt.

"I thought it might make a nice tablecloth."

"Oh, Cora." Her eyes hazed with tears. "It's beautiful." She brushed her hands over the raised flowers. "My goodness. You *made* this?"

"It's the least I could do, when you've opened your home and really made me feel welcome."

"There must be a hundred little flowers here," Skylar said, inspecting each one.

Pleased by her enthusiasm, Cora smiled down at her lap and tucked her needle beneath the next blue stitch and started another row. "I crocheted the blossoms during my travels. The coaches can be rather confining, so I was limited on space."

"Crocheted?"

The question in Skylar's voice surprised her. "A little different from knitting. Simpler, in fact. Once I get the rhythm down of the design, they go rather quickly."

"My goodness, that's because your fingers are a blur of motion."

Cora stilled her hands. A flush warmed her cheeks. "If I'm idle for more than a minute, I'm usually pulling out my crochet hook or knitting needles." She rubbed her thumb over the impression her needles had pressed into her index fingers over time, an imperfection her mother had noticed right off. "Mother thought it a nasty habit."

"I should think it rather useful."

"It has been useful," she admitted, smiling at a woman she liked more with every passing moment. "I sold a steady supply of sweaters and such while running the boarding-house, which is how I paid for my trip out here."

"I don't know much about sewing and rather wish I did. Do you think I could learn?"

"Of course."

"You'd show me how?"

"I'd love to. I have an extra hook and needles in my trunk upstairs."

Skylar pushed to her feet, and Cora realized she meant *now*.

Yes, she definitely liked this woman. They were up the stairs in a flash, kneeling before her open trunk. Skylar's eyes drew wide at the colorful display of yarn.

"Cora!"

"Well, you have to have yarn if you're going to knit."

"You must have every color," she said, sifting through them.

"Quite a few. Some fabrics as well."

"Margarete made our curtains and such. Now that I'm housebound, I'd like to do more. The depot will be getting a shipment of fabrics come the first of the month. I'd like some fancier window coverings and perhaps some pretty pillows." She lifted a small stack of white doilies from the trunk. "My mother used to have these."

"Doilies."

"Doilies," Skylar repeated, a smile on her lips.

"They're easy to crochet. We could start with those."

"I'd like that."

"I have a window swag in here I'd made for the board-inghouse." Cora tugged the pink taffeta from beneath a pile of yarn. "If you like it, the width is similar to the window in your front room."

Skylar ran her fingers over the smooth swirls of pink then drew her hand back. "You don't have to. You've already done so much."

"I don't have any use for it. If you don't like the fabric

for your window, perhaps you could use it for dresses for the girls."

Skylar bit her lip and glanced back at the lace-trimmed swag. Her blue eyes sparked with excitement as she stood with the swag and a ball of yarn for the doilies.

"Let's try it over the window."

He hadn't been comfortable in the saddle all day!

She'd done it on purpose, filling his mind with images of her smooth skin wrapped in nothing but cool sheets, when he needed to be focused on rowdy stallions.

Chance walked from the stable in the front yard, the night closing in around him. He stomped up the front steps, not looking forward to being in Cora Mae's presence. He didn't have to go further than opening the front door. One look at the parlor, a quick glance into the great room and he felt the full presence of a *Tindale*.

He pushed the door shut behind him, his gaze landing on the lacy white rag covering the small table beside the door. More were draped over the back of the sofa and the arms of the chairs.

He scrubbed a hand over his stubbled jaw, the muscles bunching in his back. This was how it started, covering the house in their fancy eastern frippery, slowly infiltrating until the house was coated in satin and echoed of nothing but bawling women and more misery than a kid knew what to do with.

He wasn't having it. He snatched up the lacy ovals and rectangles, crushing them into a wad.

This was his house. He'd built most of it with his own two hands. They didn't need her expensive eastern frills littering up the place!

His gaze landed on shiny pink fabric ballooning out from the top of the front window. Memories of pink satin wallpaper flashed in his mind, along with swags of lace and dried dogwood smothering the warm wood textures that had once been his home.

He wasn't about to be crowded out of his house by another Tindale. He lifted the rod and shook off the satiny sleeve. Wrapping the fancy swag around the pile of useless rags, he stormed up the staircase, cutting a fast route to the back of the house. She could save her lacy do-dads for the next victim.

Reaching her room, he swung the door open.

Cora Mae spun around as the door banged against the wall. She stood beyond the bed, clutching the unbuttoned bodice of her dress. "Chance!"

He'd assumed she'd be in the kitchen. Reminding himself of why he'd opened her door in the first place, he strode to the bed. She wasn't so different from her mother, bringing fancy frills and lies into his house. He dropped the pile of useless decorations.

Cora Mae sucked in a breath. Her mouth dropped open.

"I believe you misplaced a few of your things around *my* house."

He turned and slammed the door shut on his way out. She needed to get out of his home and *out of his mind*.

After washing up in the basin in his bedroom, he headed for the stairs. Cora Mae hadn't come out of her room.

He wouldn't be swayed by any Tindale pouting. He didn't care if she stayed in there all night.

Out of sight, out of mind.

As he reached the kitchen, the men were just starting to file into the dining room. He was glad to see his sister-in-law sitting at the table, looking fresh as ever.

"Isn't it lovely?" she was saying as Tucker sat beside her.

Chance spotted the web of white stretched across the table, and froze.

Holy hell.

"She crocheted all of those little flowers during her trip out here. Can you imagine?"

Every man at the table looked closer at the white weave beneath all the dishes, murmuring their amazement.

An intense heat began to creep its way up Chance's collar as he walked to the table and slumped into his chair. The cloth of connected flowers brushed his pant leg.

She'd made it? He never would have guessed.

"Cora knits, too," Skylar announced. "You should see her work the needles. She's promised to teach me. She showed me how to work the crochet hook this afternoon."

"How 'bout that," Tucker said, clearly pleased by his wife's excitement over the new craft.

"I finished a doily. Nothing fancy, but it's pretty."

Tucker drew her hand to his lips. "I want to see it."

Skylar flushed with pleasure. "We put it on the table just inside the parlor."

Oh hell.

Garret reclined back in his chair to have a look. "Table looks bare from here."

Skylar stood up to peer into the front room, and the muscles in Chance's neck knotted up.

Damnation. The thought of Skylar having had a hand in decorating the front room had never crossed his mind.

"Well, that's odd."

Cora Mae walked in from the kitchen, the bodice of her dress now buttoned up to her chin, her hands clamping bright-blue hot pads over the handles of the large stew pot.

"Cora," said Skylar, "did you move the doilies we worked on today?"

The heavy pot *thunked* onto the table. "You'll have to ask Chance." She dropped into the chair beside him. "This is *his* house."

He felt everyone's gaze shift in his direction. Cora Mae folded her hands in her lap, her downcast eyes trained on the bowl in front of her.

The heat beneath his collar rapidly climbed his neck.

"Chance?"

Skylar's voice felt like a whip crack through the heavy silence. He couldn't even look at her.

"I, uh…moved 'em."

"Why?"

"Well…I, um…" What could he say without looking like a complete ass? Skylar wouldn't be pleased to discover just how rude he'd been to her new best friend. He glanced across the table at his brother, hoping Tucker would bail him out.

"Stew's getting cold and I'm starving," Tucker said, obviously taking note of his desperate situation. "Chance can enlighten us on his decorating expertise after supper."

The hard look in his twin's eyes was anything but understanding as he folded his hands and bowed his head, cutting off the opportunity of further comments.

"Lord, we thank you for this bounty, for blessing us with a healthy family and hardworking crew. We thank you for bringing Cora Mae back into our lives, *which has pleased my wife no end*. Help us, Lord, as we struggle with tolerance and humility, and give us the wisdom to choose our battles wisely, so that we may continue to earn your grace. Amen."

Having been one of the longest prayers Tucker had ever given, Chance heard the message loud and clear.

"Garret, why don't you start serving stew and we'll pass the bowls around," Tucker suggested.

The kid stood, filled his bowl, passed it to Cora Mae and took her empty one. Without glancing up, she swapped the stew for Chance's empty bowl as others passed in theirs.

"So far the numbers look fairly good on the north end," Tucker said, taking control of the conversation. "How about the south?"

"So far so good," said Garret. "Huh, Chance?"

"Yeah." He took a basket of bread from Mitch. As he held it out to Cora Mae, his gaze focused on her hands. They weren't the delicate hands of a pampered woman. Her skin looked smooth as cream, yet showed signs of use, her short nails worked back to the quick and a callous on the inside of her thumb.

As if sensing his gaze, she curled her fingers into her palms.

A soft cry sounded from upstairs.

"I'll get her." Cora Mae surged up from her seat.

Chance was already standing. Their gazes locked and he noted the red rimming her eyes.

Oh, hell. He'd made her cry.

Remembering the only time he'd seen Cora Mae cry, a familiar surge of regret twisted through him.

"Why don't you both go?" suggested Tucker.

"No." Eyes as dry and cold as a glacier glared up at him. "I'll go."

She turned away.

Chance did about the only thing he could—he sat down and ate his meal.

Chapter Six

For the first time in the past week, the afternoon wind had died down to a mild breeze. Cora knelt to pick another yellow squash. Hoisting a full basket into her arms, she walked along the uniform rows of a lush garden she could only dream of having. The neat greens and herbs ran the entire length of the side of the house, bursting with a harvest that could keep her and Skylar busy with pickling and preserving. She pushed open the white gate, an ache squeezing her heart as she glanced past the ranch buildings nestled amongst green hills, hugged by the surrounding mountains.

It didn't matter how much she loved it here, Chance wouldn't let her stay. The past few days of pleasantries with Skylar and the others hadn't taken the sting out of Chance's blatant rejection. He couldn't have made his feelings plainer if he had packed her up and dumped her at the stage line.

When he charged into her room, his eyes revealed what his days of silence had hidden—an abhorrence of *anything* Tindale. She understood his hatred of her mother, but what had she done to earn such resentment? She'd done everything she could to distance herself from Winifred.

It wasn't fair! She only wanted to have a life free of her mother's cruelty, but still she haunted her.

"Afternoon, Miss Tindale."

Cora jumped, her gaze snapping toward a grove of fruit trees beside the garden.

Wyatt stepped forward. Sunlight separated his dark duster from the shaded grove. "How nice to see you again," he said, pulling off his hat. The light breeze caught the ends of his curly black hair. "And on such a nice afternoon."

She wondered how he came to be standing beside the garden fence, appearing casual and relaxed. She couldn't see any sign of a horse in the ripple of hills and trees stretching out behind him.

"Mr. McNealy." She glanced over her shoulder, searching for anyone standing about the yard. Wyatt's slow grin suggested he already knew they were alone. Gooseflesh rippled across her skin.

"You needn't be alarmed."

After all she'd learned about him, stealing from her stepbrothers, attacking poor Zeke, her wariness of him was a warranted reaction. And if he hadn't meant to alarm her, he wouldn't have sneaked up on her while avoiding the attention of the ranch hands.

"If you're looking for Tucker or—"

"I'd prefer not to leave here with my teeth in my hands, thank you. I figure you can relay my message." He held up a small leather pouch. "Payment for the colt Chance delivered. Can't have any ill will getting in between Chance and Salina, with her trying to snare him into courtship and all."

The very idea wedged in Cora's mind like a bur.

"Don't suppose you have any objections to such a union?" he asked. "Do you have plans to claim a Morgan for yourself?"

"Certainly not," she said, startled by his question and realizing she had bristled up at the mention of Chance courting Salina. "Chance's personal matters are none of my concern."

"Hmm." Wyatt nodded, seeming to mull that over. "I suppose I should feel the same way. Can't blame a cowboy for dreamin'." The sadness in his smile added to the chill washing through Cora.

"You have a nice afternoon, Miss Tindale." He tossed the leather pouch into the air. Cora watched as it landed in her basket, sliding between a yellow squash and a head of cabbage. When she glanced back at the trees, Wyatt was gone. She took a cautious step back, wondering if he hid in the trees or in the grass like a snake.

He was trying to frighten her, and it was working. She set the basket down and ran past the house, beyond the clothes flapping on the clothesline, toward the dust rising into the air beyond the bunkhouse and stables.

A commotion of noise and voices grew louder as she neared the end of the long buildings. The men had been talking about busting broncs when they'd come in at noon, everyone except Chance, who must have taken to eating grain with the horses.

"You're up, Ike," someone shouted over the clamor.

"I'm not getting back on that hell-raiser!"

Cora rounded the corner of a stable as a man strode toward a circular corral from a neighboring pen where other men were lassoing horses. A pair of fawn leather chaps hugged his narrow hips and flared wide across his legs with each of his long strides. Even from a side view, she knew it was Chance, the breadth of his shoulders, the power in his stride, the swirl of sensation in the pit of her stomach.

"What do you mean *back on him?*" Chance's voice rang clear above the others. "Do we gotta call the women out here to do your job? That stud should already be green broke."

"Come on, Chance," Duce called out from inside the corral, the orange bushy hair beneath his hat making him easily recognizable. "Let's see if you can sweet-talk this demon as good as Skylar."

Chance leaped onto the fence, swinging his legs up and over as his strong arms vaulted him to the other side in a single fluid motion. He jammed his hat down as he strode toward Duce and Garret, each holding the harness of a brown-and-white horse.

Cora stepped up to the corral and peered between two others sitting atop the fence as Chance took the reins. Duce and Garret made a fast retreat.

"Two dollars says he lands on his ass," Garret called out from a high perch.

Chance kept his eyes on the horse, not making any attempt to mount it. The low, silken murmur of his voice carried back on the wind. Cora had to wonder if the horse was as mesmerized as she, and as taken aback by Chance's smooth and sudden shift into the saddle.

The horse sidestepped, then lunged forward, dipping its head as the hind quarters bucked up, trying to send Chance into the air.

Cora held her breath through two more sharp kicks.

Chance shifted in the saddle and tightened his hold on

the reins, talking softly all the while. The horse glanced back at its rider. Chance tugged at the reins, and the horse turned to the right then stopped.

"Just takes focus and a little finesse," Chance said, patting the horse's dark mane.

And a mountain of muscle, Cora noted, her gaze following the muscular bulge of his arms to the flex of powerful thighs beneath his chaps.

Good gracious. Her own body felt quite tremulous.

He steered the horse in a circle. Another flex of his thighs and a slow gait answered his lead.

"See there?" The corner of Chance's mouth kicked up in a slanted grin as he reined in the horse.

She caught his gaze and was startled by a surge of sensation in the most peculiar places. His brilliant green eyes widened a fraction beneath the brim of his hat. Her breath burned in her lungs.

The horse bucked again, breaking their gaze as Chance flew from the saddle. Cora gasped as he landed hard in the dirt. He instantly jumped to his feet and glared at the horse cantering away from him.

Laughing, Garret jumped down from the fence and opened a gate. "The next bronc is mine. Come on, Boots! Bring him in." A shaggy black dog darted into the ring and began chasing the horse toward the open gate.

"Put him with the green brokes," Chance shouted, using his hat to beat the dust from his pants and chaps.

"But he bucked you off," Garret protested.

"Chance lost his focus." Duce glanced over the fence and tipped his hat. "Afternoon, Miss Cora."

Cora didn't answer, her gaze locked on the man tromping toward her. Chance lunged up, bracing his hands wide on the fence separating them, and landed before her with the grace of a mountain cat. Tingles danced across her skin as he stepped closer, towering over her, crowding her space.

Flustered by her body's reaction, the ache in her breasts, she crossed her arms.

"Do you need something?" he asked. "Some of us are trying to work here."

The impatience in his tone clipped at her nerves, reminding her she was nothing but a nuisance to him, a pest he'd like to pluck from his ranch and ship back to the East Coast.

"Truly?" she managed to say in a mild tone. "All I saw was you sitting in the dirt."

Chance arched an eyebrow as low chuckles rumbled from the men gathering on the fence behind him.

"I'm looking for Tucker," she said, thinking she'd tell her concerns to someone who'd actually listen.

"He's with one of the brood mares, three barns over. Is everything okay with Skylar?"

"She's fine. Gentlemen," Cora said to the three men now standing behind Chance.

"Miss Cora," they said, reaching for their hats as she turned away.

"I'll walk you over," Garret offered, breaking away from the others.

"Thought you were busting the next bronc," Chance called after him.

Garret grinned over his shoulder. "Duce can take it. I already earned two extra dollars today."

Chance leaned back against the fence, his gaze never leaving the gentle sway of Cora Mae's hips. The purely feminine movement stoked the surge of heat that had hit his body a moment before he'd been thrown from the saddle. In the space of a breath, his body had answered the open desire reflected in her eyes.

Be damned. He hadn't imagined the sheer, hot hunger he'd seen in her gaze.

What the hell is she playing at?

"That sure is some woman," Duce said from beside him.

Chance's grunt was neither a denial nor an agreement.

"The kind of woman it takes to flourish out here."

"How do you figure?"

"She don't bend under your dark glares for one thing."

"I didn't glare at her."

"Her pastries are sweet enough to make this cow-puncher weep," Duce said, ignoring his protest. "And I ain't never met a woman with flaming hair who didn't have a temper to match. You know what they say about a woman with a temper, they're real wild in the—"

"I'll remind you that you're talkin' about my stepsister," Chance said, shifting his glare to Duce.

"If I thought your stepsister had the slightest interest in me, she'd already have a ring on her finger."

"She doesn't," Chance felt inclined to remind him.

"I've noticed. But I'll bet my saddle I ain't the only man who feels that way."

Chance scoffed. "The kid couldn't be more obvious if he dropped to one knee and started spouting sonnets."

Duce laughed and turned back to the corral to get started with the next bronc. "I wasn't referring to Garret."

Chance's gaze slid toward the corrals, but every man had turned their attention back to their work. So why was he still standing about as though he had nothing better to do than waste his time thinking about a woman he didn't want *on* his ranch, much less consuming his thoughts?

* * *

The last bit of twilight touched the darkening sky as Chance reined in his horse in front of Zeke and Margarete's house. He and Tucker had built the older couple's home up the road from their place to afford them some privacy.

Zeke sat on the front porch, his thinning gray hair bright as a porch light. Packing tobacco into his pipe, he reclined in his chair, his boots propped up on the porch railing. "Evenin', boss."

Chance grinned at the title. "How you doin', old man?"

"Better every day."

Chance was glad to see the ripple of wrinkles around his eyes, where they should be, instead of swollen purple bruises. "How's the hip?" he asked as he came up the steps.

Zeke grinned. "I could probably dance a little jig. It's the womenfolk who are keeping me housebound. I'm ready to get back out there and earn my keep before you toss me off this place."

"You ever hear of snowstorms in hell?" Chance said, smiling as he dropped onto the rickety wooden chair beside him. They both knew that day would never come. Zeke had been the first trail boss to give two half-starved fifteen-year-olds a shot at driving cattle and had taught him and Tuck all they knew about long drives. When they hadn't been on the cattle trail, Zeke and his wife had taken them in, giving them the start they'd needed to find their own way. Chance would make sure Zeke and Margarete were looked after the same way for as long as they chose to stay.

"I'll be out there tomorrow," Zeke said, clamping his pipe between his teeth, "even if my *señora* harps at me the whole way."

"Just in time. We could use another man to bust broncs."

"I will bust you," Margarete said as she stepped through the open front door.

Chance smiled up at her, recognizing the stubborn set of her jaw. The only thing Zeke would be mounting anytime soon would be a rocking chair.

"Have you had supper?" she asked.

"No, ma'am."

"Cora brought us too much. I will fix you a plate."

"I appreciate it."

Margarete patted his shoulder and turned away, hurrying back into the house.

"This is the third night in a row you've graced our porch," said Zeke. "I'm starting to feel mighty special. Don't suppose a certain little redhead is keeping you away from your own supper table?"

Chance rocked his chair onto the back legs. "Maybe."

"I overheard something about the two of you having a scuffle."

"Wasn't a scuffle. I tried to take a stand and got put in my place…which lately tends to be the barn."

Zeke chuckled as he lit a match. "Yeah, that's about what I heard." He puffed on his pipe, the circular glow lighting up his tawny skin in the growing darkness. "Dangerous business, agitating the henhouse," he said, shaking out the match.

"Henhouse, *hell*. That house is half *mine*."

Zeke blew out a puff of smoke and shook his head. "You must be forgetting that a man's home is his castle, which we all know is ruled by the queen. You've got no queen, son. Do believe that gives Skylar full reign."

"I might as well move my clothes into the stables, then."

Zeke rubbed at his whiskered jaw. "Mind if I ask what

the problem is?" he said softly. "Was my understanding that you and Tuck had both been fond of your stepsister. Cora cooks as good as my mama did and comes off as being mighty sweet."

"It's been my experience that anything that *sweet* can be nothing but trouble."

"Or attract trouble," Zeke said, his teeth clamping down on the end of his pipe as he eased back.

"What's that supposed to mean?"

"Wyatt McNealy stopping in to pay a call to Miss Cora."

The front legs of Chance's chair hit the porch with a hard clunk. "Wyatt was on the ranch? When?"

"Round three o'clock. I spotted him there beside the garden," he said, pointing toward the ranch house, "talking to Miss Cora."

"What call would he have to be talking to Cora?"

"Can't say. Whatever it was seemed to spook her. I was on my way out the door when he stepped back into that grove of trees. Miss Cora set off toward the corrals like her heels were on fire. Wyatt was real careful picking his way off the ranch. I didn't spot him again. I suppose Cora found Tucker before you."

The hell she had. The fire he'd seen in her eyes hadn't been due to fear or any mention of Wyatt. "Did anyone else see him on the ranch?"

"Not as far as I could tell. Mitch and Tucker set off in his direction a short time later, but must have been satisfied that he'd headed back to the Lazy J."

Why would Wyatt want to talk to Cora Mae?

The image of her standing beside Wyatt in the fancy yellow dress flashed into his mind. Strange she'd be talking to him on the day she'd arrived. He hadn't thought twice about it at the time, but if there was anyone who'd be foolish and cocky enough to conspire with someone on his ranch, it was Wyatt.

He knew she'd been hiding something—he just hadn't connected it with Wyatt.

"Margarete," he called out, surging up from his chair, "I'll have to pass on the supper. See you later, Zeke."

"You don't have to rush off," Zeke called after him.

"Oh, I think it's time I had a talk with my stepsister."

Five minutes later he was tethering his horse near his front porch. He knew she'd been lying about her reasons for coming here but had never imagined they'd be linked to Wyatt. He'd have the truth now.

He pounded up the steps and through the front door. Cora Mae was perched on one of the oversize chairs in the front room, beneath her fancy pink valance. She glanced up at him and quickly stuffed something into a small basket tucked beside her.

"Chance," she said, flipping the lid shut.

"What are you doing?" he asked.

Her back stiffened like an iron rod as he approached her. "It's none of your concern."

"Everything you do while you're on this ranch is my concern. How do you know Wyatt McNealy?"

Her eyes popped wide. "I beg your pardon?"

"Wyatt. The cowpoke you were sneakin' around with in the garden today."

"*I wasn't sneaking around*. The man appeared in *your* garden."

"He had to tiptoe around a whole ranch full of men to catch you alone. I'd like to know why he found you worth the effort."

"I can assure you I don't know. I met Mr. McNealy not two minutes before you threw a horse on him."

"Right. And now he's stopping in for socials?"

Her hands fisted. "Are you accusing me of something?"

"Can you tell me why Wyatt would seek you out?"

"I should think it obvious."

"Why don't you tell me what he had to say?"

"Ask Tucker. I've already given him the message."

"I'd rather hear it from you."

Her jaw tightened with anger. "He delivered the money for your colt."

His eyes went back to her basket, and Cora surged to her feet.

"How dare you even think I would steal from you!"

"I didn't say—"

"You didn't have to! I could read the accusation in your eyes. You have a suspicious mind."

"And you have a shady past, Cora Mae."

"I believe I've asked you to call me Cora."

"Why? So I'll forget who you really are and where you came from?"

She jerked back as though he'd struck her. The pain in her expression was a blow to his gut.

"Cora Mae—"

"You caught me," she said, her features firming. "I'm in cahoots with Wyatt."

Her comment blindsided him. It suddenly struck Chance just how ridiculous the notion had been.

"Isn't that what you think?"

The lack of one lie didn't mean she hadn't told him others. "I just—"

"Why else would I be here in *your* house, talking to

Wyatt in *your* garden, if I wasn't plotting against you?" She rounded on him, forcing Chance to take a step back. *"Maybe,"* she said, jabbing a finger at his chest with a blatant defiance no man on this ranch would dare, "Wyatt just enjoyed showing you what a fool you are. Perhaps he wanted to remind you that there's no such thing as safety in a lawless land inhabited by *imbeciles!* But don't take my word for it. After all, Tindale blood pours through my veins like *venom!"*

She glared up at him, her breath labored, her cheeks flushed, her eyes alive with fire.

Hot damn. She still had a temper.

She spun in a whirl of gray skirts and stormed from the room.

Chance sat on the chair she'd risen from, his mind a tangle of confusion.

"Chance?" Tucker walked in from the dining room. "What the hell did you do to Cora?"

What had *he* done? She was making him crazy!

"What did you say to upset her?" demanded Tucker.

"Why do I keep getting blamed for her mood swings?"

"The only one on this ranch taking swings is you. What's it going to take for you to realize she's nothing like Winifred? She never has been and you know it."

But he didn't. Not really. She'd blown back into his life like a whirlwind, disrupting everything, making him feel a stranger in his own skin.

Realizing her basket was digging in to his hip, he reached over and flipped up the lid. The start of a tiny sweater lay on top. A second of the same design in green was folded beneath. She'd been busy with those knitting needles, and his nieces would look adorable in the matching sweaters.

He looked up at his brother's angry face and wondered if he really was just being an ass, blaming Cora Mae for an attraction he didn't want and a lack of self-control he wasn't used to dealing with.

Biting out a curse, he grabbed up the basket and started for the back stairs.

"Where are you going?"

"To *apologize*."

He stopped outside her bedroom door, sucked in a deep breath and knocked gently.

He waited, but didn't hear anything beyond the increasing sound of crickets in the yard.

"Cora Mae?"

"Go away!"

Instead he eased the door open. She stood just a few feet inside the room, her arms crossed over her chest.

The room smelled like her, he noted, a combination of floral fragrance and shortbread.

"What do you want?" she spat.

"You left your basket." He eased it onto her chest of drawers, not about to take another step into her room.

"Should I dump it out so you can search the contents?"

"I want to apologize for what I said. I didn't mean it."

"Yes, you did. You're a man of few words. No doubt you choose them carefully."

"I also make mistakes and can admit when I do. I call you Cora Mae because that's how I've *always* thought of you. It's just habit."

"Tucker hasn't had any trouble calling me Cora."

"Guess I thought about you more often than he did."

Her lips parted in surprise.

Chance tensed, stunned by the admission. She stared

into his eyes as though trying to interpret some derogatory connotation, or worse yet, find the sincerity he truly intended but wasn't sure he wanted to reveal.

Silence swelled between them, damn near suffocating him.

"You're handy with those needles," he said, breaking their gaze to glance at her sewing basket. "The girls will look pretty as springtime in the sweaters you're knitting."

"You *did* search my basket."

"No, I—"

"Looked in my sewing basket," she insisted, arching a single eyebrow.

Lord, she's cute. She had the damnedest effect on him. Didn't seem to matter if she was spitting mad or flashing smiles, everything about her put his pulse into double time. "The colors caught my attention," he said.

"Surprised to find pastels in my *shady past?*"

He didn't know whether to curse or laugh. The irritation burning in the depths of her eyes suggested he should leave.

"Don't worry, Chance. I've already told Skylar I'll be gone by the end of the month. I'll try to stay out of your way until then. I'm sorry you find my presence so offensive."

He was sure he should say something contradictory but was afraid to suggest otherwise.

"It was never my intention to crowd you out of your home," she continued.

The sincerity in her gaze ripped at his conscience. "Where will you go?"

"I'm quite capable of building a life for myself anyplace I choose. For your information, most people *like me.*"

"I wasn't—"

"Which is more than I can say for you." She surged forward and slammed the door in his face.

Damnation! This was not the way he wanted things to go. He wanted her gone, yet knowing she'd leave with hurt feelings only made him feel worse.

Women.

A week ago he'd have sworn marriage-minded females were the worst. He'd never imagined he'd find himself attracted to a woman who wanted nothing more than to wish him to the devil. He never could have guessed that woman would be Cora Mae Tindale.

Chapter Seven

Salina sat in her study, her mind throbbing from the past hour of staring at columns of numbers in the books spread across her desk. She'd never appreciated the difficulty of her late husband's task. Of course, when Harlan had been alive, the surrounding cattle barons hadn't been breathing down his leathery neck, trying to drive him out of business.

She needed tea. "Carmen!"

Salina eased back in her chair and rubbed her temples as she waited for her housekeeper. Thunder boomed outside. The rain pounding against the roof wasn't helping her headache. A moment later her short, stout housekeeper appeared in the doorway. Salina hoped the flush in her wrinkled cheeks meant she'd been baking.

"Mrs. Jameson?"

"Did you finish the sweet rolls?"

"Yes, ma'am."

"Bring me one. And a pot of tea."

"Right away."

As the woman waddled off, Salina was hit by a horrifying thought. If she lost her contracts, she'd be forced to fire Carmen.

Thunder rumbled through the house, rattling the window behind her, increasing her growing sense of dread. She was starting to think making Wyatt her foreman had been a mistake. She didn't doubt his loyalty, just his ability to assert any power over the crew, much less intimidate the rustlers who'd been robbing her blind with startling ease.

Glancing back at the ledger, she tapped her pencil against the page. If Wyatt's numbers were correct, they should have just enough to make the first shipment. But she wouldn't have much left for the next drive, not unless they found out who was herding away her stock, and where those steers were being held.

Chance Morgan wouldn't have allowed his competition to drive him out of business. But that handsome devil was proving to be as elusive as the cattle rustlers.

The front door slammed. Wyatt walked into her study, his hat and jacket dripping wet. "We're missing at least another forty head of cattle," he said, shutting the door behind him. "Maybe more."

Salina gaped at him. "How can that be?"

Wyatt shifted his shoulders, knocking water from his long duster onto the polished wood floor. "The farther out we ride, the more empty pasture we find."

Salina banged her hands against the open ledgers. "Steers cannot be tucked into a pocket and carted off! I want to know where they've gone!"

"Judging by the tracks we found today, I think they're stashing our steers up in the canyons on Morgan land. We'll find out soon enough."

"At this rate, I won't have to worry about shipping penalties—I'll have nothing left to tax!"

"I'm working on it." He pulled off his hat, scattering more droplets as he shoved a hand through the dark curls of his hair.

"Wyatt!" She stood to peer over her desk at the growing puddle. "You're getting my floor wet!"

"In case you haven't noticed," he said, shrugging out of his heavy duster, "it's raining out there fit to drown Noah." He tossed his damp jacket onto one of the pink striped satin chairs before her desk. "Which may give us the advantage we need. Makes the ground soft, good for tracking."

His hands began working down the buttons on his shirt, distracting her from the protest raging in her mind. The sight of his bare chest and the firm muscles of his arms sent a pounding surge of desire through Salina. He dropped his wet shirt to the floor and panic mingled with attraction.

"What do you think you're doing?"

His slow seductive smile sent her pulse racing. "Getting out of my wet clothes."

"Wyatt."

He reached for his belt buckle. The answering rush of desire closed her throat. But they couldn't! She was saving herself. For *Chance*.

"You can change in the bunkhouse."

He only grinned as he moved around the desk, sliding his belt from the buckle. "This storm isn't going to pass anytime soon."

There had been plenty of times she'd prayed for rain, just to keep Wyatt in her bed all day. "Carmen will be here any minute with my tea."

"I shut the door. She'll come back." His hand curved

around her waist, the heat and determination in his gaze crumbling her resolve. He plucked a pin from her hair and dropped it to the floor.

"You've missed me."

"If I wanted you—"

He kissed her, seducing her mouth as her hair tumbled around her shoulders. He pulled her tight against him, the rhythmic caress of his body burning through her like sensual lightning.

"You haven't wanted no one but me in a long while," he murmured against her mouth.

Returning his deep kiss, she knew it was true. Everything was so easy with Wyatt. *And exciting*. His kisses, his lovemaking, his stamina. If he was half as good a rancher as he was a bed partner, she wouldn't be in her current situation.

Why couldn't he be Chance?

Wyatt's lips moved across her throat, distracting her from her thoughts. Within moments her black dress was falling to the floor and she was trembling, straining toward his touch. Something crashed behind her as he took her down onto the desk. His mouth slid to her breast, the hand between her thighs flooding her body with overwhelming pleasure.

"*Wyatt*." She arched against the hard surface, crying out as a climax rocked through her. His mouth found hers, muffling her cries as he continued to stroke her body, rebuilding the mounting tension, making her burn for him all the more.

"Now, Wyatt."

"I don't want to stop touching you."

Salina grasped blindly at his trousers, pushing them from his hips. Wyatt groaned as she found the hard, hot length of him. And then he was filling her, tugging at her hips as he slammed into her, giving her everything she needed. She arched, meeting his thrust, wondering how she'd made it a week without having him inside her.

A while later she lay spent beneath him, listening to his heavy breaths and the steady rainfall. Vaguely recalling something crashing to the floor, she glanced over the edge of the desk. Her ledgers were strewn everywhere with papers, pencils and a spilled bottle of ink.

"Oh, Wyatt. You've made a mess of my study."

Laughing, he eased up, bringing her with him as he fell back onto her chair. He kept her pressed flush against him, her knees tucked against his hips. A deep sigh broke from his chest. "I love the rain."

Salina smiled and kissed the tender spot she knew lay behind his ear, the steady patter on the roof now seeming rather soothing.

"Stop your foolishness," he whispered against her hair, "and *marry me*."

She tensed beneath the gentle glide of his fingers tracing her spine.

"You're not going to catch that Morgan maverick," he said.

She leaned back and found his dark eyes and handsome face all too tempting. "We've been over this, Wyatt."

"If he wanted you, he'd have had you by now."

She pushed off him and turned away to retrieve her dress. "Not all men have to bed a woman to be interested in her," she said, lifting her crumpled dress from the floor and holding it to her chest.

"Sweetheart, I was interested for *months* before I ever got near you. You'd never known the tender touch of a man, hadn't had even a taste of passion until me. I worked hard to win you over, Salina. I think I've put in my fair share of courtship."

"If I lose this ranch, you lose me."

"Seems to me, I'd lose you either way."

Wyatt reached for the britches bunched at his ankles. He stood and pulled them up over his hips. Her persistence in chasing Chance Morgan infuriated him. He knew Morgan's kind well enough. The two brothers lorded around these hills, shouldering their way through the stockyard as if the world should tremble at their feet.

He didn't mind carrying out Salina's wishes against their ranch, knowing her foolish ideas of bullying Morgan into courtship would likely backfire and secure Wyatt's place by her side.

"Marriage didn't get in our way before," Salina pointed out.

Wyatt scoffed. Chance Morgan wasn't a man who'd take a pretty young bride and let her languish away in a satin palace. No doubt he'd expect his wife to be faithful. And so would Wyatt. He didn't want to be Salina's fancy man; he wanted to marry her. For years he'd loved no one but her and had been as patient as a man could be.

He'd felt some guilt over the way ol' Jameson had died, dropping dead to the floor right there in front of them. He'd given Salina the distance she'd requested. In the past year he'd stood by while she'd chosen others—but she always came back to him.

He'd outlasted them all, finally winning the sole place in her bed. Everyone on this ranch knew she belonged to him—everyone except Salina.

"You'd really choose him over me?" he asked.

Her brow puckered in annoyance. "This isn't about who I like best. If you want me, do something about it! I won't go back to having nothing, not for you, not for anyone."

"You won't have to!"

"I will if I lose this ranch! What would you have me do, Wyatt? Marry you and *then what?*"

"I'm doing all I can."

"It's not enough!"

"Hell, I've only got five men!"

She stepped into her dress, shoved her arms into the long black sleeves and clamped the bodice over her pretty round breasts. "You can't blame this incompetence on a crew *you* hired."

Frustration burned in his chest. Did she have no faith in him? "I'm getting close. I'll recover the cattle. When I do," he said, tugging her against him, "you make sure you realize it was *me* and not Morgan who saved this place." He took her mouth in a hard kiss. She kissed him back with renewed passion. If he wasn't preoccupied with catching those damn rustlers, he'd gladly oblige her all afternoon. But he'd had more on his mind than sex when he'd come into her study. She'd been too damn arousing and had kept him out of her bed for too long.

Abruptly he pulled back and set her away from him.

Salina leaned against the desk, breathing hard as she clutched at her bodice. Her expression was nothing short of crestfallen as he buttoned his fly, strained as it was, and went to retrieve his shirt.

"Where are you going?"

The pout in her voice tugged at him. He didn't dare look at her, determined not to give in. He wasn't about to give her up.

"If I'm gonna catch those damn rustlers, I've got work to do." He stuffed his shirttails into his pants and gathered his hat and duster before glancing back.

She sat in her chair, her arms crossed tightly over her unbuttoned bodice.

"I'll be back in a couple of hours. Why don't you go put on something pink for a change, so I can take it off you?"

Her teeth closing over her lush lower lip didn't hide her smile or the spark of interest in her eyes.

She was his.

Morgan would disappoint her—he was counting on it.

Chapter Eight

"You ever seen a newborn foal?"

At the sound of Garret's voice, Cora glanced up from the lemon cake she was frosting. His broad shoulders hidden by the half-opened door, Garret's white hair glowed like a beacon in the bright sunlight.

"No, I haven't."

"Would you like to?"

If anyone else had asked, she would have agreed in a heartbeat, but she didn't want to encourage Garret's attention. Strong and handsome, she was sure any other woman would appreciate the constant doting that was beginning to wear on her nerves.

"Rosie dropped her foal just about an hour ago," he said. "The Appaloosa is Tucker's favorite mare. He thought you'd want to see her."

Tucker had sent him? "Okay." She put the finishing swirl on the icing. She swiped a dab of frosting from the empty mixing bowl before setting it in the sink, then tucked her thumb into her mouth, happy with the sweet lemony flavor.

She stepped out of the back door and squinted against the bright sky. "Your hair positively glows," she said, the smooth, pale strands seeming almost translucent in the intense light. "I've never seen hair so white as yours and Josh's."

He smiled and tugged on his wide tan hat. "When we used to drive cattle out of Texas, some of the boys called my father The Viking on account of his pale hair, and likely his gruff manner." He glanced up at the sky as they set off across the yard. "This is the prettiest day we've had all spring."

There wasn't a single cloud left from yesterday's storm. "I was sure the sky couldn't get any bluer."

"We don't get many days like these, with the wind died down so we can feel that sun on our skin. The rain washed a good coat of dust off everything. Made a mess of the roads, though," he said as they reached the end of the yard.

Every pit and groove in the dirt road held a puddle of water.

Garret held out his arm. "I'll get you across."

After a few precarious steps through the saturated, slippery ground, she accepted his help and wrapped her fingers around the solid muscle beneath his blue sleeve.

"We had to move some of the mares," he said, guiding her around a large puddle. "The ground behind the stable is a bit flooded."

He led her up the road to a set of wide-open doors at the center of the stable. She stepped into the surprising warmth of a long building filled with oversize stalls. A tall, slender heater stood in the center row at each end, creating quite a cozy environment. She followed Garret to a stall holding a russet mare, her hindquarters dusted white and flecked with spots of deep amber.

"Hello, Red," Garret said to the young foal lying beside

its mother in the hay. At the sound of his voice, the small horse struggled onto its spindly legs. The only white on the foal was four socks and the hint of light flecks on the filly's backside. Her new coat gleamed.

"She's beautiful.".

"Isn't she?" Garret opened the gate and motioned for her to go ahead of him. "This one's gonna be a real prize."

Cora knelt down to pet the fluffy fur of its neck. "She does shimmer."

Garret crouched beside her, brushing his hand across its coat in a vigorous caress. "Too bad they don't keep this soft down. I'll be surprised if Tucker sells her. He sure waited long enough to breed Rosie."

"Hey, Garret! You in here?"

"Yeah," Garret answered, standing to look over the stall.

Cora rose up enough to see a head of thick blond hair step in from the bright sunlight. Tucker smiled at the sight of her, and Cora released a sigh of relief. She'd been doing her best to avoid Chance. He seemed to be doing the same. She wasn't quite sure what had come over her the other day and didn't care to explore the startling sensations she'd been feeling in his presence ever since.

"You came out."

"She's beautiful, Tucker."

He turned his attention to Garret. "Ike says he spotted the wildcat you've been hunting. Took down a calf out on the north pasture. You want to ride out or should I?"

Garret glanced back at her, indecision clear in his hazel eyes.

"Go," she said.

He hurried from the stall, saying, "I just gotta grab my rifle."

Tucker leaned against the gate, his expression thoughtful as he held her gaze. "You know, you're the only one aside from Skylar who can do that."

"Do what?"

"Tell us apart at a glance. I must get called Chance ten times a day."

Cora rolled her eyes. "I'd think anyone could sense the difference. Chance puts off a cold front I can feel a mile away."

"He doesn't mean any real harm, you know? He's just—"

"Rude."

Tucker smiled and crossed his arms over the top of the gate. "I was going to say blunt, but I suppose you're right. I guess we're all just used to him. It's nothing personal against you, I swear."

Sadness washed through her. She glanced back at the foal and ran her hand across its soft coat. "He's made it quite clear that he hates me. It doesn't get much more personal than that."

"Darlin', Chance doesn't hate you any more than he hates me."

"Could have fooled me."

"I think half the time he fools himself. I'm sure it would be a lot easier to just not care about anyone. He carried a lot of grief over leaving you behind. We both did. We left home ready to save the world and discovered we could hardly save ourselves. By the time we made it back to the farm, Winifred had sold off the land and you were long gone."

Cora's heart clenched. "You really went back for me?"

"Not soon enough. Couldn't have been an easy life, living with your mother."

"We've all had our hardships," she said, moving to stand across the gate from him. The knowledge that they'd gone back healed some of the hurt she'd been carrying for so long. "Chance mentioned you'd both been in a prison camp."

Tucker's eyes widened in clear surprise. "He told you about that?"

"Just a brief mention."

"Which is about all he's ever said to me on the subject. Since we got out, he's refused to talk about it. Not exactly highlights either of us care to rehash."

"I'm sorry. It must have been horrible."

"It was pure hell. Being a couple of smartass kids who didn't realize we were in well over our heads didn't help us any. It was Chance's rotten luck to be the instigator the night one of the guards figured out we had one real weakness."

He shifted his gaze to the foal. The pain she saw in his eyes sent a chill over Cora's skin. As silence stretched, she wasn't sure she wanted to know what that weakness had been, but she had to ask.

"What weakness?"

"By hurting just one of us, he could crush the other."

Her breath stalled. "Was Chance beaten?"

Tucker shook his head. "Not that night or during the days that followed. The guard thought he'd grabbed Chance, but after he started in on me it didn't much matter. I don't remember much after that. No doubt I would have died if a sympathetic soldier hadn't sneaked us out of camp."

"Oh, Tucker."

"I was the lucky one. I don't remember hardly any of it. Having to be the spectator sure snuffed Chance's fire. He's generally one for sticking to the straight and narrow, and tugs me back in line when I need it."

"I don't know how to take him," she admitted.

"I suspect he's having the same problem. Give him some time. As I recall, it took us a while to warm to you after our folks married. But we ended up having us a time." He smiled fondly. "Never would have guessed a girl could be so skilled at gigging frogs."

"I never had so much fun in my life as the time I spent with both of you. That hasn't changed. The past two weeks have been a blessing."

"We sure hope you won't rush off."

She didn't see any other option. The tension between her and Chance was only getting worse. "It was never my intention to stay," she said, reminding herself of that very fact. Though she had hoped to find a home with the brothers of her youth, she'd merely needed time to catch her breath, make a plan for her future. "You don't need to worry about me," she said, forcing a smile. "Like a weed, I can root anywhere."

"You're not a weed, Cora. You're *family*."

That in itself was a gift. In the past couple weeks she'd nearly felt part of a family.

"I'd better get back to work," he said, pushing away from the gate. "I'll be over in the next barn. If you need any help getting back to the house, just give a holler."

"Thank you."

He reached over and tugged gently on a stray curl, his emerald eyes gleaming with a smile. "That's what big brothers are for."

Brothers. That had been all she'd ever wanted, to have them back in her life.

Watching him leave, she stepped from the stall and glanced around the clean stable, their care and hard work clearly visible. She was proud of all they'd achieved, the life they'd made for themselves.

Rosie moved forward, sticking her head over the gate. Cora reached up and rubbed behind her stiff ears. Cora's heart ached, knowing her presence only dredged up bad memories for the one man she never wanted to hurt.

"How's my best girl?"

The warm gentle voice washed through Cora Mae like a caress. She pressed into the shadows against the stall and peered beneath Rosie's muzzle. Chance stood in the sunlight that poured in from the side door. His back to her, he reached into the first stall and patted a large fawn horse.

"Feeling neglected?" he asked.

Very.

"Soon as you drop that foal I'll have you back out there. 'Course, then you'll be more interested in looking after your colt than chasing down mavericks with me."

No wonder he hardly ever spoke around his family. He obviously saved his conversation for the horses. She watched his hands move caressingly over the horse's coat. He saved his touch for the horses, too. At the thought of his hands moving so softly over her, a tingling jolted through her body.

Good gracious.

She glanced back at the end door where a wedge of sunlight glittered across a wide puddle. Inching her way back, she stepped lightly through the water. Once around the side of the stable, she released a hard sigh of relief.

She didn't know how to take him at all, she thought. She hurried up the mucky slope. She wanted to make it back to the path before Chance left the stable. With her next step, she slipped and splashed onto her knees.

"Blast." Gritting her teeth, she plucked her hands from the cold mud. The stuff clung to her like clay as she tried to push to her feet. Finally upright, she took another step.

Her feet shot forward. With a shriek she landed flat on her back.

Drenched in cold, Cora sucked in a shuddering breath. She sat up, everything but the front of her bodice now coated in mud. Hoping to salvage a shred of pride, she tucked her feet beneath her, ready to try again.

Coarse laughter drew her gaze to the top of the rise. A gleam of sunlight outlined broad shoulders and the vee of Chance's chest. He towered over her like a Greek god. Beneath the hat tugged low on his brow, his green eyes sparkled with sheer delight, turning her embarrassment to pure rage.

"This isn't funny!"

"From where I stand, it's downright hysterical." He sauntered toward her. Chuckling, he stepped lightly through the mud. "Need a hand?"

"No, thank you." She pushed to her feet, her fingers digging into the soft mud as she stood.

"How about a bucket of water?"

His laughter died the moment he spotted her fistful of mud. He cocked a golden eyebrow. "You're a bit too old for mud fights, Cora Mae."

Mud drizzled between her fingers as she clenched her fist. She was just the right age to knock him on his overgrown, arrogant butt. "How many times must I tell you to call me *Cora?*" she said, taking aim at his annoyingly handsome face.

"I wouldn't do that if I were you. You're far too prissy to end up facedown in the mud."

"Which shows how little you know me," she said, and slung.

Mud slapped him across the face and splattered against his blue shirt. His stunned expression forced a laugh past her tight lips. Expecting him to rage, she took a sliding step back. His swift smile caught her completely off guard.

"Oh, you're in for it now." He tugged off his hat, tossed it to safety, then reached toward the ground.

Cora rushed back, sliding as she groped for another fistful. Mud struck her dress. She screamed and pelted him in the chest.

"You little—" He collided against her. Cora screeched as she went down, splashing into the mud. Laughing, Chance landed on his knees beside her. He glanced up, his eyes alive with mischief.

"I warned you." He stood and dumped a handful of muck on her head.

"My hair!" she sputtered. She grabbed ahold of his booted ankle and tugged.

Chance went down with a mighty splat. He pulled her into the mud right beside him.

"Heathen!" she shouted, twisting against his hold as he wrestled her over the top of him.

"Girl!" He pinned her beneath him, her face an inch from black water. "You do know I could drown you in this stuff if I wanted to?"

She peered up at him through the grime dripping from her hair, her grin so wide her cheeks ached. "Big words for a mudskipper."

Deep laughter leaped from his chest and his hold loosened, giving Cora the advantage she needed. She lunged up, tackling him back into the mud. They sloshed in a mad struggle to subdue the other. Overtaken with giggles, Cora lost her grip and he slipped from her grasp. He rolled her to the ground, thoroughly soaking her.

"Chance!"

"Yield!"

"Never!"

"What the hell's going on!"

Chance released his hold just enough for her to look up. Tucker stood outside the second stable, his eyes wide with horror.

Chance rolled away from her and sat up. "Hey, Tuck."

"Chance? *Cora?* My God, are you…okay?"

"Is *she* okay? She nearly drowned me." A wide smile parted the mud on his face.

Cora laughed, quite proud that he currently bore no resemblance to his twin.

"Do you two have any idea what you look like?"

"This is your brother's dirty work," she said, struggling onto her knees.

"She started it." Chance nudged her shoulder.

Cora pushed away from her muddy opponent and got to her feet. Chance grabbed the back of her dress and tugged her into the mud as he stood.

"Oops."

"You big—"

"Here, let me help you up." Chance grabbed her hand and tugged her to her feet. His green eyes shone with laughter.

Startled by a sudden stir of awareness, Cora's breath caught. Even coated in grime, he was breathtaking.

"You've both lost your minds," said Tucker, shaking his head as he turned away. "I hope you don't plan on walking into the house like that. Skylar's likely to have heart failure at the sight of you."

The house. Cora glanced down at her mud-soaked dress. "Oh my goodness."

"What's the matter? You just realize you're too filthy to get to the tub?"

"I don't see what you're grinning about," she said as she trudged her way to a patch of semidry ground. "You are just as muddy."

Chance was beside her in a few easy strides. "You still know how to swim, don't you?"

"I suppose I—" His arm closing around her cut off her words.

"Good," he said, cradling her against his chest.

"Chance!" Her arms locked round his neck. "Put me down!"

"In a minute."

"I'm too heavy!"

He jiggled her, making her cling to him. "Are you calling me weak?"

His wide smile mesmerized. Her heart started that wild cadence. "No," she said, her gaze locked with his. "Never that."

She could feel the ripple of his muscles as he moved. A shudder stole through her. It wasn't fear. Surprisingly, it felt quite nice to be wrapped in his brawn, the intensity of his eyes stirring a warmth deep inside her. She felt as though she were melting into his embrace. His face moved closer, and Cora's breath stalled.

"Cora?"

"Yes?"

"Hold your breath." With that, he *dropped her.*

She splashed into the pond and the bite of freezing water. She came up shivering and sputtering for breath. "You…are the biggest…*bully!*"

"Am not." He dove off the end of the dock. A moment later he surfaced beside her. "I'm just helping you get cleaned up." He reached for the wooden deck above them. Muscles flexed, and he was standing on the dock. He turned, smiling as he crouched low. "Give me your hands."

She reached up. The warmth of his fingers clasped over hers. With one tug she was out of the water and colliding against his firm chest. His arms banded around her to keep her from falling back into the pond. His body gave off an amazing amount of heat.

He turned her toward the center of the dock, then gripped her shoulders and set her roughly away from him.

"No hard feelings?" he asked, his expression wary.

"*You're* the one with hard feelings."

Chance couldn't deny it. After the way she'd looked at him before he'd tossed her into the water and rubbed against him just now, his hard feelings were about to bust through his fly. A condition that only worsened as Cora Mae reached back to gather the length of her sopping hair.

Her dress clung to every dip and curve in her body. The light gray fabric did little to hide the rosy-tipped evidence of her chill.

Desire swept through him.

Cora gasped, just before she wrapped her arms around her chest, hiding those hard peeks.

"*Chance*. I can't go up to the house like this."

"No, you can't," he said, taking in the curvaceous view that was guaranteed to keep him awake for nights on end.

"*Chance!*"

His gaze snapped up to Cora Mae's wide eyes.

"Stop gaping and get me something before I freeze!"

He turned away before she could see the proof of his stray thoughts strained against his britches. He stepped into the boots he'd taken off before diving off the dock and went to fetch a blanket from the clothesline.

When he came back, Cora Mae was shivering beside the tree a few yards beyond the dock. She flashed a timid smile, and he couldn't help wondering if she'd taste as sweet as she looked.

He swung the blanket around her shoulders, then used it to pull her against his body, and she let him, pressing flush against his chest.

"Thank you," she said, a sigh breaking from her lips.

He tried to tell himself she was cold and was only seeking his warmth, but his body wasn't listening.

"Cora Mae—"

"Cora," she corrected automatically, taking a small step back, making him wonder if she'd just noticed the intimacy of her body pressed to his. He smiled, and felt a shudder sweep through her that had nothing to do with being cold. He saw desire in those brown and copper depths.

"Cora," he said, making sure he got it right, just before he leaned in and brushed his lips against hers. She stiffened. His hand slid into her hair, preventing her from pulling away. She gasped and he deepened the kiss, gliding his tongue across hers in a fleeting caress, drawing a sugary sweetness into his mouth, and the faint taste of lemon.

Dear God. She tasted better than in his dreams.

He returned to the satin sweetness of her mouth for a full sampling. She stood in the circle of his arms, letting him kiss her, but not quite participating. Coaxingly, he flicked her tongue.

Kiss me back, Cora Mae.

She shivered against him. Her tongue moved lightly against his, and passion burst through him, dragging out a groan of suppressed desire.

The blanket dropped away as he smoothed his hand down her back. The most arousing sounds rose from her throat. Every timid stroke of her tongue kissed him into oblivion.

By the time he drew his mouth away from hers, she was relaxed in his arms, her breathing as sporadic as his own. He smiled into her wide, passion-filled eyes and pushed a long auburn curl away from her face, tucking the damp strands behind her ears.

"Chance?" Cora tried to catch her breath, her mind a haze of confusion as she blinked up at him. How could her muscles have turned to melted butter while her heart raced fit to burst? "I'm dizzy."

He hugged her close and laughed against her lips. "Me, too."

Cora leaned into his soft lips, eager for the closeness they'd just shared. She reached up, her fingers twisted into his hair, holding him closer as his taste and the heat of his embrace surrounded her.

He lifted her against him. Her wet skirts didn't hide the ridged evidence of his masculine body. He shifted again, and the feel of his body pressed so intimately to hers ignited a hard surge of panic. Her mind flooded with the memory of being held down, the sharp stab of pain between her legs.

She shoved against him. *He…he wouldn't.*

His grip tightened, his hand flexing on her buttocks,

trapping her against the bruising strength of his body. Fear streaked through her, overpowering a rush of wild sensation.

With a shriek of protest, she wrenched herself away from him and stumbled back.

"Cora." Chance moved to pull her soft warmth back against the fire twisting through his body. The stark fear in her eyes stopped him.

She backed away, her narrowed eyes hazing with tears. "How could you?"

"Cora Mae—"

She turned and ran toward the house.

Chance stood there in stunned silence. What the hell had just happened?

He licked his lips, her taste still lingering there. He slumped against the tree and glanced down at a body honed to do a lot more than just kiss. He'd been ready to throw her to the ground and relieve the desire that had been pulling at him since she arrived.

Good God— He'd all but attacked her.

He scanned the ranch, making sure no one else had witnessed his lack of restraint. He didn't see anyone. The shock and betrayal in her eyes filled his mind.

What have I done?

She wasn't some promiscuous widow out getting her kicks; she was *Cora Mae*, and he'd just scared her half to death.

Damnation. He'd scared himself.

Chapter Nine

The chair beside Chance sat empty. He didn't have to look up from his plate to feel the angry glares aimed in his direction. Skylar had already cornered him in the kitchen, asking if he knew why Cora had run into the house in tears and hadn't been downstairs since. He'd lied straight to her face, claiming he didn't have a clue.

When Skylar walked into the dining room with a plate of lemon cake, the thought of Cora Mae's lemon-tinged tongue rubbing against his had him out of his chair in a heartbeat. He headed for his study, hoping to find some peace and solitude.

Over an hour later he sat in the solace of the one room that didn't bear any hint of her presence, yet all he could see as he stared at his ledger were Cora's wide frightened eyes gazing back at him.

He eased back in his chair and blew out a pent-up breath. He wasn't sure if he should go to her and say... *something*.

The door squeaked open, letting in the sound of a

fussing baby. Chance straightened in his chair as Skylar stepped inside, a crying bundle in one arm, a carrying basket in the other.

"Shhh," she soothed, patting the swaddled baby on her shoulder as she kicked the door closed behind her. "Hush now, Em. Don't wake your sister." She glanced up and drew to a halt. "Oh! Sorry, Chance. I didn't—"

"Come on in," he said, rising from the cushy chair she clearly needed more than he did. "I was just heading out."

"Tucker fell asleep on our bed while reading to Joshua. We came down here so we wouldn't wake them." She slid the basket onto the desk. "I know it's just after seven, but you've all been working so hard."

"You can nurse those angels anywhere you please," he said, glancing into the basket at Grace wrapped up tight in a new pink blanket. "I see Grace's color is now pink."

Skylar smiled as she eased into his chair. "I had planned yellow beforehand in case these two were boys. Luckily Cora had a supply of pink yarn and ribbons."

Of course she did.

Emily let out a sharp cry from beneath the blanket draped over Skylar's shoulder, just before she found her source of nourishment. That was all it took to initiate a similar protest from the basket. Skylar released a hard sigh and rocked the basket while cradling Emily against her with her other arm.

"Can I hold her?"

"Yes. Thank you. They're such piglets."

Chance lifted his fussing niece and tucked her into the bend of his arm. A few gentle pats on her bottom and she quieted, cuddling against him. He picked up his ledger and took it back to the bookshelf.

"You certainly have a knack with babies."

All females should be so simple, he thought, sliding the ledger into place. "Can I get you anything, Skylar?"

She glanced up from her daughter and smiled in appreciation. "A glass of water would be grand."

He and Grace left the study and returned a few moments later with her drink.

"Thank you," she said as he set the glass on the desk. "I feel like a permanent feeding station. I've been so thankful for Cora's help. I would have gone mad this past month trying to adjust to feeding schedules and keeping up with Joshua and everything else."

Chance sat down in the chair on the other side of the desk and kept his gaze on Grace.

"She's agreed to watch the girls and Josh for a couple of hours tomorrow. My horses have probably forgotten me."

"Not likely." Skylar was one of the finest horse trainers he'd ever seen, when she wasn't heavy with child. But she and Tucker seemed to have their own selfish plans to fill this house up with kids. Damn cute ones at that, he thought.

He sure hadn't planned on children running through this house when he'd built it. He and Tuck had had a plan: start a horse ranch and avoid the marriage trap. He figured Tuck must have been out of his mind when he'd fallen for Skylar. But Chance had to admit, life hadn't been bad. Skylar settled his rambling brother and brought a level of comfort to their home. Joshua's arrival had been like a miracle. The boy knew how to hit every soft spot left in Chance's heart.

He brushed his finger across Grace's plump rosy cheek. Kids were something special. Maybe his brother had it figured out.

Or maybe Chance just needed to remind himself that Tucker had a way of coasting through life on God's graces, whereas he tended to trip over them. Disrespecting Cora Mae the way he had certainly hadn't been a smooth course of action, and damn sure wasn't going to earn him any graces.

"I hope my girls aren't keeping you awake at night."

Chance glanced up. "No." The only girl keeping him awake was the one upstairs wishing him to the devil.

A smile eased across Skylar's lips, making him wonder if she could hear his thoughts. "Want to talk about it?" she asked.

"No."

"I didn't think so." She stood and placed her sleeping infant in the carrying basket. As if on cue, Grace began to fuss in his arms.

"Piglets," said Skylar, grinning as she approached him and relieved him of her fussing daughter.

"Can I take this bundle upstairs for you?" he asked, looking into the basket at Emily.

Skylar settled back into the soft desk chair. "Yes, thank you."

He lifted Emily from the basket and started for the door.

"Chance?"

He paused in the doorway, glancing back at her.

"Whatever your grievances are with Cora, I hope you two can work them out. I'd hate to see her go."

"Did she say she was leaving?"

Skylar nodded, her expression heavy with concern. "At the end of the week. I don't think she has anywhere else to go."

"Did she say that?"

"No. But she's a lot like you in that respect."

Chance frowned. "How do you mean?"

"She doesn't share her burdens."

Problem was, Chance knew he was one of those burdens. "I'll talk to her."

"I'd appreciate it."

He nodded and headed for the stairs.

It wasn't hard to see that nearly everyone on the ranch preferred Cora Mae's company to his. He'd be a selfish bastard to chase off Skylar's first real friend.

He stepped lightly into Tucker's bedroom. His brother was asleep against a stack of pillows, an open book on his chest. His son slept soundly beside him. Tucker woke as Chance laid Emily in the cradle.

"Playing nursemaid?"

"Seems that way. Sky's downstairs with Grace."

Tucker leaned over the side of the bed and smiled at his daughter. He reached over and stroked her soft tufts of blond hair.

Leaving the room, Chance felt a sharp stab of jealousy.

It all seemed to come so easy for Tucker—marriage, kids, ranching.

The sudden thought stunned him.

He had never begrudged the happiness Tucker had found with Skylar. He'd never wanted any such thing for himself. He only wanted to run his ranch and be left alone.

Cora Mae was driving him out of his mind!

He stopped before her room. *What the hell am I supposed to say to her? You stay and I'll go? Give up the only life that had ever meant anything to me?*

He rapped on the door. "Cora?"

She didn't answer, but he knew she was up. Light seeped through the cracks around the door.

"Would you talk to me?"

He waited another minute.

"Please, Cora."

Another moment passed. Something scraped on the other side of the door before it opened, just wide enough for her to peer out at him. No doubt her foot was braced against the door to keep him out.

Chance stared down at the scuff marks on the wood floor leading to the chest of drawers she'd clearly just shoved from the doorway. *Good God.* Did she think he'd attack her?

Glancing up at the caution in her darkened eyes, he assumed so.

"What do you want?" she asked, her cold tone adding to the guilt building inside him.

"To apologize," he said, telling himself he shouldn't notice the way the lamplight lit up the clean shiny curls of red and copper that swirled around her shoulders. "I'm sorry, Cora. I was out of line."

Tears glistened in her eyes. "I didn't…I wouldn't have—"

"You didn't do anything other than trust me. I've been feeling lower than dirt all evening for breaking that trust."

She sniffed, blinking back her tears. "I get the message," she said, her tone hard. "I'll leave."

He stared at her a moment, stunned by the implications of her statement. "You think that's why I kissed you? To get you to *leave?*"

"Why else? I've told you I have no interest in marriage. Perhaps I should have expanded that to *paramours.*"

"I admit my actions were disrespectful. It won't happen again. But I sure as hell didn't kiss you to try and scare you off."

Her poignant expression didn't change.

"I swear it, Cora Mae," he said, the distrust in her eyes killing him. "I went too far, and I hope you can forgive me."

"Of course. I care for you as a brother."

His eyebrows shot up. *"A brother?"* She'd just accused him of trying to make her his lover and now he was supposed to think his actions had been somehow incestuous? "Can't we at least be *honest* about this? The way you kissed me back was hardly sisterly."

Her eyes flared. "I didn't ask you to kiss me!"

"Maybe not, but after the way you kissed me, you can't deny the attraction between us." The memory of her tongue moving tentatively over his burned through him. She'd filled his arms perfectly, her warmth pressed against him, her softness beneath his hands. She'd all but melted into him, kissing him back with…with the inexperience of a virgin.

Hell. Her timid exploration had set him on fire, and he'd taken her from her first taste of passion to grinding against her.

"I'm not saying what I did was right," he said, reminding himself he'd come to her room to apologize. "I could taste your innocence, and I—"

"Good night!"

He pushed against the door before she could shut it. "Cora Mae, I'm trying—"

"I don't want your attention," she shouted. "I don't want these feelings!"

The door slammed shut.

Chance shut his eyes and leaned against the door frame. What had he expected?

Judging by the solid rise in his trousers, an invitation

into her bed would have been a start. He wanted her until he couldn't see straight.

He couldn't have her. He *wouldn't* take her. What was more, she didn't want him.

At least, *not now*.

The sound of the chest being shoved back in front of the door confirmed that notion.

Damnation!

All she'd wanted was confirmation that he'd keep his hands off her, and he hadn't been able to even give her that much.

He walked into his room, telling himself he should be thankful she had the sense to resist him. *Hell*. If Salina affected him half as much as Cora Mae, he'd have found himself standing before a preacher by now.

His skin prickled at the thought, dread overpowering every other emotion in his body. He walked across his dark room and glanced out of the window in the direction of the Lazy J.

Maybe he was just fighting the inevitable. His options seemed plain enough. Celibacy or marriage. Clearly his long bout as a celibate was driving him out of his ever-loving mind, to the point of shaming Cora Mae. Hadn't everyone pointed out the same thing? Cora Mae wasn't the problem here—*he was*.

He had to get out of this house.

Chapter Ten

Eight-thirty was too early to be in bed, but Salina didn't care. Feeling quite decadent, she lifted a mug of hot chocolate to her lips and leaned back, sinking into a pile of pillows that still smelled of Wyatt. He'd seemed awfully confident before he'd ridden out this evening, although he always looked confident while lying naked in her pink bed linens.

She smiled at the thought. Whatever his plans, she hoped he would succeed. She could not afford another large loss.

A light knock sounded on her bedroom door.

"Yes?"

The door squeaked open. "Mrs. Jameson?"

"What is it, Carmen?"

"Mr. Morgan is here to see you."

Salina sat up, hot cocoa sloshing across her hand as she clutched at her loose wrapper. "*Chance* Morgan?"

A wry smile flittered across the old woman's lips. "Yes, ma'am."

Good gracious! "Well…offer him some refreshments and tell him I'll be right down."

"Yes, ma'am."

Salina raced to her wardrobe and rummaged through her black dresses. Hurrying into one, she swept her hair up into a coil and secured a wide hair comb. After buttoning her shoes, she drew a deep calming breath and assessed herself in the mirror over her vanity. Everything seemed in place. She pinched her cheeks to give herself a bit of color.

Perfume.

She couldn't go downstairs smelling of Wyatt. She picked up her perfume bottle and coated herself in a rose-scented mist.

Perfect.

She started downstairs, anticipation bubbling. She'd known Chance would come to his senses. Her breath caught at the sight of him filling up her parlor. He stood, hat in hand, taking in the sophisticated elegance of her home. His broad shoulders stretched nearly the width of her small hearth.

"Good evening, Chance."

He turned and tucked his hand into his pocket, his expression stern. "Evening, Salina. Hope I haven't stopped in at a bad time."

"Not at all. Indeed, your arrival is a lovely surprise. Please, sit."

Chance glanced at a pink upholstered settee. "All right."

Not certain its spindly legs would take his weight, he eased onto the dainty sofa and dropped his hat to the polished dark-wood floor. Surrounded by pink-and-white wallpaper and a menagerie of glass dolls, he felt like he was sitting in a little girl's doll house.

Salina wedged in beside him, her brown eyes shining with pure feminine appraisal as she smiled up at him. His gaze landed on the two white mounds bubbling up from her bodice, the scent of rosewater damn near choking him.

What the hell am I doing here?

It had seemed clear enough during the long ride over. After all Skylar had done for him and Tucker, he supposed he needed to step up and do something to benefit the ranch. If courting Salina could fix all their problems, what the hell did he have to lose?

"Didn't Carmen offer you refreshments?" she asked.

"She did."

"You declined? You simply must have a sweet roll."

"Did you make them?"

Laughter trickled from her throat. "Surely not."

"Don't you cook?"

"I find there are far more appealing ways to spend my time than sweating in a hot kitchen." Her hand flexed on his knee.

The woman sure didn't beat around the bush. The sensual glint in her dark eyes suggested this would be a good time to take her into his arms.

She smiled and leaned into him.

It wasn't as though he lacked experience in seducing women, but as he curved his hand around her waist and pressed his mouth to hers, he realized he lacked the urge. Not that it mattered—Salina latched on to him, her mouth all but devouring his. Her arms banded his neck as she pressed against him. His hands moved up her slender back before sliding to her waist and hips, but all he felt was bony woman—no hint of the lush softness he'd felt with Cora Mae—

Damnation. Hadn't that been why he'd come here, to get Cora off his mind?

Salina sucked his tongue into her mouth, her breath hard against his face as she pressed her breasts against his chest. To his sheer annoyance, he didn't feel a damn thing as she wriggled her way onto his lap.

Did she expect him to bed her right here in the parlor, with her housekeeper in the other room?

He broke away from her kiss and practically had to peel her off him.

"Salina," he said, easing back on the settee, feeling rather suffocated. "I'm not one for mincing words, so I'm going to come right out and ask."

"Yes?" she said, licking her lips as her face lit with a smile.

"Are you looking to be courted or do you just want a quick tumble?"

Her eyes widened. A flush rose into her cheeks as she eased away from him. "To be courted."

"I'm no expert on the matter, but I'm pretty sure that starts with some talking."

"Well, I suppose I've never truly been courted."

"Ol' Jameson didn't woo you with candy and flowers?" he asked, amused by the notion. He'd only met Harlan Jameson on a few occasions. The weathered rancher had struck Chance as a tough hombre if he'd ever known one.

"Harlan rode into the yard where I was hanging the wash and said he was looking to take a wife. He asked. I accepted. We were wed that afternoon."

"Love at first sight, huh?"

"He did ride in like a savior," she said, her lips quirking with a smile. "I'd never been off the farm, much less had the opportunity to meet any suitors."

"You were raised on a farm? I wouldn't have guessed."

"My mother was a school teacher before she birthed enough children to fill a schoolhouse. We were well educated, and dirt poor. I might have only been seventeen when I met Harlan, but I knew freedom when it knocked on my door."

"Freedom? That's not a term I've ever equated to marriage."

"It was for me. I grew up in a sod house with eleven other siblings. I always knew I was meant for better things. Harlan gave that to me. I intend to hold on to it."

She didn't hide her motivation for wanting his name. "I can respect that," he said, thinking this might indeed be the solution he needed. She wasn't looking for love, and neither was he. If he was going to take a wife, he didn't need a mess of emotion to go along with it.

He stood, picking his hat up from the floor. "I should be going."

Salina surged up beside him. "So soon?"

"I think we've made a good start, and work comes early."

"Am I to assume we're courting, then?"

He stared into eyes the color of mud, and couldn't help but think of Cora Mae. If she wanted reassurance, he'd give it to her. "I suppose so," he said, tucking a finger beneath Salina's pointed chin, tilting her face up as he leaned in to kiss her. He touched her lips lightly with his, then backed toward the door.

"Can I expect to see you again soon?"

"Doubt it."

Disappointment darkened her eyes. "Do you intend a long courtship?"

"I'm not one for rushing into things, and we're in the midst of spring roundup. This is a real busy time for us."

She nodded, her brow pinched in a frown. "I understand. Things are quite busy for me as well."

Taking that as an agreement, he turned to leave. As he opened the front door, a sudden question sprang to his mind. "Salina," he said, glancing back, "what's Wyatt to you?"

"He's my foreman," she said, smiling gently.

"Should things work out between us, he'll have to go."

The instant tension in her delicate features wasn't an agreement. "He's the most experienced cattleman I have."

"There are men on my ranch who've worked cattle longer than he's been tugging on his own boots. Men I trust. If we merge our land I'll likely put a couple of them in charge of ranging while we smooth out a system."

"But…we'd live *here,* wouldn't we?"

He glanced around the Victorian-style house that suited him like a summer rash. "None of this needs to be decided right away," he said, sliding his hat over his hair. "You have a good evening."

Chance made his way down the front steps, trying to assure himself he was doing the right thing for everyone. Stepping up into his saddle, he glanced around the quiet yard. Could he live here, over an hour away from his own ranch?

His gut burning, he guided his large buckskin toward home.

As Star ambled through Lazy J pasture, toward the canyons leading to his valley, Chance couldn't shake another truth. Sitting in that house only emphasized everything he admired in Cora Mae. The way she felt wrapped in his arms, how she fit so easily into their family, the way she smelled of sweet scents from the kitchen. Not to mention how pretty she looked coated in mud. She'd certainly been a worthy opponent in the mud fight.

He grinned at the thought. If he wanted to be honest with himself, he'd realize Cora Mae as a woman wasn't so different from the Cora Mae he'd loved as a kid. Maybe he *had* been letting his hatred toward her mother sour his perception.

Soured perceptions didn't have a damn thing to do with his attraction to her. Every time he felt himself getting close to her, his mind and body went haywire. Having an attraction he couldn't control was playing havoc with his temper.

Star sidestepped and nickered, the warning jerking him from his thoughts as something landed around his shoulders.

Oh, hell.

A rope cinched tight, yanking him straight back out of the saddle. He pounded against the ground. His stomach lodged in his lungs, a dozen hands descended upon him.

Son of a bitch!

An ambush.

Chapter Eleven

P̲innned down, the rope around his shoulders tightened over his neck as another burned the skin of his wrists.

"Light the torch!"

Even with his face pressed to the grass and a ringing in his ears, Chance recognized Wyatt's voice. A torch hissed, the flash of light blinding him.

Released, Chance sat back on his heels. Squinting against the orange glow, mindful of the rope chafing his neck and trailing down his back, he tested the binding around his wrists. Four wide-eyed cattlemen stood around him, their bandannas still pulled over their mouths and noses like a bunch of bank robbers.

"Ah, hell," one muttered. "He's a Morgan."

No wonder Salina's place had been so quiet. Her crew had been out playing cowboys and bandits. And he'd been the fool strolling through the moonlight with his head lost in the stars.

Wyatt stepped into the circle of light, his expression nothing short of gleeful. "Well, well, well. Look what we have here." He glanced around at his crew, who didn't seem to share his excitement. "Told you boys we'd catch us a rustler."

"Rustler?" Chance shifted up, onto his feet.

The group before him took a step back. Cowards, the lot of them. He continued to tug discreetly at the rope binding his hands, checking for weakness. Unfortunately, Wyatt's cowhands seemed to have a talent for tying secure knots. No doubt the noose around his neck had been tied to perfection.

"How do *you* like being attacked without any warning?" asked Wyatt.

"What are you talking about? When I found you in town, I called you by name before I knocked you on your ass."

"You're not so tough now," Wyatt scoffed, taking a step toward him.

"Yeah?" Chance growled through clenched teeth. "Keep walking and we'll find out."

Wyatt didn't take another step. "Maybe we should drop you from a tree branch and test that noose."

Chance glanced at Wyatt's confused crew.

"He's not the rustler, Wyatt," one of them said, still hiding behind his bandanna.

"He's on Lazy J land," said Wyatt.

"No kidding. How else am I supposed to get to Salina's ranch? Even if I was out here looking for cattle, they're likely to be mine! You've been skimming off our herd for months."

Wyatt's eyes narrowed. "Why would you be at the ranch?"

"That's between me and your boss."

"You went to see Salina?"

"I did."

A stillness came over Wyatt, one that Chance recognized immediately. The cold rage in Wyatt's eyes told him what Salina hadn't.

She had lied to him.

"Put him on a horse," Wyatt ordered.

With a noose still tight around his neck and trees rooted all around? *Like hell!* "Save them the trouble and cut me loose."

"I don't think so." Wyatt shook his head, a slow smile tilting his lips. He strolled forward, keeping his voice low. "So goddamn smug. Riding around these hills like you're God's gift to the world."

Chance didn't know what he was talking about. He rode around these hills trying to make a living, just like every other man.

"I've enjoyed it, you know. Getting paid to knock you down a few notches. If you think you're going to ride in and just steal my woman, you're sadly mistaken."

"If she's your woman, why's she hunting me down like I'm the last man in Wyoming?"

Wyatt stiffened as though lashed by a whip.

"She still won't want you, you know. Killing me won't make you any less of a penniless cowpoke."

"She can't get enough of me! Hope that's a comfort to you while you're burning in hell."

"Don't fool yourself into thinking I'd be going alone. My brother wouldn't rest until he'd killed every last one of you." The truth in those words sent the pain crashing through Chance. Tucker didn't deserve to have more bloodshed on his hands. He didn't deserve to continually suffer because of Chance's mistakes.

"I said put him on a horse!" Wyatt shouted.

The men standing behind him in the circle of light didn't rush forward.

Ira Preston, son of a shopkeeper in Slippery Gulch, pulled his bandanna from his mouth. "Wyatt, *he's a Morgan*."

"I know who he is! Get him on a goddamn horse!"

Chance tensed as one of the men followed his orders and fetched his Palomino. Wyatt wasn't the first man eager to stomp Chance into an early grave, but as four men closed in on him, this was all starting to feel too damn close for comfort.

"I don't know about this, Wyatt." Ira stood back, holding the torch, his frantic eyes searching the darkness for signs of backup Chance dearly wished had been there.

"You won't get away with this," Chance said with exaggerated impatience, carefully watching the men circling him like a pack of wolves. He twisted his wrists, fearfully aware of the pile of rope near his feet and trailing down his back. "We're on Lazy J land."

"It's a big ranch," said Wyatt. "We get all kinds of trespassers through here."

Watching the men at his sides close in, Chance shook his head. "Your inexperience is gonna get you all killed."

"His brother really was a man hunter," said Ira.

"And nothing's easier to track than sloppy vermin."

"*Shut up!*" Wyatt shouted.

Two sets of hands closed over his arms. Chance stood stiffly in their grip. One of Wyatt's men, Nigel, led a tall palomino toward him.

Seeming confident his cronies had a hold on Chance, Wyatt stepped close. "Mount up."

Chance shoved back with his feet, letting the men

beside him support his weight as he planted his boots in the center of Wyatt's scrawny chest. Wyatt flew back and landed flat on the ground. Twisting in the grip of the others, Chance slammed his forehead into the nose of the man on his right, rattling his own skull as the man's nose cracked. Blood gushed as he yelped and staggered back.

With his next step, Chance slammed his knee against the third man, doubling him over as his family jewels ricocheted into his gut. His hands slid from Chance's sleeve as he fell to the ground, coughing and gasping.

Chance stumbled back. Three men on the ground, the fourth trying to calm his skittish horse, Chance glanced at Ira.

The cowhand threw the torch into the grass. "I quit!" The flame hissed in the damp grass and went out, leaving them in darkness. "I don't get paid enough for this," Ira shouted, his boots beating a hard path toward their horses.

Chance stared into the darkness, listening to the groaning of one man, the faint whispers of another.

Something jerked him back, yanking him upward. The coarse fibers of the noose burned into his throat, pinching off his windpipe.

"Tug, damn it!" Wyatt shouted, and he realized Wyatt had gotten hold of the rope and tossed it over a branch. "There's more than one way to hang a man."

Chance's body strained up, his heels leaving the ground. Blood pounded in his ears as he tried to draw a breath, but couldn't.

He couldn't die like this, his throat slowly crushing, the ground just beneath his feet.

Somber brown eyes and shimmering red curls flashed in his mind. He couldn't believe their last words would be ones of anger. More than anything, he wished he had treated Cora Mae differently, had treated her *better*.

His lungs were burning for air, his heart was filled with nothing but regret.

An explosion sounded in his ears, and suddenly the tension released. His boots hit the ground. His hands bound and the noose cinched tight, he fell forward into the grass. Unable to breathe, he couldn't do anything but fight the darkness steadily closing in around him.

Fingers dug into his neck and tugged at the rope cutting off his windpipe.

Chance sucked in a wheezing gasp of air. His cheek against the cool, wet grass, he felt the vibrations of retreating hoofbeats as each blessed breath eased the burning of his lungs.

Frantic to get the noose from around his neck, he pushed up and realized his hands had been cut free by someone. His gaze landed on a pair of fur boots barely visible in the pale moonlight as he released the noose. Maggie Danvers's black pelt coat blended her with the night. He was surprised to see the reclusive mountain woman.

"Mag," he croaked, clutching his burning throat. He tossed the rope to the ground in front of him.

"Morgan." Crouching low, she struck a match. She held it high and leaned close. The hiss of breath through Mag's teeth confirmed what the ring of fire around his neck had already told him. The noose had burned a bloody trench into his skin.

He tenderly fingered at his throat, each breath coming in a bit easier. "Good thing I have a thick neck," he wheezed, his rattled throat still rebelling against the vibrations of his voice.

Mag shook out her match and stood. "Might want to keep it out of a noose for a few days. Let those burns heal up."

Her dry tone forced a laugh through the fire. As his breathing improved so did his sense of smell. Maggie's odor made him wonder if she'd gutted the bear before slinging its pelt onto her back.

"You reek."

Her smile was another surprise. Shining white teeth revealed a cleanliness he knew she hid beneath the smell of rotted carcasses. "I should think it a pleasant scent, considering you were a second away from breathing nothing but brimstone."

"Can't argue with that." He pushed to his feet, rotating his stiff shoulders as he stood. "I owe you, Maggie."

"No. Now we're even."

He didn't see how. The first time he'd come across Mag in the high country she'd guided him through the passes and led him to the valley Tucker had described to him. That was after he'd helped her bury her husband.

"Well, you have my gratitude," he said.

"I've got no use for gratitude. You can keep it."

Just because they'd helped one another out didn't mean they were friends. "Fair enough." Spotting his hat a couple of feet away on the grass, he went to retrieve it. "I suppose I should have suspected Wyatt would be waiting for me."

"He wasn't waiting for you," Mag said with certainty.

"You?" he asked.

Her laugh was quick and cold, much like the rest of her. "Wyatt McNealy tracking *me?* That'll be the day. It's taken him six months to pick up the trail of the man stealing his cattle."

"Someone's been stealing Lazy J cattle?"

"Like the Pied Piper led rats from a village. Your little rendezvous probably cost him his best chance at catching the man who deserved that noose. Stroke of bad luck for everyone."

Story of Chance's life. He and Tucker had been sure the men taking their stock had come from the Lazy J, and Tuck was one of the best trackers around. "We were certain Wyatt was the one stealing from us," he said to no one in particular.

"He was," Mag called back from somewhere in the darkness. "But not as fast as he's losing 'em."

Chance glanced at the spot where Mag had been standing. How the hell did a mountain shrew know so much about the local livestock? And why hadn't Salina told him she'd been having a problem with rustlers?

He whistled for his horse. A moment later, Star trotted toward him, her coat breaking free of the shadows. She nudged his chest as he reached for her halter.

"I'm fine. Let's get home." He shifted into the saddle, and noticed his rifle was missing from the scabbard. *Thieving bastards!* The light breeze stinging against his neck, he spurred Star toward home.

As he rode back, he recalled Salina's comment from a few weeks back:

"The highwaymen who call themselves a cattle association."

He hadn't given it too much thought. It was common knowledge that the larger outfits taxed the stockyards and controlled the railheads.

No wonder she's so set on merging their ranches. As with most anything, the bigger beasts of the industry tended to run roughshod over the more vulnerable ranchers. With Jameson gone, Salina was vulnerable.

Hopefully her *foreman* could handle the heat, if he lived long enough. Once they'd finished with the roundup, Chance would even things up with Wyatt, right after he got his rifle back.

Chance dismounted and led Star into the stable. By the time he'd climbed the back steps, his energy had been sapped, his body ached and his neck blazed like the fires of hell. He pulled his heel against the toe of his other boot and stepped out of the stiff leather.

Leaving both boots on the porch, he eased the door open. The last thing he wanted was for Tucker to see him in such a state, covered in grass stains, a ring of blood around his neck. He stepped lightly inside and carefully shut the door. The rush of warmth and sweet-scented air dashed his hopes that everyone would be upstairs sound asleep. The oven door clanged shut.

Cora Mae looked at him from across the kitchen, a tray of freshly baked pastries in her hand. She'd swept her hair up at the sides, the way he liked it, creating a cascade of curls down her back.

"Evening," he said, his voice still gritty.

Her gaze landed near his collar. She gasped, and Chance suppressed a groan.

"Chance? *What happened?*"

He didn't want her sympathy. "It's nothing," he said, quickly stepping into the pantry to grab the whiskey. If he didn't douse his cuts, they'd become infected for sure. When he came back to the kitchen, Cora Mae hadn't moved an inch. Her wide eyes gazed at him.

"You've been hurt."

"I'm fine. Good night." He turned and started up the stairs. He slowed in the hall long enough to grab some rags from a cabinet then continued into his dark room. He set his supplies on the bureau then lit the lamp. Turning back, he spied Cora Mae standing in the doorway.

"Where did you go?" she asked. "What happened?"

What was he supposed to tell her? That he'd ridden out with the intention of bedding another woman in an attempt to get her off his mind? "I was…just…out. Ran into the wrong people. Could you shut the door for me?"

"How did you…" Her voice trailed off as he pulled his shirt over his head. "You're bleeding," she said, her voice escalating. "My God, Chance, is that a rope burn?"

"Shh!"

"Don't you hush me," she said, planting her hands on her hips. "Someone's tried to hang you!"

"It's not the first time, and likely won't be the last," he muttered to himself. "Go to bed, Cora."

She took a timid step toward him, then stopped.

She actually feared him. The reminder stabbed at his pride.

"Not until I know who's done this to you," she insisted.

"One of the imbeciles you'd warned me about." He poured some water into the washbasin and uncapped the whiskey, knowing the sting in his neck was only going to get worse.

Cora Mae continued to hover just inside the doorway.

"Listen, I've had a rotten night. As much as I know I deserve it, I'd rather you not watch me flinch as I clean this burn."

She strode into his room looking ready to slug him. To his amazement, she took the cloth from his hand and pointed at the end of his bed. *"Sit."*

"You don't have to."

She looked at his neck and her eyes flinched. "I want to help." She picked up the basin from the dresser. Chance did as she'd said, settling onto the end of his bed, his pride cracking further as she approached him. Her brow creased as she looked closely at his injury.

"Good Lord, Chance. I should wake Tucker."

"*No.*"

She touched his chin and he looked up, giving her better access. The sympathy in her gaze only made him feel worse. He tried not to flinch as she pressed the cool rag against his burning skin.

"It's not as bad as it looks," he said.

"I haven't doused it with alcohol yet. Does your throat hurt?"

Only when he swallowed. "A little."

"You sound as though you've been gargling sand." She dunked the bloody rag into the basin and continued to rinse his skin. "Chance, I really should go get Tucker."

"No," he said, clenching his teeth through the pain. If Tuck knew Wyatt had had him dangling at the end of a noose all hell would break loose. And for what? Because Salina was playing games with both of them? He wasn't going to risk a ranch war over a woman. Tucker had his family to look after and they both already had all the work they could deal with. He'd bide his time and deal with Wyatt his own way.

"You're really hurt," she said.

"This doesn't involve the ranch."

"How could it not? One of your neighbors has tried to kill you!"

"Shh!"

"How can you—"

"This wasn't over a ranch quarrel."

"What else could it be?"

"Jealousy." He shook his head. *"My own stupidity."*

The concern in Cora's eyes ripped at his conscience. "I doubt Wyatt would have tried to kill me if I hadn't told him I'd paid a call to Salina."

She blinked. "Wyatt did this?"

"Seems he's not real receptive to the idea of me courting his mistress."

Cora felt her jaw drop open and was powerless to pull it shut. *He couldn't be serious!* "You're…" *Dear God.* She could barely get the words past her throat. "Courting Salina Jameson?"

His wide, bronze shoulders shifted, drawing her gaze to the firm planes and sculpted muscle of his chest. A wave of heat rushed through her body, sending a flush into her cheeks.

"Figured I'd give it a shot," he said.

She returned her focus to the task of rinsing the bloody gash in his skin, thinking she must not know Chance at all. If he was interested in a woman like Salina, he had more brawn than brains. How could he be fooled by a woman so blatantly like her mother!

"Ouch!" Chance flinched away, and Cora realized she'd been sponging his neck a little too hard.

"Sorry." She dabbed the strip of raw, welted skin once more then turned back to the bureau for the whiskey. Drawing a deep steady breath, she tugged at the high collar of her dress, slightly flushed beneath. Despite his injury, the sight of his partially clothed body was having an alarming effect on her. Gathering her senses, she turned back to the shirtless man behind her.

Chance gazed up at her through his tousled hair, watching

her with a combination of curiosity and caution. She couldn't decide what she wanted more, to smooth those golden waves back with her fingers, or gag him with the rancid cloth. Gagging would be the smartest option, she decided.

"You don't like her," he said as she moved beside him.

"I don't know her." *No more than she wanted to.* "This is going to sting."

It did. Air hissed through Chance's teeth, every light touch of the cloth setting fire to his skin. "Try not to have too much fun."

She stopped, halfway across his throat, anger flashing in her eyes as she pressed the backs of her hands to the curves of her hips. "I would *never* wish for you to be hurt."

He smiled despite the pain. "I was teasing."

Her frown deepened. "Oh."

"Used to do that all the time."

"Yes, well…we used to be friends," she said, glancing down at the rag in her hand, hiding her gaze. But he heard the sadness. She turned back to the dresser and poured another round of whiskey onto the cloth.

She didn't meet his gaze when she returned. "Look down."

Chance followed the command.

"I think we could be," he said at length, the pain in his neck becoming nearly tolerable.

"Could be what?"

"Friends."

She stepped back. The tension in her expression suggested otherwise. He knew it had taken a lot for her to come into this room and help him. Compassion wasn't trust and was far more than he deserved.

"We came awfully close earlier today," he said, remembering the short time he'd let go of his anger and mistrust.

Her lips twitched with the start of a smile, and Chance's heart leaped. He wanted to put her at ease with him.

"Or maybe you just like to play in the mud," he said, forcing a grin.

"Maybe I do," she said, arching an eyebrow.

She sure had sass. *She always had,* he reminded himself. Perhaps Tucker was right. When he really thought about it, she hadn't done anything to cause his distrust. Nothing other than accomplish what he couldn't— bringing them together without the threat of Winifred hanging over their heads. He couldn't have hoped to hear better news than of his stepmother's death, that Cora Mae had found a life she'd enjoyed, away from her mother's cruelty, a life she had given up to find him and Tuck.

Looking into her pretty face, he knew it was more than memories of Winifred that tainted his feelings toward Cora Mae. It was Cora Mae—the woman he never imagined she would become, a woman who could stoke his desire with an ease that troubled him. Mostly because she didn't even try. All she had to do was stand there, and he could sense her sweetness and the fire inside her he'd already caught glimpses of. A temptation snared with all the trappings of love and marriage—he certainly had no right to touch Cora Mae unless he was interested in both. Old warnings surfaced in his mind.

Love is a trap. Nothing else could weaken the mind and shatter the spirit with such efficiency.

"Look up," she said.

He remained silent as she finished.

"Should I do your wrists?" she asked.

"I can get it." He took the cloth from her. "Thanks."

She moved back as he stood and walked to the dresser.

He washed his hands then picked up the whiskey bottle and doused the mild rope burns on his wrists.

"Will you tell me what happened?" she asked from behind him.

He released a sigh as he grabbed a towel, not thrilled with the idea of sharing how foolish he'd been. "On my ride back from the Lazy J, I was too busy stargazing to realize I was being ambushed."

"Why would Wyatt ambush you?"

He turned and was surprised to see Cora Mae sitting on the end of his bed.

Don't get sidetracked. He was lucky she was even talking to him.

"Apparently he's having trouble with cattle rustlers and I triggered his trap. When he found out I'd been to the ranch to see Salina, he decided stealing his woman carried the same penalty as rustling."

"He could have killed you."

"He *nearly* did. I'm sure I'd be quite dead if it hadn't been for Mag."

Cora's eyes popped wide. "The trapper's woman?"

Realizing his slip, Chance could have bit off his tongue. "Yeah," he said with some hesitation. "I guess she spotted the lynching and felt inclined to help me out."

"Does she live so close? I've heard her mentioned by the other men on a few occasions. They said she passes through the area every now and again, but I assumed she lived high up in the mountains."

"Her place is closer than anyone thinks. Might even be on Lazy J land, not that it should matter to them. Halfway up the first mountain peak between our ranches is still wild country, and no place to graze stock."

"You're friends?"

"I don't think Mag has use for friends. We met during my first ride into this valley. I was lost, if you want to know the truth of it," he said with a slight smile. "She knows these hills and mountain passes better than I know my own ranch. I helped her out with something and she showed me around."

"And the trapper?"

"He's even less social than Mag," Chance said, thinking that was an understatement. Danvers had been dead for a few days before Chance had come upon Maggie trying to dig a grave in frozen ground. He'd already told Cora Mae more about Mag than he should have, more than he'd ever told anyone. He wasn't about to break his vow of silence about Danvers's death. "Anyhow, she helped me out, and I'm fine."

"Fine?"

"Close enough."

Cora could hardly believe his nonchalance. "Chance, this is serious!"

"And I'll deal with it. In my own time, in my own way."

Was he trying to protect Salina? Could he really care for her? Her mind rebelled at the thought, but the question still escaped her mouth. "Do you still intend to pursue Salina?"

"If I took over the Lazy J, I'd control the crew."

"That's a reason to marry?"

"More reason than some have for getting hitched."

"But…you don't love her."

"Exactly."

"You don't want to love the woman you marry?"

"I never wanted to marry at all." Again he shrugged. "But life's like that sometimes."

He deserved better. He deserved the warmth and caring she saw between Tucker and Skylar. "Who says you have to marry?"

"It's been suggested. It could be ideal when you think about it."

"Please, enlighten me."

Chance found himself fighting a grin as he stared at her stern expression. He couldn't win. Here he was, trying his damnedest to convince her he was averting his romantic intentions away from her—and she was getting mad at him. "I've thought about the things you said earlier, and you were right. My actions were disrespectful this afternoon, and I'm sorry. I meant it when I said I wanted us to be friends."

Her tremulous smile lasted a moment and wasn't entirely convincing. "I'd like that."

"Me, too, Cora," he said, knowing it was a lie even as the words left his lips.

She deserved to be part of this family. His physical frustrations were *his* problem. "You're safe with me. I swear it. I don't want to chase you off. Though I haven't shown it, I *am* glad you came."

Cora listened to him saying all the words she'd wanted to hear, while talking in the low baritone voice that turned her insides to jelly. She couldn't take her gaze off his mouth, the mouth that, for a time, had felt so nice against hers. She wasn't so sure it was Chance that she didn't trust.

"I'm going to bed," she said, standing and edging toward the door. "I still think you should tell Tucker about Wyatt."

"Cora?"

She stopped in the doorway.

"Can you forgive me for my actions, the things I've said?"

The concern in his gaze only increased the chaos raging inside her. "I already have," she said, her voice barely audible.

He smiled and shoved a hand through his tangled hair, relief shining in his green eyes. Yet all Cora could think about was the taste of his wild kisses, the feel of his solid chest pressed against her, his heart beating as erratically as her own.

"Thanks for fixing me up," he said, but Cora was already closing the door of her own room, and trying to tamp down the surge of sensation that had stolen her breath.

His apology couldn't take away the memory of his kisses, or the cravings she knew better than to want.

Chapter Twelve

Sounds of laughter drew him from the stable. Visions of fall rooted him in place. A shimmer of red and copper curls danced on the breeze as Cora Mae chased his nephew across the back lawn. She latched her arms around Josh and lifted him off his booted feet. The delighted giggles carrying across the wind suggested his nephew had clearly wanted to be caught.

Smart kid.

Something inside Chance warmed at the sight of them.

The past week of *being nice* hadn't been so bad. He'd discovered sitting in a warm kitchen with Cora Mae to be a real treat. He was even starting to get used to the flushed cheeks and heated gazes she did her best to hide from him whenever their eyes caught and held for a few seconds too long. Somehow, knowing she struggled with the same desire that had been tearing at him for weeks gave him the edge he needed to be able to control his own.

We're friends. Who happen to spark like flint to stone.

Skylar's voice called Joshua back into the house. Cora

Mae released the boy, and his nephew scampered up the back steps. Cora Mae picked up a wicker basket and strode toward the clothesline where linens waved like white flags in the wind.

He had to get back out to work. His branding crew needed the coils of rope he had let slide from his shoulder. Tucking his gloves into his back pocket, he headed for the clothesline. He approached, watching the shadow of Cora Mae's shapely body as she reached for the clothespin.

I've got a few minutes to be nice.

The white drape fell away, and Cora Mae jumped at the sight of him standing on the other side.

"Chance!"

"Can I give you a hand with that?"

She seemed lost for words, so he grabbed the end of the sheet flapping in the breeze.

"Thank you."

"No sense in you wrestling with this big sheet in the wind."

Cora didn't tell him she'd planned to fold them inside. She simply followed his lead, folding the linen in half, then stepping toward him to fold it across the middle.

"Breakfast sure was good," he said.

And all it had taken was his near death to get him to sit at the breakfast table and come in for a noontime meal. Her gaze slid to the red bandanna secured around his stubborn neck, hiding his rope burns. "I think you're making a mistake," she said, voicing her concern as she had in previous days.

He glanced down at the sheet they'd worked into a fat rectangle. "If I'm doing it wrong—"

She laughed, despite her irritation. "I mean by not telling Tucker about Wyatt."

He grinned and passed the bundle to her. "Don't worry. Wyatt will be dealt with, in a way that won't blow our chances for meeting our contracts. We haven't had a speck of trouble with the Lazy J in the past week. You can bet they're spooked. And they should be." He took another sheet off the clothesline while she placed the folded linen in the basket.

"How would telling Tucker affect meeting your contracts for horses?"

He flapped the sheet toward her. "A ranch full of dead cowhands would attract an inquiry."

Cora gaped at him from across the sheet. She hadn't thought of Tucker retaliating, but now she remembered his warning the morning he'd told her about Salina's crew stealing their stock. She supposed either of the twins would seek vengeance against anyone who raised a hand against the other.

"Salina's not worth the bloodshed, and my brother has seen enough killing to last a lifetime. I'll deal with Wyatt on my own."

He stepped forward again. Their fingers brushed as he passed her his end and reached for the bottom. The light caress was like a static shock, the current rippling up her arms to the peaks of her breasts. She was certain Chance felt it, too, his gaze hot on hers.

Silence stretched as they folded the next two sheets.

"You're a man of many talents," she said as she placed the last of the linen in the basket.

"Don't tell Skylar. She'll add beating rugs and pinning clothes on the line to my list of chores."

His smile was slow and lethal, making the ache in her breasts spiral throughout her body. *Dear Lord.* She wasn't sure she didn't prefer his brooding moods to the smiles and charm he'd been displaying lately. His relaxed presence, the sight of his dark hands on the white linen—*stop thinking about it!* She only wanted a brother, and he deserved a real wife.

"You and Skylar seem to be getting along real well," he said.

"Oh, Skylar's lovely." She'd never felt a stronger friendship with a woman.

"So are you."

Chance tensed as his words echoed back on the light breeze.

Where the hell had that come from?

Cora Mae laughed off the compliment and lifted the basket of folded laundry. "Thank you for the help."

She turned and walked back to the house.

Chance hadn't complimented a woman since he didn't know when. And she'd simply shrugged off his words.

"Have you changed your mind?" he called after her.

"About what?"

"Leaving."

She stopped at the base of the steps, her expression wary. "It was never my intention to stay here, Chance. But I'll help out as long as Skylar needs me."

"Hell, Cora, we all need you. You won't find a soul on this ranch who wouldn't beg you to stay."

Her instant smile warmed him from the inside out.

"Thank you for saying so."

"Nothing but the truth." The truth felt damn good. "Well, I should get back. You have a nice afternoon."

"You, too."

When he reached the stable doors, he turned and

glanced back. Cora Mae stood where he'd left her, staring after him. Even at that distance he could see her startle at being caught. She turned and quickly hustled up the steps.

Chance smiled as he turned back to the stable. *Yes, sir. Being nice felt real good.*

"Done with the laundry?"

Garret stood just inside the stable doors, the rope Chance had dropped slung over his shoulder. Anger sparked in his hazel eyes.

"I was just helping out a bit."

"Uh-huh. Lately, it seems like every time I look sideways the two of you are huddled up together, whispering."

All that whispering had been Cora Mae's insistence that he tell Tucker about Wyatt, and Chance's flat refusal. None of which was any of Garret's business. "What? Are you jealous?"

"I liked her first!"

Chance couldn't help but laugh. "Kid, I am not in competition with you."

"You think I don't see the way you look at her?"

Damnation. He'd hoped no one had witnessed the way he'd been looking at her. But then, Garret had been watching Cora Mae with the possessive eyes of a love-struck kid.

"Plenty of men marry at my age."

"Marry? *Cora Mae?*"

"Sixteen is old enough to marry," he insisted.

"First you have to find a woman willing to marry a sixteen-year-old *kid.* Let me save you some humiliation. Cora Mae isn't that woman."

"I say she is." Garret squared his broad shoulders and puffed his chest out. "And I think it's about time you stopped calling me kid."

"First you'll have to stop acting like one," Chance said, true anger clenching his muscles. "Don't gripe at me because you're not man enough to win the woman you've set your sights on."

"The hell I'm not! I'm every bit the man you are!"

Chance wasn't about to deny the fact. Garret shouldered the same workload as every other man on the ranch, and did so without complaint. But a grown man would have picked up on Cora Mae's disinterest in him by now. It wasn't any fault of his that *she* didn't blossom under the kid's attention. The realization nearly brought a smile to Chance's lips.

"So what are you worried about? Seems to me you should be focusing on your courtship tactics. Maybe you ought to run out and pick her some more flowers."

"Maybe I should help her fold sheets," Garret suggested in a biting tone.

"Or maybe you could take a good look through those grown-up eyes and notice that she's flat not interested in you."

Garret's eyes narrowed to slits. "We'll see about that," he said, stomping toward his horse with the rope.

"Don't say I didn't warn you."

Chance shifted his shoulder and realized his body was a mass of knotted tension. The kid was setting himself up for heartache. Cora Mae wouldn't succumb to his attention.

Chance wasn't one for sitting around the house at night when there was work still to be done. On a ranch their size, there was always something that needed doing, and he'd never wanted to crowd his brother's time with his family.

Tonight he found himself curious about everyone's evening activities. For the first time, he opted to bathe directly after supper.

Tucking in a clean shirt, he headed for the front stairwell. The murmur of conversation filtered up from below. Halfway down the stairs he spotted Cora Mae, one of the girls nestled in her arms as she sat beside Skylar on the sofa. Skylar held a long wooden needle and a handful of yellow yarn. Tucker sat on the floor, reclined against the sofa, a baby lying in the cradle of his folded legs as he stacked a block onto a tower. Josh sat on his knees near the growing castle, his blue eyes dark with concentration.

Another step down and his gaze landed on Skylar's brother standing before the hearth. Garret's hazel eyes hardened at the sight of him coming downstairs.

This was *his* house. If he wanted to sit inside for some evening conversation, he damn well would.

"Evening," Chance said, walking into the room. He dropped into a big chair across the room from Cora Mae.

Tucker eyed him curiously. Skylar's hands fell idle on the yellow weave as she stared at him.

Damn. Couldn't a man sit in the company of his own family?

Josh looked over his shoulder at him. "Hi, Unco 'Ance."

He grinned at his nephew who instantly turned back to his building.

"Would you tell them I don't need payment," Cora Mae said, breaking the uncomfortable silence.

Judging by the stubborn set of her jaw, they'd all been having a heated debate. His curiosity piqued, he crossed his ankles and eased back in the chair.

"Payment for what?"

"Slaving away in a hot kitchen from sunup to sundown," said Tucker. "Not to mention all the chores in between."

"I'm not taking your money."

"Like hell," Tuck countered.

Skylar's knee bumped his back.

"I mean *heck*," Tucker amended, glancing at his son, who didn't seem to notice anything beyond his towers.

Chance grabbed a newspaper from the floor beside him and shook it out, figuring his brother had all the experience when it came to handling stubborn women.

"You've been working from dawn to dusk for weeks," Tucker continued.

"It's true," Skylar added. "We would have had to hire someone to help out after the babies were born."

"Not to mention all the pretty needlework you've done for the house," said Garret.

"That's right," Tucker agreed. "You've been an asset to the household."

"And *you* have fed and sheltered me these past weeks."

"We feed and shelter the men in the bunkhouse too," Tucker informed her. "Yet they don't complain about taking their pay."

Chance smiled into the blur of newspaper print. Tucker was right. Cora Mae had worked just as hard as the rest of them. She deserved wages.

"I had rather hoped you thought of me as family," she said softly. "Not a hired hand."

"Exactly," said Tucker. "This *family* runs a business. We all work our tails off and we all take our cut."

Cora was running out of words, *and patience*. It didn't feel right to take even a cent from them. She hadn't come here looking to profit from them. She glanced toward the newspaper and long denim-clad legs crossed at the ankles, which was all she could see of Chance. His accusations on the day she'd arrived hadn't faded from her mind. She wasn't looking for a handout.

"It's really not necessary."

"Cora Mae?"

The sound of her full name spoken in Chance's deep drawl could have been a caress for the way it jolted her senses. All it took was the smooth rumble of his voice for her body to react.

Smiling green eyes glanced at her from over the newspaper. "You won't win this one, darlin'. You're outnumbered four to one."

Her breath lodged in her throat. Certain she was red from her chin to her hairline, she glanced at Skylar.

"He's right," she said. "You could use a new spring dress and I know for a fact that a shipment of fabric comes in tomorrow. Those women in town are like vultures," Skylar said bitterly. "They'll have the general store picked clean by sundown. I had hoped to ride along, but I'm not ready to leave the girls."

"You could ride along, Cora," said Tucker. "You've got an eye for fabric and could do some shopping of your own."

"I'd be very appreciative if you'd go," Skylar added. "My girls will need clothes before the next supply of fabrics comes through."

She supposed it would be nice to pick up a few things for herself. "All right. I'll go along. But I'm still not comfortable about taking wages."

"You'll get used to it," Chance said from behind the paper.

"I could ride along, too," said Garret.

"No can do," Tucker countered. "We've got corrals full of horses and a deadline looming. I can't spare two men for half a day."

"I leave at daybreak," said Chance. "Not sunup. *Daybreak*."

She was going with *Chance?* She glanced around, half hoping someone would rebuke his remark.

Garret stomped toward his room, clearly mad about not being able to go, though she now wished Tucker had relented. Her gaze was drawn to the newspaper Chance held up across the room.

Her heart constricted at the thought of spending the day alone with the man hidden behind the headlines.

Chapter Thirteen

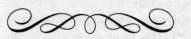

"Good morning, Mr. Morgan," said a soft feminine voice.

"Morning," came Chance's cool reply.

Cora tried to keep her focus on the bolts of gingham and lace piled on a makeshift table as Chance did his best to gather other supplies while practically tripping over women nudging others out of their way for his attention.

"Mr. Morgan," said another breathless harlot.

"Morning."

"I've a mind to make a new spring dress. I just can't decide on the color. Perhaps you can suggest one?"

Of all the impertinent…!

"Well," said Chance.

Cora glanced up, quite curious to hear his suggestion.

A pretty girl with light hair and eyes smiled up at him. He did look dashing in his dark hat and long range coat. The heavy canvas concealed the double holster hanging at his hips. She'd been surprised by the gunbelt this morning, but after his experience two weeks ago, she couldn't blame him for traveling armed. Since they'd arrived at the general store, she'd begun to wonder if he'd strapped on his guns to defend himself from the local women.

He caught Cora's gaze from across the room. The irritation chiseled across his features was as plain as the nose on his face. Cora bit her lip against a laugh. She nearly felt sorry for him. His instant smile awakened the butterflies that had been living inside her lately. He winked at her before turning back to the ever-attentive young woman standing before him.

"Why don't you ask my stepsister, Miss Tindale," he suggested. "She has far more experience with such things."

"Oh." The woman spared a quick glance her way. "Well...thank you."

Chance glanced back at Cora Mae and found her smiling.

"I'd be delighted to help," she said. Her fingers held the end of an apricot-colored fabric she'd been eyeing for a time. He could envision a summer dress, the soft color a perfect contrast against her pale skin.

He continued toward the side counter and hoped the other ladies flocking around the fabric table had gotten the message—he wasn't in town to socialize.

"Heard you had a woman out on your place," said Andrew Stone as he stepped up to the counter. "Sister, huh?"

"Stepsister," Chance amended.

"You ought to bring her by next weekend for the town social."

"Since when does this mining depot host town socials?"

"Since my wife decided to throw one together."

Mrs. Stone, a stern-looking woman of sturdy build, didn't seem the tea-toddling type. She stood amid the flutter and bustle around the fabric table, sheers in one hand, her sleeves pushed up over her thick forearms. Sweat glistened on her wide brow as she measured out yards of fabric.

"She figured this shipment of material will have the ladies sewing up a storm and looking for a place to flaunt their new outfits."

"A regular husband roundup, huh?"

"Or wife, depending on how you look at it," Stone retorted.

"I take it you're charging a fee for this town social?"

"Just for the refreshments," he said with a grin. "Spring's in the air, you know? The cold of winter will be on us before you know it. Winters can be awful long without a woman to keep you warm. She's nice lookin'," he said, sizing up Cora as though she were a prize mare. "Bet she has an offer within the first hour."

The last thing Cora Mae needed was to be ogled by a bunch of lonely miners. "I'll mention it to my crew."

"You do that," said Stone.

By the time he had all the supplies loaded in the wagon, Cora Mae had made it through the line of women waiting to have their fabric measured and cut by Mrs. Stone. Cora Mae seemed to be enjoying herself. He figured it must have taken three dozen pins to get her hair up in the tight, twisted coils at the crown of her head. Long curls hung around her face, knocked loose during the ride to town. She chatted pleasantly with the other women, yet somehow stood out from the plain faces of the other young ladies and older biddies crowded around her.

It's the light of her smile—pure as sun spray.

Realizing he was staring, he turned his attention to the candy jars on the counter. As he picked out an assortment of sweets for Josh, Cora Mae approached with a stack of cut fabric. Right away Chance noticed something was missing.

The apricot.

"Have you forgotten our agreement?" he asked.

"What agreement was that?"

"That you'd purchase some supplies for yourself. Surely you could use a spring dress or two."

Color tinged her cheeks. He didn't see why. It wasn't as though he'd suggested she needed new bloomers. Though she probably did.

"Mine is on the bottom," she said.

Chance glanced back at the stack and noticed the dark muslin beneath the folded pieces of green, pink, white and blue gingham.

"The brown?"

Her brow puckered with a frown. "You don't like it?"

"You do?"

"I don't have a brown dress."

True enough. She also didn't have an apricot dress, but he was sure that pointing that out would be borderline inappropriate. "A brown dress will be real nice," he said, wanting to ease the concern he'd put in her gaze, figuring brown wouldn't look bad. Though it wouldn't look much different than the dark gray she wore now or the black dresses in her wardrobe. There was nothing wrong with having a little variety.

"That apricot was real pretty, too."

"The chiffon?" She shook her head. "Too expensive, and the lighter fabric would take more yardage."

He didn't care how much it cost, he wanted to see her in apricot. "Have you gotten all you need, then?"

"Yes. I finished Skylar's list before sorting through the material."

"Why don't you walk down to the depot while I settle up here, see if any packages have arrived for Skylar?"

"Okay." She turned away.

As Cora Mae reached the door, Salina stepped inside. Chance's gut soured at the sight of her.

"Miss Tindale," Salina said, her smile clearly forced.

"Mrs. Jameson." Cora Mae's tone carried the same underlay of steel. She continued past her and started across the busy road.

Chance made his way to the fabric table. Spotting the long spool of apricot, he reached into the pile and pulled out the soft fabric.

"Mr. Morgan?" said Mrs. Stone, looking away from her line of ladies. "Shall I cut some for you?"

"Nope. I'll take the whole thing."

The woman blanched. "The entire bolt?"

A dozen envious eyes glanced at the fancy fabric.

"The whole thing," Chance confirmed, and carried it to the counter. "Wrap that up for me, would you, Stone?"

Mr. Stone's eyebrow shot up. "Sure thing."

"Aren't you the sweetest brother-in-law." Salina smiled brightly.

Considering she'd walked up to him without a trace of hesitation, he could only guess that her foreman hadn't filled her in on all of his recent activities.

"Though not quite the color I'd choose for Skylar."

"I'm not buying it for Skylar."

Her smile widened. Did she think it was for her?

"Here you go," said Mr. Stone, placing his paper-bound parcel on the counter.

"Did you hear about the town social next week?" asked Salina.

He was about to suggest she go with her *foreman* when he caught sight of Cora Mae through the shop window. She charged across the street as though running from a pack of wolves.

He tugged a pouch of coin from his pocket and tossed it onto the counter. "That ought to cover it, Stone. If not, put it on my tab." He grabbed the pile of sweets and fabric and rushed to the door.

"Chance?" Salina called after him.

He met Cora Mae on the boardwalk. "What's wrong?"

"Do you have everything?" she asked in a rush.

"Yeah, but—"

"Can we go? I really want to go."

Her body trembled. Something had scared her.

"Please, Chance," she begged. Cora's heart pounded in her throat. If Mr. Grissom spotted her, he'd drag her back to Delaware.

Chance held her gaze for a moment.

Fear mingled with frustration as she fought the burn of tears.

He wrapped his arm around her shoulders and guided her to the wagon. He placed his parcels in the back and turned to help her onto the seat. "What happened to upset you?"

Mother must have sent him. The man might dress as a gentleman, but Mr. Grissom was a mercenary to the bone.

"I—" From the corner of her eye, she spied the tall black carriage coming down the road, and the wide shoulders of Mr. Grissom's steel-gray suit. She whipped toward Chance, trying to hide herself.

Chance saw the stranger as Cora Mae reached for him,

pressing her face toward his neck. If she intended to use him, he'd damn well make it worth his while. Sliding a hand under her chin, he tilted her face up and pressed his lips to hers. She gasped, and he deepened the kiss, letting his tongue delve into her mouth as his arms locked around her.

The moment he felt her arms sliding around his neck, her body leaning into his, he lost his mind in a blur of desire. He kissed her until she sagged against him.

Fighting for restraint and sanity, he pulled away.

Cora Mae stared at his mouth. The combination of shock and awe he saw in her expression made him want to pull her right back to his lips.

"Oh…*my goodness*," she gasped.

"Time to get going," he said, turning her around and lifting her up onto the wagon seat. "I think we've created enough town gossip, and as much as I'd like to spend the afternoon kissing you, we have a long ride back."

"Guess he won't need to bring his stepsister to the social after all."

Salina stared out of the store window, her stomach rebelling at the image still burning in her mind. *How could he?* He was supposed to be courting *her!*

"Disgraceful," snipped the woman standing beside her.

Hit by another wave of morning nausea, Salina clamped a hand over her mouth. An ailment she couldn't blame on Chance. Just like Chance, her body had betrayed her.

After a week of nausea, she couldn't deny the severity of her situation. She had hoped the unpleasant turn of events would help her speed along their courtship. She only needed to get Chance into her bed. *Just once. And soon.*

And then she'd be through with men. She would not become her mother! But without Chance...*Dear God.* She'd lose everything, and be left with a child she didn't want.

"Oh, Salina," said Mrs. Curry, the wife of a coal miner, "I'm so sorry, dear. Weren't you just saying how Chance Morgan had been courting you?"

"Yes," she said, letting her sorrow seep through, the concerned gazes of the women around her distracting her from her shock. "I dare say, he will have some explaining to do."

"I should think that kiss explained it quite well," said Mrs. Stone. "You bes' come to the social next Friday."

Salina bristled. One kiss did not mean he'd chosen that sow over her! She'd just not tried hard enough. But she would. Wyatt would not trap her into her mother's life! She'd have Chance Morgan and Wyatt would never be the wiser.

The door opened again. Salina turned and felt the loss of her breath. The finest specimen of a man she'd ever seen filled the doorway. A man every bit the size of Chance Morgan, and ten times as refined. He smoothed his gloved hands across the front of his gray silk jacket as he strode inside. He lifted a small black hat away from the dark hair slicked back against his scalp.

Impeccable, wealthy and clearly new to the area.

He glanced around the store before his gaze settled on her.

"Good afternoon," he said.

Seemed he also had good taste.

Salina flashed her best smile. Perhaps her options were not so desolate. "Good afternoon."

"I'm looking for Miss Tindale."

Hell and damnation! Rage flared into her cheeks. Had the world gone mad?

"I was told she was in here," he said.

"You just missed her," said Mrs. Stone over the snipping of her shears.

"Haven't seen you in here before," Mr. Stone called from behind the counter. "What can we do ya for?"

"I've come to retrieve Miss Tindale. I've been informed she's staying at the Morgan Ranch."

"What do you want with her?"

"I've come to escort her home. Her mother and fiancé are anxious for her to return to Delaware."

"You her fiancé?" asked Mr. Stone.

Impatience tightened the chiseled features of the stranger's face, showing he wasn't appreciative of their questions. "No, sir. My name's Grissom. As I said, I've been sent to safely escort her home."

He wasn't dressed like a messenger. He carried himself with the easy stealth of a…*a Morgan*.

"Can you point me in the direction of the Morgan Ranch?" he asked.

"If you was sent," Mr. Stone said with a scowl, "you should know where you're going."

The snipping of fabric halted as a quiet settled over the store.

Grissom smiled.

Not a comforting gesture, Salina noted.

"Good day, then," he said mildly, sliding his hat on as he turned to leave.

Salina followed him outside. "Mr. Grissom?"

He turned, his lips curling with the hint of a smile. "Madam?"

"I couldn't help but overhear your mention of Miss Tindale's fiancé."

"Yes, ma'am. He's quite worried about her. Would *you* know the way to the Morgan Ranch?"

"Yes," Salina said, her mood brightening considerably. "Yes, I do."

Chapter Fourteen

Chance drove the first five miles surrounded by the sound of wind and horses and the accusations steaming through his mind. Cora Mae didn't offer any explanations for the scene they'd created in town. Before she'd curled around him and kissed him with enough passion to melt the sun, something had put the fear of God into her. And that *something* wore a fancy gray suit.

"Who is he?"

Wide brown eyes glanced up at him. "Who?"

"The man you were hiding from."

"I haven't a clue what you're talking about."

He bit back a swear word. "Your lies are catching up with you, *Cora*. Why is he after you?"

"Honestly, Chance."

"If you're going to talk about honesty, you might try practicing some! The tall fancy man, *who is he?*"

Cora didn't know what to say. She didn't want to involve him. To acknowledge the way her mother had shamed her would make it all too real. Cora shook her head, blocking the memory from her mind. It was nothing more than a bad dream. She wouldn't relive it. She'd leave.

"I don't know what you mean."

Chance jerked the wagon to a stop. Cora stiffened as he set the brake and turned to her.

"You didn't recognize the man driving the black carriage?"

She shook her head.

Disappointment darkened Chance's eyes. Her heart clenched. She hated lying to him, hated that he sensed her dishonesty. But just as he'd said about keeping his secrets from Tucker, no good could come from the truth.

"Then I can only assume you must have wanted me to kiss you." His eyes focused on her mouth.

"*What?* No!"

"Why else would you jump right into my arms, your mouth all but seeking mine."

"That wasn't my intent!"

"You didn't complain while I was kissing you, Cora. In fact, I know damn well you enjoyed it. There's no shame in admitting you want me."

Heat rushed to her face. "Chance!"

"What? It's about time we got it out into the open, and after the way you kissed me in front of half the town, you can't deny it. I had to *pull you* off me."

His arms locked around her and hauled her tight against him. "We're free of onlookers. Or do you prefer an audience?"

"That's not—"

"Then kiss me." He bent to her mouth, his eyes hard with anger.

She turned away, his firm grip increasing her fear. "Please stop."

He turned her face to meet his gaze. The fingers against the back of her neck were gentle yet may as well have been a vise for the hold his gaze had on hers. "You wanted that kiss as much as I did. Admit it."

"I will not. I was simply…"

"Caught up in the moment?"

The intensity in his eyes frightened her. "Y-yes."

"The rush of desire, so strong you can't think? Is that how it is for you?" His thumb brushed her lower lip, sending a tremor through Cora that shook both of them. "You can lie to me all you want, Cora Mae, but your body tells the truth."

"Why are you doing this?"

"Because I can't fight it. *I've tried.*"

"You're scaring me."

Chance looked into her eyes and knew, for the moment, that she spoke the truth. She had so much passion in her, enough to burn the two of them, but it didn't outweigh the fear buried deep in her gaze.

He hissed a curse and let her go.

"What is it with you! You damn near melt into me one moment and then tense up the next. I shouldn't even want you!" he raged, furious with himself for fighting feelings he shouldn't have in the first place. "You've done nothing but lie to me since you arrived!"

He snapped the reins.

Cora intended to fix that the moment they returned to the ranch. She drew a shuddered breath, her gaze fixed on the mountains in the distance. She recalled Chance's mention of the trapper woman who knew the mountain passes the way he knew his ranch.

Halfway up the first peak.

She had money in her pocket. She could get to a railhead without the risk of running into Grissom.

The moment Chance led the team to the stable, Cora rushed up to her room. She was thankful Skylar had taken the children to Margarete's so that she could ride out with Tucker to look at their stock.

The time it had taken to unload the supplies had felt like an eternity. She wouldn't waste time with a trunk; there was no time. Skylar would make good use of the yarn. All she needed was her carpetbag and some clothes.

Hastily she packed a few dresses, her hair brush and set of needles. She would pick up a loaf of bread on her way out.

Snapping the bag shut, she turned to leave.

Chance filled her doorway.

She gasped and took a step back.

"Cora?" His eyebrows pinched as his gaze locked on her bag. "What the hell are you doing?"

She tightened her grip on the wooden handle. "I never intended to stay this long."

"Tell me what you're running from."

"I *can't*."

"I care about you, damn it! If you're in trouble, I can help you."

She shook her head. "I have to go. I can send for my things."

"Like hell!" He stormed into the room. "Didn't you hear me? *I care about you.* How many women do you think I've said that to?"

"I can't stay."

"Cora Mae…tell me it's not me you fear."

"It's not you," she said on a shallow breath.

"Then stay."

She stiffened as his hand framed her face. His lips touched hers in the lightest caress, tormenting her with a wild torrent of emotions.

"Can you tell me you don't feel that?" he asked.

"I don't want it," she said, tears spilling down her cheeks.

"Why not?" His hand moved tenderly through her hair, and Cora felt her resolve slipping, succumbing to the pleading in his gaze as steadily as the hairpins falling to the floor. But she had nothing to offer him, not with the past closing in behind her.

"Please, don't. Just let me go."

His fingers tightened in her hair. "I did that once. I'm not about to make the same mistake twice. There was a time when we told each other everything. Tell me what's going on. Let me help you."

It was too late. If he found out her mother was alive he'd only hate her all the more. She didn't want that. She didn't want any of this.

"Chance…"

"Why can't you be honest with me?"

"Because honesty doesn't always fix what's been wronged!" she shouted, desperate to get away from him. "Did you tell your brother Wyatt nearly killed you?"

"It wouldn't have served any good. I can deal with Wyatt without starting a war that would hurt everyone else."

"Exactly."

His eyes widened with an understanding that only increased her fear. "What are you trying to protect me from, Cora?"

The truth. She was trying to protect both of them. She didn't want to deal with the past any more than he did.

She eased away from his light hold. "I have to go."

Chance glanced past her toward the window. The distant sound of approaching horses filtered into the room.

Oh, God. Cora's heart dropped to her stomach at the sight of the black carriage moving along the road lined with fencing, leading toward the front yard. Mr. Grissom snapped his whip to pick up speed.

"I believe you have a caller, Cora Mae."

Chance glanced back at her and found all the color had drained from her face. Damn if she didn't look ready to faint. "What does he want with you?"

Her knuckles white on the handle of her carpetbag, she backed toward the door. "Please, Chance, tell him I'm not here."

"Tell me what he wants with you!"

"He works for my mother!"

"Your *mother?* But…" *The little liar.* "Holy hell." He'd known she'd been lying from the first day. But he'd softened, he'd let her sweet smiles blow over him like a blinding fog.

"Cora Mae, if your mother put you up to coming out here so she could try and sink her claws into our ranch, you'll regret the day you stepped foot on it."

"She's not after your ranch! It's *me* she wants."

Tears gathered in her eyes and, God save him, they tore at his gut. "Why?"

She shook her head. "There's no time!" She tried to push past him. "Just tell him you haven't seen me, or that I've left."

He braced his arms on the wall, pinning her in. "Why should I lie for you?"

"Send him away and I'll leave. I won't bother you again."

Not bother him? Didn't she know what she'd done to him? He was bothered to the root of his soul!

He turned and started for the stairwell. "I won't lie for you."

"You promised to protect me," she shouted, staying on his heels as he descended the stairs. *"You promised!"*

Her words echoed through the kitchen and grated over Chance like salt on an open wound. He turned, bringing her up short. "I'm standing right here! I'm through running. From you, your mother—all of it!"

She wasn't. The past held nothing for her but pain and shame. "Chance, *please.*"

"It's time to own up, Cora."

Her heart clenched as he stormed through the dining room. She closed her eyes and silently prayed Mr. Grissom would leave without a fight…and without re-vealing too much.

Chance jerked open the front door as the tall fancy carriage pulled to a stop. Custom built, Chance observed, noting the ornate carvings of rich wood. The man stepping down from the driver's seat glistened with the same overpriced polish. His tailored waistcoat and silk necktie spoke of money.

"Afternoon," Chance called out, walking to the end of the porch.

"Good day, sir. I'm looking for Mr. Morgan?"

"Then you're in luck. I'm Chance Morgan."

"Mr. Morgan, I'm searching for Miss Cora Mae Tindale. I've been informed she's staying here."

"She is."

Chance heard the hard rush of breath from beyond the open front door. If she had dealings with this man, it was best to get them over with while he *could* protect her, rather than to keep running from him.

"Come on out here, Cora Mae. You've got company."

She inched into the open doorway, her wide eyes dark with fear as she looked out at the man in the yard.

"Miss Tindale," said Grissom, removing his hat.

"Hello, Mr. Grissom."

"Your mother has been quite worried about you. I've come to escort you back home."

She stepped beside Chance, trembling like the last leaf of autumn. "I won't go."

Grissom flashed a smile that was about as warm as a snake's belly. "Miss Tindale, I must insist." He took a step forward. Cora Mae flinched, clearly ready to run.

"That's far enough," Chance warned, not liking Grissom's intimidation tactics.

Grissom paused, his eyes flickering toward Chance's holstered revolver before meeting his gaze. "Is it your intent to stop me from returning Miss Tindale to her mother?"

"Not at all. Cora Mae is free to come and go as she pleases. But I believe she just declined your invitation."

Grissom looked back toward the coach, and Chance tensed. God help him if Winifred was inside that carriage.

"Oh, no," whispered Cora. *"Please, no."*

The sheer terror in Cora Mae's hushed voice drew Chance's attention. He didn't recognize the woman trembling behind him. He heard the carriage door open, but couldn't look away from the stark fear blackening Cora Mae's wide eyes.

Chance slid his arm protectively around her trembling shoulders, her expression bringing back a flood of childhood memories; Cora Mae running through the house in a flutter of satin and ruffles, terrified, seeking shelter from her mother's frequent tirades.

"Come along, Cora Mae."

Winifred's familiar crisp voice put a pinch in Chance's spine. Glancing back at the yard he was disappointed to see that time hadn't pruned her up as much as he'd hoped. Tall and sleek, she stood with her chin poised high, her posture stiff. Her black dress and black bonnet suited the tight contours of her face. Severe as she looked, it was plain to see she had the makings of a beautiful woman, spoiled by an ugliness that came from within.

"Really, Cora Mae," she said, disregarding Chance's presence. "We've had quite enough of your foolishness," she said with calm politeness. "Get down here at once."

Cora Mae vigorously shook her head, loose curls swaying, her complexion frightfully pale.

"You've already created quite a scandal, running off on your engagement night."

Engagement?

"You had no right!" she shouted. "I won't marry him."

Damn right, you won't! Chance tightened his hold on her, stunned by the notion.

"Foolish talk," snipped Winifred. "Of course you will. You should be thankful he is still willing to marry you after the fiasco you've caused."

"The fiasco *I've* caused?"

"We have all tired of your games!"

Winifred's shrill voice increased the fine tremble in Cora Mae's body.

"Now, get down here and into this carriage at once!"

Chance tucked Cora Mae tight against his side. She

wrapped her arm around his back. Her fingers clutched the side of his shirt, and Chance felt an odd sense of possession. They were no longer children at the mercy of this snake of a woman.

"She's not going anywhere she doesn't want to go."

The wrinkles in Winifred's face increased with her scowl. "Chance."

"Winifred," he answered in the same flat tone.

Her lips pursed at the informal title, although not nearly as informal as other titles echoing in the back of his mind.

"Cora Mae, you have burdened your stepbrother long enough."

"Cora Mae isn't a burden. She's a delight. And she's welcome to stay here as long as she likes."

Again she ignored him, her gaze remaining fixed on her daughter. "Laird Ambrose Campbell has been quite patient."

"Laird Ambrose Campbell can take a running leap straight to hell."

Winifred's mask crumbled into angry creases as she whipped her narrowed gaze toward Chance. "Surely you have eyes. Cora Mae isn't a spinster and unwed because ugly thick-boned women are highly sought-after."

Cora flinched, and Chance was reminded just how deep hatred could run through his veins. "Don't listen to her," he whispered.

"I have worked very hard to secure her marriage agreement, and have already paid a handsome dowry to ensure her place in an upstanding family."

Bullshit. Chance had no doubt Winifred intended to use her daughter for her own personal gain, whether it be wealth or social connections.

"Would you ruin her only chance at marriage, her last opportunity to become a lady?"

"Winifred, I can assure you Cora Mae doesn't need any fancy titles to know she's a lady. Fact is, she's been fighting off suitors for weeks. So you can run along and tell your laird that Cora Mae is no longer in need of his *generosity*."

"You can't hold my daughter here against her will!"

"Don't you mean against *your* will? What are you expecting to gain from this marriage *agreement?*"

Her eyes narrowed. "It's clear to see that Cora Mae is too frightened by you to be sensible."

Chance glanced down at the woman trembling against his side. He slipped his hand beneath her chin. "Cora Mae, are you afraid of me, sweetheart?"

Despite her unease, Cora knew she trusted Chance more than she had ever trusted anyone. She slowly shook her head.

"I didn't think so. Don't panic," he whispered bending toward her. "I'm gonna kiss you."

His lips brushed across hers in a light caress, and she embraced the rush of sensation just as she had by the pond and in town, letting her fear fall away as his warmth filled her. When Chance released her mouth, his gentle smile was another source of strength. He winked, nearly bringing a smile to her lips before he turned to look out at her mother.

The look of utter shock contorting her mother's face was another boost of confidence.

"I hate to spoil your plans, Winifred," Chance said in a mournful tone. "I really do. But as you can see, your daughter has taken quite a shine to me. You can rest assured that Cora Mae has found a man who feels damn fortunate to have her in his life. No payoff required."

"Then you should know she is likely to be heavy with child."

"Mother!"

Cora swayed beside him, and Chance tightened his grasp.

"Don't try to deny it, Cora Mae. I know full well the agreement was consummated."

The pain in Cora Mae's tear-glazed eyes cut him clear to the bone. He didn't believe it. There was no way in hell she would have opened her body to another man—not willingly.

My God.

He turned her in his arms, away from her mother.

"The marriage is all but sealed," said Winifred. Her lips tipped into a cold, victorious grin.

Chance was certain he'd have slugged her if she'd been within arm's reach. "Lady, I'll give you to the count of three to get off my land."

Winifred's eyes drew wide. "Didn't you hear me?"

"One."

"She is likely carrying another man's child!"

"Two."

"Do not stand there as if—"

"Three." Chance drew his Colt and shot a fancy carved bird from the top corner of her carriage, the spray of splintered wood scattering in all directions.

Winifred squawked and fluttered. Her fancy footman rushed to open the carriage door.

"This is not over!" she shouted as Grissom urged her inside.

He squeezed the trigger. Another bird burst into splinters. "You better hurry, Grissom. When I run out of birds, I'll be aiming for an old bat."

Grissom boxed her inside. Unrushed, he climbed up to the driver's seat. A slow smile tightened his lips as he touched his fingers to his hat in a parting gesture before gathering the reins.

Chance fought the urge to shoot the man from his perch, just for the hell of it. He held Cora Mae as the carriage sped down the road. He wasn't quite sure what to say.

"I'm so sorry," Cora said against his shirt, her arms tight around his waist. "I didn't think she'd find me. I never thought she'd come."

"Honey, look at me."

Cora drew a shuddering breath but couldn't ease her hold. Her mother had meant to humiliate her.

"Cora Mae," Chance said softly.

The emotion in his voice washed over her like a soothing caress, forcing her to meet his gaze.

"Is what she said true? That man, Campbell, did he hurt you?"

Staring up at his eyes filled with concern, she was hardly able to breathe, much less reply.

Chapter Fifteen

"Answer me," Chance insisted. "Did that bastard steal your innocence?"

"I...I couldn't stop him," she managed, hardly breathing. "She let him in when I was asleep, and I...I couldn't—"

Chance swore beneath his breath, the hard words a clear contradiction to the gentle fingers brushing her tears from her cheeks. "What a tangle."

"I had to leave."

"You could have told me."

She gave him a shuddered look. "I only wished to forget it."

"The past seldom stays where it belongs."

"I only needed some time, and I wanted to see you again—I didn't think...*I'll leave.*"

"Like hell!" He folded his arms around her. "You're staying right here. Where you belong."

More tears burning for release, Cora buried her face against his chest.

"Don't cry, sweetheart," he soothed. "I won't let her take you."

Chance glanced about the yard, counting a dozen gaping expressions. He wouldn't allow Winifred to shame Cora Mae this way. He'd set it right. With child or not, she belonged here. With *him*.

"Y'all can get back to work!" he shouted.

Cora Mae drew a long, steady breath. Chance hugged her close, her body warm against his. He breathed in the sweet scent of her hair, liking the way she fit so perfectly in his arms, her head tucked beneath his chin.

"We need to get married. Tonight."

"What?" Cora jerked away from him. "Chance, *no*."

"I'm keeping my promise."

"To protect me, not to *marry* me."

"If you're carrying his child..."

"I'm not pregnant. *Just fat*."

"You are not! I just had you in my arms and I happen to have loved the feel of every smooth curve!" He rubbed a hand over his face. "I should have been full-on courting you long before now."

"Courting," she choked out. "Don't be absurd."

"Sweetheart, we just went over all this. You've been driving me wild since the moment you arrived, and you won't convince me that you're not attracted to me. So why would the idea of me courting you be absurd?"

"Because it was a mistake! You swore it wouldn't happen again."

"I take it back. My only regret was that I'd frightened you. Now I see why. You have to know I'd never hurt you like that."

Cora could only shake her head. She didn't want to find out.

"You kiss me with enough passion to set fire to stone. *We're getting married.*"

She stared at him, wondering how he could be so sweet and endearing one moment and such an utter brute the next. "You can't just—"

"We heard gunshots!" Tucker rode into the yard from a side pasture, a cloud of dust in his wake. Skylar reined in right beside him as Tucker leaped from his saddle.

"Who was here?" he asked.

"Winifred."

Tucker froze halfway up the steps. He turned to look back at the departing carriage. "No fooling?"

"Would I joke about something like that?" Chance asked. "She came for Cora Mae. She can't have her. I'm going to marry her."

"What?" Tucker all but shouted.

"I can have John here within an hour to perform the ceremony," he said as he walked down past his brother.

"Chance, this is insanity! I just told you there's no need."

"You heard your mother, Cora Mae," he said, his purposeful strides steadily putting ground between them as he neared the barn. "She's coming back."

"But I'm not with child!"

He stopped and turned back. "And when she finds a judge who can be bribed into ordering your return until your claim can be confirmed, what then? You'd be at her mercy, and *his.*"

Dear God. She hadn't thought of any such possibility.

"We're getting married. Tonight." Chance disappeared into the barn.

Cora turned to Tucker standing on the steps. "He's serious."

"With child?" Tucker's gaze locked on her stomach. "What the hell is going on?"

"Let's discuss this inside," Skylar suggested, hurrying up the porch. "Cora doesn't need an audience."

A blush stung Cora's face. Men stood along the fencing and at the side of the house, clearly drawn by the sound of gunfire and shouting.

Humiliation poured through her.

Cora stood near the front window, watching Skylar and Tucker walk toward Zeke and Margarete's house to retrieve their children. Not even they seemed convinced by her refusal to marry Chance. She wasn't about to sit around and wait for Chance to sweet-talk her into something she knew would be a mistake. She had long since started taking care of herself.

"Cora?"

She turned as Garret came in through the dining room. He held his hat in his hands and offered a sheepish smile.

"I overheard what happened. And I want you to know you don't have to marry Chance."

Finally! Someone who spoke reason. Perhaps he'd be kind enough to saddle a horse for her.

"I'll marry you."

Cora stared at him a moment, hoping he hadn't just said what she could have sworn she'd heard. "Garret—"

"I mean it, Cora. I love you."

Oh, good heavens. How do I deal with this?

"Garret, that is so sweet. But I—"

"I'm not trying to be sweet! Chance didn't give you a moment to turn him down, and if you don't care for him—"

"It's not that I don't care for Chance. I just don't want to marry. *Anyone.*"

"But…if it was between me and him."

"But it's not. I care for both of you. You're such a charming young man. I know you'll find a young lady who's perfect for you."

"I'm not so young," he protested. "I think *you're* perfect."

Cora's heart twisted. "I'm flattered, Garret. Truly. I'm very fond of you, but I don't care for you *in that way.*"

His expression fell as hurt darkened his eyes. "But you do toward Chance?"

"I…I don't know." She only knew she wasn't going to marry. Not Garret, not Chance, not anyone.

The longer he'd thought about Cora Mae, the more Chance realized marriage was the perfect solution. A solution to Winifred's demands, and the desire he couldn't seem to contain when Cora Mae was in his arms. He *wanted* her, he had since the moment he'd set eyes on her. He'd wanted her more with every moment he'd spent in her company. He was suddenly dying to see her, to make sure she'd settled in to the idea of marrying him.

Not finding her in the house, he left Reverend Keats in the parlor and went to the stables. Mitch was brushing down one of the mares.

"Have you seen Cora?"

"Nope. But I just rode in a few minutes ago. How'd it go in town?"

"Just fine."

As Chance made his way around the side of the house, he spotted Tucker and Skylar walking arm in arm, coming back from Zeke's house. Perhaps they'd all walked over.

"Did you fetch the preacher?" Tucker asked as they met in the front yard.

"He's inside."

"What did you tell him?"

"That Cora Mae has agreed to marry me, and we needed a preacher."

"*Agreed* might be too strong a word," offered Skylar. "Are you sure about this?"

"I've never been more sure of anything." Something inside Chance warmed at those words, bringing a smile to his lips. "Is she up at Zeke's?"

"No," said Skylar. "When we left to check on Josh and the girls, she'd gone to lie down."

Chance tensed. "How long ago was that?"

"Near an hour," said Tuck. "Skylar nursed the girls and Margarete opted to watch them until this evening so Skylar can help Cora with the wedding."

"She's not in the house," said Chance, his gaze moving across the distant fields. "Or the yard."

"Zeke and I were on the porch the whole time. We'd have seen her if she'd tried to leave."

"Not if she went out the back." Chance glanced toward the rear of the house and the ready supply of green-broke mounts, a number of them bridled and harnessed. His gaze shifted to the rise of mountains separating their place from the Lazy J.

"Oh, hell."

"No," said Skylar. "She wouldn't ride up into that wild country."

The one time he'd willfully broken a promise…if Maggie found out he'd told Cora Mae, she'd likely try to skin him alive.

"She's not that stupid," said Tucker

"No, she's that smart. Skylar, can you bake us a cake? I want this to be a real wedding," he said, backing toward the house.

"Chance, at the moment, you don't seem to have a bride."

"I will." He turned and ran to fetch his saddled horse.

Tucker stayed on his heels. "Why the hell would she ride farther into the mountains?"

"Because of my fool mouth!" Chance led his horse toward the stable for a fresh mount. "I have to reach her before she finds Maggie."

"Who's Maggie?" Tucker asked, following him.

"Danvers."

"Who?"

"Mad Mag," Chance clarified with impatience.

Tucker's eyes widened beneath his hat. "That crazy trapper woman?"

Was marrying him such a horrible option that she'd track down a mountain shrew she'd never met? A few flashing thoughts of how he'd treated her over the past month answered his question.

Damn.

"Why would she seek out someone like that?" Tucker moved ahead of him and led Star from her stall as Chance released the cinch on his saddle.

"I told her how Mag helped me out of a tangle a few weeks ago."

"She did? Why didn't you say anything?"

"Didn't come up," he hedged.

"Did you happen to tell her Mag is a lunatic?"

"Have you ever actually met Mag?"

"As close as I ever hope to get. Don't take more than a half mile to catch her scent, a quarter mile to draw her bullets, and I reckon a sight less for her to hit her mark. That wild woman and her man are just as likely to shoot her off the mountain?"

"Maggie's not crazy. She's just mean, but not mean enough to kill someone in cold blood." He *hoped*.

"How would you know?"

"She led me to this damn valley on my ride in," he said, oblivious to his brother's shock, his focus on the saddle he was securing to his large buckskin.

"That couldn't have been pleasant."

Chance glanced at his brother, seeing his shudder of revulsion at the thought of getting so close to Maggie. "I'll be back with Cora," he said, about to mount his horse.

Tucker stopped him, grabbing Star's harness. "When you find her, you should remember she ran because she wants to protect you."

"From what?"

"*Marriage*. I gather it's a loathing you two have in common. With Winifred as a role model, I can't say I blame her. I hope you realize you can't force her to marry you."

"I can and I will. If Winifred catches her, we've lost."

"*We've* lost? If this is some kind of vindictive move to get back at Winifred, I won't let you use Cora Mae. She doesn't deserve it. What's it gonna take to convince you she's nothing like her mother?"

"I know that! Why do you think I want to marry her?"

"How the hell should I know? Your attitude toward her these past weeks hasn't led me to believe you have a fancy for big-boned women and flaming red—"

"One more insult," Chance growled, his hands fisting at his sides.

"I'm not insulting her. I was just saying—"

"I know what you were saying! There isn't a damn thing wrong with Cora's shape or hair color. I happen to think she's perfect and damn attractive just the way she is!"

Tucker stood in stunned silence as his brother's boisterous admission echoed through the barn.

"I *want* to marry her!"

"You do?"

"I might as well," he grumbled. "I can't sleep for thinking about her. She just…she…"

"Let me guess. She becomes more beautiful by the second, consuming your thoughts until she's all you see, eyes open or shut?"

The sheer misery in his twin's expression answered Tucker's question. "Holy hell," Tuck said, shaking his head. "I can't believe it. You're in love with Cora Mae."

"I never said that."

"If you plan to marry her, you'd better get used to saying it. I do believe proclamations of love are words most women want to hear on their wedding night."

"Like you said to Skylar on your wedding night?"

"Go ahead and take shots if it'll make you feel better. But like you, I was too damn scared to tell Skylar I loved her when I should have. I've since wised up. I love my wife. I don't have any qualms about telling her so. In fact, I make a point of it."

"Not all folks gush like the two of you."

"True," agreed Tucker. "Just the lucky ones."

Chance glanced up at his twin, pain pulling at his chest. He'd never had Tucker's dumb luck. Or maybe he'd just been too blind to see his good fortune when it was staring him right in the face, kissing him into oblivion.

How could he convince Cora Mae?

He didn't have a clue, but he'd damn well try.

"Don't let the preacher leave," he said as he swung into his saddle. "I'm bringing her back."

Chapter Sixteen

The horse had thrown her. Chance spotted two patches of ground where the horse's hooves had dug in, sending its rider into the dirt and scrub. What had she been thinking? Riding out on a half-wild horse. She'd certainly taken his direction literally, practically making a beeline straight up the mountain. Unfortunately, he'd given an accurate description of Maggie's location.

A quarter of a mile from Mag's cabin, a second set of tracks joined Cora Mae's. He wasn't sure if he should hope they were Mag's, or someone else's. When both sets of tracks disappeared fifty paces later, he knew Cora Mae had found Mag, or more likely, Mag had found Cora Mae. The mountain shrew had done a fine job of covering their trail, but Chance didn't need any hoofprints to find his way up to her place.

A hundred yards from her cabin, the double click of gun hammers stopped him cold, just before a cool feminine voice sounded from the scrub behind him.

"Lose something, Morgan?"

Chance held his hands out, not doubting the threat in her easy voice. "You ever thought about giving a proper hello?"

"And give you the advantage? Why, no. I'm not inclined to give any kind of greeting to a man who can't keep his word."

He glanced back slowly and spotted her crouched on a boulder, a shotgun trained on him. Her tan hat and jacket were decent camouflage against the rock and scrub. She held the long gun with an ease that told him it wouldn't take more than a reflex for her to fill him full of buckshot.

"She's the only one, Maggie. And I didn't tell her everything."

"Enough for her to march right up to my door, asking directions like I'm some damn trail guide!" She lowered her gun. Her crisp blue eyes sparked with anger. "How did you think I'd greet that?"

"Maggie?"

She swatted tangled strands of black hair away from her pale cheek as though suddenly bothered by it. "You think I want some woman flouncing around these parts spreading gossip about me?"

"Where is she?"

"Devil if I care. You're the one who cut her loose."

"If I'd have known—"

"Exactly! Arrogant bastards, *all of you.* Always thinking the world will bend to your will. You gave Cora information you had no business revealing because you didn't think she'd have the sand to use it."

"Wrong. I knew she'd never use it *against* you."

"So now *you* decide who I should trust and who I shouldn't?"

"I just want Cora."

"Yeah, well you can want in one hand and sh—"

"Damn it, Mag! *Where is she!*"

Maggie rocked back on the heels of her boots, seeming to ponder whether or not she should tell him. "That bay's got fine lines," she said, her gaze moving over his horse. "Want to sell her?"

His jaw popped beneath the strain of his clenched teeth. *"Maggie."*

"I left her inside my cabin so she could tend her wounds." *"What wounds?"*

"Don't you glare at me! That gnashing bastard she was riding tore her up a bit."

"Thanks, Mag," he said, spurring his horse. "I owe you!"

"Damn right you do!"

The rotted wood hovel Maggie called a home looked like a haven as Chance reined in and stepped down from his saddle. The bark-covered door squeaked as he pushed it open.

Cora Mae sat on a bed against the side wall in a cabin no bigger than his kitchen. She pushed her skirt down and glanced up through a wild mess of curls. A bowl of water sat on the bed beside her. She held a blood-stained rag. Chance's gaze locked on her ripped gray skirt coated with dirt and thorns. He could only imagine the condition of the delicate skin beneath.

"My God. You wanted to get away from me that badly?"

The stark fear in her eyes kept him lingering in the doorway when he would have gone to her.

"Why are you afraid of me?"

"You shouldn't have come."

"You're hurt."

"I'm fine," she seethed.

Cora looked down at the snags and ground-in dirt on her

skirt and silently cursed the unruly horse that had sent her crashing to the ground.

"I should whip that horse," he said, crouching before her.

"It wasn't the horse's fault."

"You're right. *I* should be whipped for driving you to do something so foolish."

"Chance—"

"I'm sorry for being short with you, Cora Mae, but I'm not the man who raped you."

"I know that!"

"Then let me help you," he said, reaching for her skirt. "You know I won't hurt you."

"But *you do*."

His finger released the gray wool. "*How?* How do I hurt you?"

"In ways I can't even explain."

"I'm not trying to."

Tears hazed her vision as she shook her head. "I don't have any defenses with you."

"I think we're even in that respect." A smile touched his lips. "Let me help you."

"It's just some scrapes. I've already cleaned them."

"Can I see?"

She held his gaze for a long moment before nodding. Her breath stalled as he nudged her skirt up, revealing her torn black stockings and scraped knees.

"What do your hands look like?" he asked, his voice thick with emotion.

Reflectively, she curled her fingers into her scraped palms. She'd already picked out the stickers and gravel.

"Cora Mae?"

Biting her lower lip, she held out her hands.

His eyes flinched at the sight of her bloodied palms. "Anything else hurt?"

Touched by the pain so clear in his eyes, she shook her head, not trusting herself to speak.

Chance blew out a breath. "Thank God." His hands slid around her hips as he fell forward, shocking her as he dropped his head to her lap, hugging her tight in the same motion. "If I ever do anything that stupid again, don't run. Promise you'll rage at me."

Unable to deny herself, Cora slid her fingers into the golden hair curling up from his collar and shared his tremors as she leaned in to kiss the golden crown of his head. "Okay."

He eased back, his green eyes shimmering with moisture. "Can I sit beside you?"

Hardly able to breathe, she gave another nod.

He moved onto the bed. His arm slid around her. His hip pressed tight against hers, and his long legs maneuvered them back on the bed until he could recline against the wall, inadvertently lifting her feet off the floor.

As if realizing the dominating move, his lips tipped into a wry smile.

"Sorry. I'm just exhausted."

Cora smiled too and leaned against him, not minding his weight and warmth. Being crushed against his side was rather soothing. "So am I."

"You've got to forgive me, Cora," he said after a time.

"For what? I'm the one who arrived uninvited, who lied to you."

"I haven't treated you as I should have."

"I understand that I've been a disruption to your life."

"I don't want to lose you. *Please stay*."

She stared up at him, knowing they'd reached an impasse. And now was the time for truths. "I can't. I'm afraid of the way you make me feel," she admitted.

His laughter surprised her. "So am I," he said.

"You don't really want to marry me."

"*Yes*, I do. The fact is, I think you're ten kinds of wonderful."

That stunned her.

"You're partial to me, aren't you?"

"Wanting to kiss you isn't a reason to marry," she said, flustered by the rush of warmth in her cheeks, and *other places*.

"It's a good start."

"Chance!"

"Well, it is," he insisted. He lifted her hand from her lap and pressed her palm to his chest. "Feel that?"

How could she not? His heart was doing its best to pound out of his chest, the same as her own.

"You do that to me. The sight of you, the thought of you—"

His words added to the rush of sensation flooding her body. "Chance, *stop*." She pulled her hand away.

"Don't you think I've tried? Hell, I was prepared to court Salina to try and get you off my mind!"

Tears slid hotly across her cheeks. She'd been ready to let him.

His hands framed her face, his thumbs brushing away the wet trail and setting off a rush of shivers. "I'm crazy about you."

The rich timbre of Chance's voice moved through her like a lulling caress. "You make me want to believe you."

"It's true. Your mother's the one who told you lies, Cora Mae."

"She was unkind, but I am quite aware of my shortcomings. I only wish to live a life where they didn't much matter."

"What shortcomings?"

She rolled her eyes and looked away from him. "Do you think she's the only one who's made disdainful comments about my hair color or referred to me as having a *sturdy* build?"

"Not every woman is meant to have the shape of a riding crop."

A frown tugged at her lips. "Yes, I know."

"I happen to find every smooth curve of your body damn appealing. In fact, I've never been more attracted to a woman in my life."

Oh, Lord. She couldn't catch her breath.

"And I love your hair color." He slid his fingers through a mass of curls. "Reminds me of fall leaves. Did you know fall is my favorite time of year?"

"Yes."

His grin widened. The hand resting on her hip slid up to the curve at her waist, then slowly back down, leaving a trail of sparks in its wake. "Glad I'm not the only one taking notice. You do fancy me, *don't you?*"

"You're not short on admirers, Chance. The women in town were practically jumping into your pocket."

The warm rumble of his laughter intensified the bursts of heat caused by his words and his touch.

"Marry me. I won't hurt you, Cora Mae. I promise. You trust me to keep my promises, don't you?"

She knew now it wasn't Chance who hadn't kept his promise, but her mother who'd kept her away from him.

Even after she'd lied about her mother, Chance had kept his promise. He'd stood by her. "I trust you."

"Marry me."

His gaze implored her for an answer, but she didn't have one. The clash of attraction and emotion only added to her confusion.

His fingers brushed her cheek in a light caress. "Would it be all right if I kissed you?"

Loving that he had asked permission, a smile eased across her lips. "I...suppose."

Her breath stalled as he leaned closer. His lips brushed lightly against hers, once, then twice. She trembled as the tip of his tongue glided across her lower lip.

She reached up, wanting to feel the pressure of his mouth, the demand of his tongue, the shimmering bursts of heat breaking through her, burning away the rest of the world.

He gave it to her, melding his mouth to hers, his fingers moving tenderly through her hair, against her back.

She loved being lost in the stir of sensation he made her feel.

Startled by the realization she pulled back, breaking the kiss.

Chance didn't seem offended by her sudden retreat. He didn't release his hold on her, but watched her with patient green eyes.

"I don't know what to do," she said.

"What does your heart say?"

She loved him, but she'd always loved him. That didn't mean she wanted to *marry* him. "I never intended to marry."

"Me, neither." He kissed her forehead. "Yet here I am, *begging* you to be my bride."

"We could have the marriage annulled after Mother leaves."

"No."

His instant denial surprised her. "Why not?"

"I'm asking you to stand with me before God and our family. If I say those vows, I intend to keep them."

Yes, he would, she thought. "You wouldn't want t-to—"

"I want you until I can barely stand for the thought of having you."

A combination of fear and fascination flooded Cora's body.

"But I won't take you, Cora. Not until you ask me to, plain as day. You have my word on that."

His fingers brushed a tangle of stray curls away from her face as he traced her jaw, making her tremble.

"I could have you buck-naked on top of me," he said, "and I'd still stop if you asked me to."

Cora felt her mouth drop open.

"Want me to prove it?"

His mischievous grin made her smile despite her distress. "No!" He'd just proven he could easily make her want him.

"Can you tell me what happened? What he did to you?"

She shook her head. She didn't want to remember the humiliation, or her own ignorance. "I should never have gone back," she said, glancing down at her lap. "She sent Mr. Grissom to Massachusetts to bring me home. I had hoped…" A sigh of regret broke from her chest. *"Foolishness."*

Chance's arm tightened around her shoulders. His lips brushed over her hair. She closed her eyes and let his warmth wash away the chill beneath her skin.

"Hope isn't foolish, Cora Mae."

"Perhaps not, but *I* was. I should have run then."

But she hadn't. She'd been caught up in the promise of attending a family ball, the chance to be included. Cora didn't lack social graces, she only needed a chance to prove herself. But once again, her mother had lied. She hadn't intended to present her to the family—she'd intended to announce nothing short of a family investment. The Tindales wanted ties to a Scottish nobleman, and she'd been the bartering tool.

"I never suspected. Even while she kept me locked up in that house for weeks, I never dreamed…I couldn't have imagined her intentions. She said there was to be a family ball. Family I'd been unfit to be around all my life. I was to tell them I'd been off teaching at a women's college. Imagine the scandal if they knew a Tindale had been a common mill worker?"

"They believed you'd been off at a college?"

"I never got to see them. It was the night before the event."

"He attacked you?"

Tears pricked her eyes.

"Cora Mae?"

"He came to my room," she said.

"Did you call for help?"

"Would it have mattered? The Tindale estate is enormous with too many servants to know them by name. Besides, who answers the cry of a prisoner?"

"No one," Chance said, pulling her close.

She didn't resist, but rested her head on his chest as she curled into his warmth, needing his comfort. "I had no reason to be on guard. My bedroom door was locked, bolted from the outside, as it had been since I'd arrived. To benefit *me,* of course. Mother didn't want me 'sneaking food from the kitchen and puffing up like a toad.'"

"How did he get in?"

She didn't want to believe the truth that had haunted her for two months. "I woke to a great weight bearing down on me, the smell of bourbon in my face. Before I could register what was happening, the pain of it stole my breath."

She shuddered at the memory.

"I'm sorry, Cora Mae."

"It was over as quickly as it had begun. He spoke as he pushed off of me, though I didn't make out the words. But as he left my room, *I heard her*. She had been just outside the door."

A haze of tears slid from her eyes as her mother's voice played in her mind. *I trust our bargain is sealed?*

"She had to know I'd never consent. She sent him. She gave me away."

"No," Chance said, tilting her face up to meet his gaze. "You've never belonged to her, Cora Mae."

"She never wanted me."

The pain in Cora Mae's eyes ripped at his heart. His hatred doubled for a woman who'd been given the sun, but was too selfish to absorb its warmth. When he looked at Cora Mae, he saw beauty, sunlight, the promise of enough heat to melt his heart.

"Sweetheart, she's never *deserved* you." He gathered her close and felt a wave of relief as she embraced him, her arm banding around his waist.

"Cora, I won't hurt you."

"But it *does* hurt," she said, her voice muffled by his shirt.

Chance caressed her back as rage clawed through him. God save him if he ever came face-to-face with Winifred and her laird. If he hadn't yet earned his spot in hell, what he'd do to them would carve his name into the brimstone.

He drew a steady breath and strove to keep a neutral tone. "Did it hurt when I kissed you just now?"

She peered up at him, her chin resting on his shirt. Her slow smile set off a burst of warmth inside him.

"No," she said in a whisper.

He tugged on an auburn curl, loving the feel of her in his arms, her relaxed weight pressed against his side.

"How did it make you feel?"

"Warm and safe and...wonderful."

He couldn't fight his smile. "Me, too. I've kissed quite a few women, Cora Mae, and it's never felt that way for me. Not until *you*."

Her eyes widened, emphasizing flecks of gold and amber amidst many shades of brown. He slid his finger along the inside of her wrist. Watching her tremble from the light touch, his body coiled with mounting desire. "You feel that?"

She nodded.

"That's passion."

"When did this happen?" she asked.

Laughter broke from his chest. She delighted him in ways nothing ever had. "For me, it started when I realized the attractive woman who stole my attention the moment I spotted her on the boardwalk was the girl I'd been missing for most of my life."

Cora's breath caught. The gentle smile on his lips swelled her heart to the point of bursting.

"You like being in my arms."

She couldn't deny it. "Yes."

"You fit perfectly against me," he pointed out, glancing down at the length of them.

They did seem to mesh well together. "Yes."

His eyes darkened as he leaned and kissed her nose, then her lips. "This is how it will be between us," he said. "No pain. Only passion." He kissed her forehead. "And pleasure." His lips brushed hers. "And trust."

The words were nothing more than his breath on her lips before he deepened the kiss, teaching her the meaning of all three. By the time she eased away from him, her breath was coming fast and hard. She felt weak and excited all at once.

"I'm not used to feeling this way."

"Me, neither." He lifted a lock of her hair from his chest and let the red coils slide through his fingers. "Since you arrived, my days begin and end with thoughts of you. I crave your smiles, your company."

It was the same for her. When he looked at her as he was now, his eyes shining like green embers, she couldn't imagine being anywhere else, with anyone else.

"Stay with me."

"Okay."

"Marry me."

The urgency in his gaze increased the tantalizing stir of her body.

Marry Chance. She had never dared to dream.

Hadn't it always been Chance and his wild ways, daring her to be bold, bringing her the joy she'd never known to seek?

"Is that a dare?" she asked, a smile tipping her lips.

His slow smile added to the wild surge of excitement building inside her.

"Oh yeah," he said, his mouth seeking hers once again. "A triple-dog dare."

Chapter Seventeen

It had been damn hard, leaving the comfort of Cora Mae's arms and the quiet serenity of Mag's cabin. He could have sat huddled up on the small bed for the rest of the night, listening as Cora Mae told him about her days at the mill, the work she'd done, the friends she'd made—interrupted by intermittent kisses and light caresses. In that hour, an ease settled over him, contentment reflected in Cora Mae as she relaxed to his touch and shared his kiss.

Only when Chance realized darkness would soon be impeding their travels and Mag would likely want her privacy back, did he force himself to get up from the small bed and lead Cora Mae into the surrounding grove and the chirping of birds. He helped her onto his saddled bay. A short way down the trail he found the stallion Cora Mae had taken tethered to some tree branches.

As they neared the ranch, the sparkle of pond water caught Chance's attention. Surrounded by green, the tall grasses spotted by wildflowers, it seemed the perfect location. The sun would be setting soon, painting pink hues across the sky, giving them just enough time to get married.

He glanced at Cora Mae. Disheveled and dusty, her hair a wild array of colorful curls streaming out behind her shoulders, she'd never looked more beautiful to him.

"How about we get married in the meadow, near the pond?"

She followed his gaze, her eyes sliding toward the tree where he'd first kissed her. A smile bowed her pink lips.

"What do you think?"

"That would be wonderful."

Yeah. He was thinking it would.

Reaching the back porch, he dismounted and went to help her down. He could see she was trying to figure out how she could dismount in her skirts while maintaining her modesty.

He reached up and grabbed her waist. "Kick your leg over the back end," he suggested. As she did, he lifted her and set her on the ground. "When's the last time you rode astride?"

"When I was nine," she said smiling up at him. "With you."

"And you took that stud?"

"I got to where I was going," she said, making the most of her five feet as her jaw took on a familiar stubborn edge.

"You did," he agreed.

Recalling Duce's comment about Cora Mae being the kind of woman to flourish out here, he decided the man had been right. Chance wasn't sure why that came as such a surprise. For all her soft beauty, Cora Mae had proven to have will and drive to match his own. As he tucked her beside him, he noted how she complemented him to perfection—soft where he was hard, generous with her affection when he yearned to show more.

He wanted to kiss her, but decided he needed to start implementing some of the restraint he'd surely need to make it through the night.

"Cora!" Skylar walked onto the back porch. "Are you all right?"

Cora felt a pang of guilt at the sight of Skylar's concern, her blue eyes widening as she spotted her torn skirt. "I'm not hurt," she assured her.

"Just some scrapes," Chance said as they ascended the steps.

"Sorry if I've worried you."

"I'm just glad you're all right." Skylar's gaze moved between them. "*Is* everything all right?"

Chance glanced down at her, and Cora realized anew how very tall he was. The top of her head didn't quite reach his shoulders.

"Are we all right?" he asked.

"I think so," she said, smiling. "We're going to be wed in the meadow," she said to Skylar.

Skylar blinked in surprise. "Then it's a good thing I've just finished frosting the wedding cake."

"Wedding cake?"

"Chance isn't lacking in confidence," Skylar said, smiling at her brother-in-law before she turned to go inside. "He asked me to bake the cake before going after you."

Following her into the kitchen, her breath caught at the sight of a tall white cake sitting on the table, three tiers stacked on top of each other. A pile of small pink flowers lay on the table, clearly a decoration Skylar intended to use.

"Nothing fancy, to be sure."

"It's beautiful," Cora said, moisture springing to her eyes.

"Thanks, Sky," said Chance.

"My pleasure. Margarete took care of supper. You can look forward to a traditional Spanish meal."

After he wed Cora Mae. Chance ushered his bride toward the dining room. As they neared the front room, she heard the murmur of Tucker's voice and spotted him sitting on one of the chairs. Realizing a guest sat in the parlor across from Tucker, she hesitated. Chance's hand on the small of her back urged her forward.

"Preacher," he whispered near her ear.

The older man stood with Tucker, his silvery gray hair sleeked over his scalp. A gentle smile lifted a network of wrinkles in his tawny skin. "Found your bride, I see?"

Cora flushed, certain her appearance was quite ravaged.

"Yes, sir. Reverend John Keats, this is Cora Mae Tindale."

"Reverend Keats," she said.

"Miss Tindale, it is a fine pleasure to meet you."

"Is there a church nearby?" she asked.

"Do believe the mining depot is the closest," he said. "I've been retired for some years, but am glad to be called upon when needed. I'd be honored to perform your marriage ceremony, if that's your wish."

The reverend glanced to his side and Cora noticed Tucker's tense expression

"Yes," she said. "I've agreed to marry Chance."

"We'd like to exchange vows out by the pond," Chance said, "if that would be all right. I don't have rings—"

"Not a problem, my boy. By the pond will be splendid. Shall we proceed?"

"We're ready if you are," said Chance.

"No, you're not," Skylar piped in, just when Cora feared Chance intended her to be wed in a torn and tattered dress. "Cora needs time to prepare."

The disappointment in Chance's eyes brought a smile to her lips. "I won't run," she said in a teasing tone.

His answering smile put a kick in her pulse. "How long do you need?" he asked.

She was tempted to marry him right here and now, more than ready to feel his arms around her, his lips against hers.

"Thirty minutes," Skylar answered for her. She took her by the arm and tugged her toward the stairs. Once inside her bedroom, Skylar shut the door and pinned Cora with a hard gaze.

"How are you feeling? Really?"

"I'm not certain." Her insides were a mess of jitters and excitement.

"Is this what you want, Cora?"

"I think so."

"Do you love him?"

"Ever so much."

Skylar smiled. "Then let's get you ready."

"What should I wear?"

"The gown you wore the day you arrived would be lovely."

Cora frowned, recalling Chance's scowl as his gaze had roved her attire on the day of her arrival. "I had the distinct impression Chance didn't like it."

"Oh, I believe he cared for it more than he was wanting to. You get to the tub. I'll warm the iron."

"Do I have time for a bath?" she asked, the idea of easing into warm clean water sounding good enough to make her groan.

"They can't start without you. *You* are the bride."

Cora sucked in a deep, quivering breath.

She was the bride.

* * *

Thirty minutes later Chance stood beside Reverend Keats and his brother, wearing the stiff, collared shirt and snug black suit he'd borrowed from Mitch so as not to disturb Cora Mae. The wind had actually died down, the pond mirroring the pink-streaked sky. Their wedding guests stood behind the two kitchen chairs that had been brought out for Zeke and Margarete. The couple smiled up at him, each holding a baby. Garret stood with the other ranch hands, Joshua in his arms, a scowl on his face.

Chance shifted nervously as he glanced again toward the back of the house. Tucker tapped his sleeve.

"You still got time to change your mind."

Chance didn't hear him, his gaze locked on the vision of sunlight walking through the meadow. Her hair had been swept up. Tiny white flowers had been tucked into the cascade of auburn curls. Her pale cheeks flushed to the color of sunset as she walked toward him, the soft rustle of her fancy yellow gown dictating the slow, painful thump of his heart. She held a small bouquet of wildflowers, the stems bound in a white satin ribbon. He thought of the frayed satin tucked into a pouch upstairs, all the time he'd searched for a thread of goodness in life, and thought of *her*. It had always been Cora Mae, his beacon of light, keeping the darkness from claiming his spirit.

Tucker muttered something near his ear. Cora Mae's dark eyes locked with his, and Chance's heart bucked hard against his chest, knocking the last of his breath from his lungs. She looked utterly terrified. He tried to smile as she drew near, but just trying to draw air was too much effort.

She stepped beside him, and he rubbed his palms against his slacks.

"It's the nicest dress I have," she said, her hushed voice barely reaching his ears.

He managed a slow smile. "You look…" He swallowed against the lump in his throat. "I don't even have words…"

The gruffness of his voice brought the burn of tears into Cora's eyes. He'd never looked at her with such clear emotion. He took both of her hands into his large palms, and all her doubts evaporated.

She was marrying this man.

Cora suddenly found herself impatient for the minister to finish the proceedings. Yet even as she stood there, the warmth of his hands holding hers, a colored sky stretching out behind him…it didn't seem real. She'd never believed in fairy tales, yet she was quite sure, in this moment, she was living one. He looked so dashing in the dark suit, his golden hair flipped up at the collar.

"Cora Mae?" he whispered, leaning close. He nodded toward the preacher.

"*Oh!* We've started."

Low chuckles rumbled across the meadow. Reverend Keats stared at her expectantly.

Heat flared in her cheeks as she leaned closer to Chance. "Did he ask me something?" she whispered, hoping no on else could hear.

"Yeah, darlin'. He asked if you'd be my wife, in sickness and health, and—"

"*Yes.* I will. I do," she said to the man smiling at them.

"Well then, by the powers vested in me, I now pronounce you man and wife. You can kiss your bride."

Chance's arms slid around her, and Cora rose onto the tips of her toes to meet the soft caress of his lips.

The whooping and hollering of their guests crashed

through the tranquil moment. Cora stepped back and was instantly surrounded by ranch hands, each nudging the other out of the way to be the first to congratulate the bride.

Chance watched the playful spectacle with a wide smile.

She was his. Even building his ranch hadn't felt half this good.

"Hot damn!" shouted Duce. He slapped a hand against Chance's shoulder. "Best wedding I ever been to."

"Won't argue with that," said Mitch. "Let's eat."

The sun quickly dropping behind the mountains, everyone began to walk toward the house. Chance held his hand out to Cora Mae. Her smile was the brightest light he'd ever known. As she moved against his side, he wondered why it had taken Winifred's arrival to make him see what had been there all along.

As they all gathered in the dining room, Chance spotted Garret walking through the front room, his arms loaded down with clothes.

Ah, hell. He hadn't given a lot of thought to Garret's reaction to his marrying Cora Mae. Garret hadn't stuck around with the others to offer any congratulations. Clearly, the kid didn't see their marriage as worth celebrating.

"Garret?" called Skylar. "What are you doing?"

He glanced toward them, anger etched across his face. "Moving into the bunkhouse." He walked out of the door and slammed it shut with enough force to rattle the window.

The alarm in Cora Mae's eyes sent a surge of irritation through Chance. He knew the kid was sweet on her, but that was no reason to upset her on her wedding day.

"I'll talk to him," he said, pulling a chair out for her.

She took him by the hand and dragged him into the parlor. She curled her finger, beckoning him to lean in. Chance grinned and leaned toward his little wife. "What?"

"He offered to marry me."

Surprise stole his grin. "Garret did? When?"

"Just before I left."

Well, hell. The kid had gumption, and not much else when it came to women. "So, were you tempted?"

"*That's not funny.* I feel horrible about hurting his feelings."

"More like his pride," Chance muttered. "I tried to warn him."

"About what?"

"That he wasn't your type."

"When did you do that?"

"Yesterday. He tried to stake his claim and told me to back off."

Her eyes widened. "Off what?"

Chance smiled. "*You.* I tried to point out that your taste in men wasn't sixteen-year-old boys."

"He's been nothing but sweet to me. He looked so hurt when I declined his offer."

"You're his first real crush. He'll get over it."

Cora glanced at the door.

"I'll talk to him tomorrow." He drew her hand to her lips. "Let's go have supper, Mrs. Morgan."

Her heart fluttered at the title. *Mrs. Morgan.*

It still didn't seem real.

Two hours later Cora carried the last of the cake plates to the sink basin as Chance and Tucker saw John out to his wagon. Duce had agreed to accompany the older man home. With everyone having gone to their bunks and Skylar tucking Joshua in upstairs, the house was unnervingly quiet.

"Cora, get away from that wash basin," Skylar said, coming into the kitchen as she grabbed the dishcloth.

"I'm just cleaning up a bit."

"No dishes."

"Can I help you with the girls?"

"Both are fed and sound asleep, for the next few hours, anyway."

"Thank you, Skylar, for the cake and the flowers. You really helped to make everything so special."

"If I've learned anything about Chance in the last few years, it's to take him *literally* about everything. Once he sets his mind to something…well, that seems to be a Morgan trait," she said, her warm gaze looking out of the window.

Cora spotted their husbands standing in the yard.

"They do have their similarities," said Skylar.

"Bullheadedness being one of them," Cora agreed.

"I've seen a change in Chance, lately," Skylar said, walking back to the table. "A *good* change."

"Do you really think so?"

"I'm certain everyone on the meadow could see it while he was looking at you. He'll be a good husband." Skylar picked up a parcel that had been sitting on the table and held it out to her.

"For you. Sorry it's not wrapped. I wanted to at least get a ribbon around it, but…"

Cora stared at the white box.

"A wedding gift," Skylar clarified.

Shocked, she accepted the present. "Skylar, you didn't have to give me anything."

"It's not much."

Lifting the lid, Cora found that wasn't true. Something made of a fine, exquisite lace lay inside. "Oh, my goodness." Cora touched what appeared to be a gown. "Skylar…" Realizing the bodice consisted of nothing but sheer lace and a satin ribbon threaded up the center, her voice dried up.

"I've never worn it," Skylar said. "I was swollen with child when Tucker brought it home from a trip to a rail town."

"I couldn't," she said.

"We want you to have it."

Cora swallowed hard as she stared at the expensive and frightfully revealing gown. "I'm not sure it will fit me." Realizing she sounded rude, she quickly added, *"But it's lovely."*

"I'm sure it will fit. And it has the wrapper, if you're worried about catching a draft."

Cora lifted the delicate lace to see the white cotton wrapper beneath. "Skylar, this is much too nice. I just can't."

"Of course you can. A bride deserves a little luxury on her wedding night. Besides, I've already hemmed the bottom of the gown and the wrapper."

Oh, goodness. She must have had to cut off more than a foot of fabric.

"There's no need to be nervous," said Skylar.

"You would wear it?" she asked.

"Absolutely." Skylar leaned close, her voice barely a whisper. "With Tucker, I'd wear far less."

Cora had noticed that Skylar was highly affectionate with Tucker. He also seemed to be rather tender with her.

But that didn't mean things stayed all rosy behind closed doors. She trusted Skylar to tell her the truth.

"He doesn't…*hurt* you?"

Skylar's startled expression sent a flush to Cora's cheeks. She was about to retract the rude question when Sky said, "Not at all. Quite the opposite. I know you've had a bad experience, but it's not the same. Not when you're with someone you love, a man who cares for you."

"He's agreed to not…t-to wait."

"That's nice. But I wouldn't wait too long."

"Really?"

"Truly."

"And you think I should wear the gown?"

"Most definitely."

Cora drew in a deep breath and replaced the lid, thankful Chance had agreed to wait and she didn't have to decide on the gown for tonight.

Chapter Eighteen

Chance stopped in the hallway, surprised to find Cora Mae in her room wearing one of her black dresses. Though she was digging through her trunk, her bed was turned down as though she intended to sleep apart from him.

"Cora, what are you doing?"

She closed her trunk as she stood. "Going to bed. I'm quite exhausted."

"You're in the wrong room, honey."

Her eyes flared wide. "But you said—"

"I said we didn't have to consummate our vows. I didn't say you wouldn't be sleeping in my bed."

"Is that necessary?"

"*Necessary?* You're my wife. You'll sleep in my bed. *Our* bed," he amended.

"Oh. I hadn't thought about it like that."

"I intend to keep my word. Would you like me to help you collect your things?" he asked, wanting to ease the anxiety clear in every line of her face.

"My things?"

"Or don't you intend to wear nightclothes to bed?"

He smiled as red splotches rose in her cheeks. He'd take the blush over her stricken pallor. "If you don't have a nightdress," he said recalling their conversation on the subject a few weeks back, "I—"

"I do. I can collect my own things," she said, her hands clasped so tightly he was sure she'd lose circulation.

"All right. I'll leave you to it." He went to his room, wondering if she planned to pull on ten pairs of bloomers. He didn't care what she wore, as long as she was next to him.

He lit the lamps beside his bed, then decided it wouldn't hurt to turn the covers down. As he tugged the blankets back from the pillows, he realized his own palms were sweating.

Holy hell.

He was really going to sleep in this bed with Cora Mae. He glanced around at what was essentially a big empty room. Aside from the bed, a couple of pieces of bare furniture and the stove in the corner that he'd never bothered to light, the room was rather lifeless. He imagined that would change.

Too late for cold feet, he thought as he sat on the bed. He tugged off his boots. As he placed them next to his bureau, he spotted the bolt of fabric propped beside it, still wrapped in the brown paper.

Perfect.

He picked up the package as Cora walked into the room, draped in white from her chin to toes. He'd never seen the crisp white wrapper. He was pleased to see her hair down. She'd brushed the tight curls into loose waves of autumn fire.

"Come and sit down," he said, walking toward the bed.

He sat on the side of the mattress and patted the spot beside him. "I have something for you." He held up the brown parcel. "A wedding gift."

Her eyes lit with surprise. "When could you have gotten me a present?"

"This morning."

She sat beside him and he slid the package onto her lap.

"I didn't have the forethought to get a ring. Hopefully this will do until we have the time to ride down into one of the rail towns."

She simply stared at the long present, her eyes slowly hazed with tears. "Oh, Chance. *You didn't.*"

He supposed the rectangular shape gave it away. "Open it," he urged.

He'd never given a gift to a woman, and discovered his own heart thumped with excitement just to see her pull that fabric from the paper.

"I've got a pocket knife," he said, reaching toward his belt.

Her arms shot protectively over the paper and twine. "Don't you dare!"

Chance sat back, enjoying the light in her eyes as she began to carefully untie the knotted rope. She folded the long string into a neat pile before searching for the edge of the brown paper. You'd think the paper was made of silk for the care she took in peeling it back.

"My God, woman, I could have branded a dozen horses in the time it's taking you to undo that bit of paper."

She only smiled. Even though she knew what was hidden beneath the wrapping, she seemed surprised when the soft apricot fabric was finally revealed, inch by tiny inch. Her lips parted as she brushed her fingers over the smooth cloth.

"I saw you touching it just like that in the store," he said.

"You bought *all* of it." She glanced up, her eyes bright with moisture. "It must have cost a fortune!"

"Do you like it?"

"I *love* it," she said, her tears twinkling like stars in the lamplight as they spilled over her cheeks.

"Then it was worth every cent."

"Thank you."

He kissed her lightly on the lips. "You're welcome."

"There's enough here for all of us. The girls and Skylar. We'll have to start making patterns."

"Tomorrow," he said, lifting the material and setting it aside. When he turned around Cora stood, glancing cautiously at the bed.

"Here," he said, moving behind her. "I'll take your robe." He slipped his hands over her shoulders and pulled the white cotton from her arms before she could protest. He said they wouldn't consummate the marriage. That didn't mean they couldn't enjoy each other.

The gown he found underneath made him second-guess his tactics. Tight sheer lace hugged every smooth curve from her shoulders, to her waist, to the flare of her hips where a white satin skirt draped to the floor. She turned toward him and Chance forgot how to breathe. A satin ribbon threaded up the center kept the full swell of her breasts bound in the delicate lace. Pink buds pressed against the bodice, the rosy tips rising to a point beneath his appreciative gaze. Had the lace gone lower than the dip of her navel, she'd have brought him to his knees for sure. As it was, standing had become rather painful.

"Another wedding gift," she said, nervously crossing her arms. "Skylar gave it to me."

What the hell was his sister-in-law trying to do to him? He forced his gaze up past her chin. "It's…nice."

Her sigh of relief seemed to vibrate through the room. If she took one step closer, he could relieve any further doubt of just how attracted he was to her, but he imagined that sort of proof would send her screaming from the room.

"You're beautiful." He kissed her blushing cheek.

"Chance?" she said, her voice husky with a desire he knew she was just starting to recognize.

"Don't be afraid of me," he whispered, and pressed his mouth to hers. Her lips parted beneath his. He kissed her slowly, deeply, until she trembled and leaned into him. He placed his hands on her hips, carefully keeping distance between their bodies. Biting back a groan of regret, he eased away from her.

"Why don't you go on and get into bed," he said, quickly looking away from her, needing a chance to cool down.

"Which side should I take?"

"Doesn't matter." If things went the way he was hoping, they'd be sharing the middle.

Conscious of her eyes following his every move, he pulled his belt from the loops, set it on the bureau, then began unbuttoning his shirt.

"Should I turn out the lamp?" she asked as he shrugged off his shirt.

"If you want to." He reached for the strained closure of his trousers.

"Chance?"

He glanced over his shoulder and fought the urge to laugh out loud. Covers pulled up to her chin, she gazed up at him with wide brown eyes.

"Yeah?"

"What do you intend to sleep in?"

He looked away from her as he popped open the buttons, nearly groaning at the instant relief. "I believe we had this conversation a few weeks back in the kitchen. I don't own any pajamas, and I usually sleep in all that God gave me."

He heard a flutter of bed covers, just before the room went dark. Chuckling, he tugged off his trousers and realized the darkness could definitely work to his advantage. He wouldn't have to worry about the hunger revealed in his gaze as he snuggled up to her. Touching would only add to his suffering, but he wasn't new to torture, and he wasn't going to win over his bride by keeping distance between them. As much as he wanted to see his hands on her soft skin, it was just as well that he couldn't—not yet.

He slid beneath the covers and kept inching until he found the warm woman huddled on the far side. He curved around her small form. She stiffened against him.

"Relax, Cora. I just want to hold you."

A hard breath broke from her lungs. "Hold me?" her voice squeaked.

He kissed the shell of her ear. "Do you mind?"

Her hair tickled his cheek as she shook her head. His arm slid around her waist as he settled on her pillow.

After a few moments he realized she wasn't breathing. He stroked her lace-bound stomach, and the breath broke from her lungs.

"We're just holding each other, Cora Mae," he said, smiling into her hair. He breathed in her sweet scent. Despite the hunger gripping his body, he was happy just to have her in his arms. He'd wait as long as it took to gain her trust.

Cora trembled despite the warmth of his chest against her back. His hand tucked beneath her breasts was creating a heat all of its own. His warm palm shifted again, sliding across her belly and she choked on a breath.

"Should I get another blanket?"

Good heavens, she was about to catch fire.

"Cora Mae?"

"No," she said, laughing. *Nervous tension*, she thought. He'd touched her like this up at Mag's cabin, and she'd very much enjoyed it. Of course, they'd both been fully clothed, in the light of day.

Chance slid his arm beneath her pillow and gathered her closer. Cora released a long breath, forcing herself to relax in his arms, knowing he'd never hurt her. She wished she hadn't put out the lamp.

"I thought this evening went rather well," he said conversationally. "Not bad for a shotgun wedding."

The vibrations of his voice against her back increased the tantalizing stir of her body.

"What did you think?" he persisted, his hand sliding over her hip.

Now he's talkative?

"Cora Mae?"

"Yes," she said, smiling at the thought that he'd need reassurance about their wedding ceremony. "It was lovely."

He nuzzled her hair. "*You* were breathtaking," he whispered near her ear.

A surge of pleasure shimmered inside her. She'd been so nervous. To her surprise, the dress had actually fit quite nicely.

"Will you let me kiss you?"

"*Now?*"

"I can't think of anything I'd like more, but only if you

want to." His lips brushed the shell of her ear, sending a wave of tremors clear to her toes.

Drawing a deep, silent breath, she shifted. As she turned toward him, the hand on her hip slid across her stomach to the small of her back. His other arm slipped beneath her head, the warmth of his skin branding her cheek as she settled into the new position. His breath dusted her face, sending tendrils of sensation shooting up from her belly. She wished she could see him.

"If I do anything you don't like, I want you to tell me. Will you do that?"

"Yes."

His lips touched hers, lightly, tentatively. Again she wished she could see him.

When his mouth returned, it seemed only natural to open to him. Her tongue met his, and bursts of tingling heat shot through her. She slid her fingers into his hair as he caressed her side, her belly…her *breast*.

"Chance!"

"I won't hurt you," he said, his thumb brushing across the sensitive peak, leaving sparks beneath her skin as his mouth stroked her throat. "I just want to kiss you. I want to kiss you all over."

She couldn't deny that what he was doing felt incredibly good. Her body hummed as his lips moved down her neck to her shoulder.

"Do you mind?" His breath dusted the skin between her breasts.

Cora couldn't have answered him if she'd tried. He kissed her straining nipple through the delicate lace, dragging a moan from deep in her throat as pleasure blossomed beneath her skin. His tongue circled and teased, the warm moisture of his mouth stealing her breath. He hovered above her, though nothing touched her but his hand stroking her sides and his warm, wonderful mouth on her breast.

As his lips slid back up to her neck, she hardly noticed the gown sliding off her shoulders. Only when her fingers were forced from his hair did she protest, a protest that died the moment his mouth returned to her breast—this time no lace to dull the sensation of his tongue. Her back arched off the bed. He drew her into his mouth and pleasure pulsed through her body.

"Chance!" She strained her eyes, wanting to see him.

"I won't take you."

Distracted by the desire building inside her, she barely registered his words.

"Just kisses," he whispered, kissing a trail to her other breast, treating her to the same tantalizing torment.

She twisted against wild sensations ravaging her body, the sweet ache welling between her legs. His lips carried sparks of fire across her belly, and Cora groaned, flexing against him.

Again she opened her eyes. Again she saw only darkness. *"Chance?"*

"Trust me," he breathed against her skin. His hands stroked down her bare legs, and she realized her gown was bunched at her waist.

"Only pleasure," he whispered. His palms smoothed up her inner thighs, opening her to him as his lips carried fire to her very core. "I promise."

"Oh, my goodness," she breathed, the air sizzling from her lungs as his mouth claimed her. She arched against the new surge of desire. Pleasure spiked as his tongue circled and stroked. She gripped at the sheets, crying out as bursts of sweet lightning ripped through her, stripping away everything as Chance consumed her with wild wonderful pulses of sensation and light.

Her mind lost in a haze, her lungs burning for breath, Cora realized with a start that Chance had released her.

Opening her eyes to darkness, she surged up. His arms closed around her, bringing her back down on the bed. Fear stamped out the last of the sensations that had consumed her just moments ago as the memory of being held down in the dark flashed in her mind. She tensed as he drew her close.

"What's wrong?" he asked, loosening his hold.

"I can't see you," she whispered, knowing it made no sense. She knew it was Chance who held her, Chance's kisses that had driven her to delirium. "I need to see you."

"You want me to light the lamp?"

"Would you?"

"Sure."

Chance hesitated, uncertain as to how she'd react to her state of undress, or the evidence of his violently aroused body. "If that's what you want."

"Yes, please."

"All right." He moved to the side of the bed.

"Wait!" Her fingers closed over his arm like steel talons.

"I'm right here." He reached for her even as she collided against him. She damn near scampered onto his lap. "Honey, have I frightened you?"

"No," she whispered. "I don't like the dark. I shouldn't have put out the lamp. I kept trying to tell you."

If she had, he sure hadn't noticed. He'd been wholly focused by the passion welling beneath his lips. She'd enjoyed his intimate kisses, and he'd damn sure enjoyed kissing her. But the tremors shaking her body as she clung to him now weren't derived from passion. "I'm sorry, honey."

She smiled against his neck. "You did a good job of distracting me."

He kissed her bare shoulder, relief breaking through him. He moved back against the headboard. "Ease back, darlin'," he said as he reached toward the side table.

She sat back, her skin warm against his thighs.

"I'd hate to accidentally light your hair instead of the wick."

Her giggle danced through the room and under his skin as he lit the lamp.

"How's…" His voice dried up, his words forgotten as his gaze collided with the flawless curves in his arms, straddling his lap. The wild flames of Cora Mae's hair glittered in the lamplight. The pink crowns of her breasts peeked through long auburn coils. The gown he'd unlaced hung loosely on the sweet curve of her hips.

Want pounded through him with such force he didn't know what to do first. So he simply stared.

"My God. You're beautiful."

A blush began to creep up from her breasts to her pretty white cheeks.

"Feel better?"

She flashed a shy smile. "Yes."

Chance was afraid to move, the hard proof of his arousal precariously hidden beneath the white ripples of her gown. "Honey, I don't want to frighten you."

"You don't."

Cora licked her lips, her fingers tingling at the thought of smoothing across the firm muscles of his chest. Golden light twinkled through the hair on his chest with his deep breaths.

"Do I get to touch you, as well?" she asked.

His eyebrows shot up, and she was quite certain she'd surprised him. His slow grin put a tingle in every place on her body he'd kissed.

"As much as you want," he said, easing back against the pillows.

More than eager, she flattened her hands against the ripple of muscles in his torso and made a slow ascent. The bursts of pleasure she felt at just touching him shocked her. The sheer power of his body was startling. Yet she'd never felt more secure.

She glanced up at green eyes that smoldered, and felt the loss of her own breath. She wanted more of him. She wanted to make *him* feel all that he'd given her, sweet lightning coursing through his body, making him cry out in pleasure.

"Can I kiss you?"

"Hell *yes*."

Smiling, she rose up on her knees and pressed her mouth to the tender pink scar at the base of his throat. "I wanted to do this the night you were hurt."

He groaned as her lips followed the trail of new skin. Her fingers tested the resilient muscles of his arms as she kissed his shoulders, his collarbone. She delighted in the salty taste of him, the violent tremors of his body as she moved over him.

Chance didn't know how much more he could stand. With every shift of her body, the gown bunched at her waist brushed over his erection, stripping away his control. If she moved a fraction closer, he'd lose it for sure.

Her lips branded his chest, and his hips flexed in response, the sting of pleasure dragging a groan from deep inside him, stripping away his restraint.

"Cora Mae," he said in a hoarse whisper. "You're making me weak."

"I don't think that's possible." Finding the flat disk of his nipple, her tongue teased and circled, mimicking what he'd done to her.

A sweat broke out over his body.

Holy hell! He was supposed to be teaching her the pleasures of her body, not vice versa.

Her teeth raked over the surprisingly sensitive peak.

"Cora…Mae," he choked out.

She moved up his body, her kisses light, teasing, barely dusting his skin. Reaching his mouth, her arms slid around his neck, her hips shifted against his and Chance nearly shouted from the jolt of desire. He framed her face with his hands, his tongue mating with hers, linking their mouths the way he desperately wanted to link their bodies.

She rocked against him, rumpled satin and lace the only barrier between his hungry body and the sultry heat burning him through the layers of fabric.

Chance broke the kiss. "Honey, *stop.*"

Cora flexed her hips against the ridged heat of his body, shivering from the shocking spiral of sensation.

His hands closed around her waist, stopping her movements, even as his body strained against her. She wanted to give him everything he'd given her, to caress the part of him that was most male. She slid her hand over corded stomach muscles. Her fingers followed the line of golden hair, uncovering the satiny steel of his body.

Chance's eyes flew open.

She brushed her open palm over the smooth length of him, intrigued by the satiny softness of something so hard. His breath broke. His hand closed over hers before she could repeat the caress.

She leaned up to kiss his lips. "I want to give you what you gave me."

"I can't...take it," he said in a broken breath.

"But it's possible?" she asked, watching pleasure take him as her fingers closed over him, measuring him.

His fingers locked around her wrist. "I'd be taking the pleasure I should be giving you."

"But I feel it just the same. Deep inside me. An ache that's more pleasure than pain."

Her words burned Chance as deeply as her caress had, knowing she took such joy in touching him. She was a wonder. He knew they'd have passion between them, but he couldn't have guessed that it would exceed anything he'd ever experienced.

"Do you still?" he asked.

She stared at him in silent question.

His hands flexed on her hips, increasing the heat in her gaze. "Do you still ache for me?"

Her instant blush answered his question, even before she gave a slight nod. Her innocence was humbling. Her trust touched him to the deepest depths of his soul. "When we make love, it will be the same, *even better,* both of us pleasing each other. No pain."

"I want that," she said in a quivering breath.

"Lift your arms," he said, gathering up the bottom of her gown.

Her eyes widened, uncertainty flashing in those rich brown depths. She still straddled his legs. Without the gown, there'd be nothing but the sleek heat of her body between them.

"Remember my promise?" He kissed her lips. "Bucknaked on top of me. You say the word, and I'll stop."

Holding his gaze, she raised her arms over her head with the elegance of a ballerina. Chance slid the gown up the ivory curves of her body, lifting her hair away from her breasts as he passed over them. He leaned down, kissing each rosy tip, smiling as she trembled in response. As he tossed the gown to the floor, her hair flittered back down, but it was the deep auburn curls arched over his thighs that held his attention.

He glanced up and found Cora's wide eyes on the proof of his arousal. He closed his arms around her and pulled her to his chest, impatient to feel her skin pressed to his. She went willingly, curving her arms around his neck.

"Oh, my goodness." A sigh unraveled from her lungs as she settled against him.

"You are a wonder to touch," he said, stroking her from her shoulders to the lush curve of her backside. "So smooth and soft."

Overwhelmed by the tender intimacy, tears burned at Cora's eyes. She hugged Chance's gentle strength against her, hardly able to believe where this day had brought them. She sniffed as tears leaked from her eyes onto his broad, beautiful shoulder.

"Cora Mae?"

Hearing the concern in his voice, she smiled and kissed his neck.

He eased her back, his brow furrowing at the sight of her tears. "Honey, if you're—"

"I love you," she said. The surprise in his eyes brought

another smile to her lips. "I love the sound of my name on your lips."

"It's a beautiful name."

"I've always hated it," she said, watching her hands move over his chest. She marveled at the feel of his skin beneath her palms, how safe and unabashed she felt sitting with him like this. "You give me so much."

His mouth slanted over hers, and Cora welcomed his wild kiss. Her breath caught at the feel of his hardness pressed against her sensitive flesh.

To be joined so intimately with him will be worth the pain.

His hands curved around her buttocks as he repeated the caress, and Cora arched back, stung by a lash of intense pleasure. Her hips moved in response to the desire coursing through her.

Chance needed to be inside her more than he needed to breathe. Her body was burning him like liquid fire as she pressed against him.

Slipping his hand between their bodies, he caressed the delicate bud of her passion in the same languid rhythm. She cried out, her movements becoming urgent.

"Chance!"

Straining for control, he fought the urge to tumble her back on the bed. She rocked against him, her mouth seeking his. She moaned, her fingers delving into his hair as she kissed him. The feel of her breasts against his chest, her tongue possessing his mouth, her heat spilling into his palm…

"Let me make love to you," he said against her lips, needing to hear her say the words.

"I want—" her breath broke as he stroked her softly.

"What do you want?"

"You," she said simply. "I want *you.*"

"I'm yours." He gripped her hips, tugging her up until his shaft met the slick molten heat of her body. A groan broke from his chest at his slight penetration. Cora Mae tensed.

"Cora—"

"It's okay," she whispered. "I want this, I want *all* of you."

That was exactly what he wanted to give her. A kind of pleasure he'd never known. He'd never given all of himself to any woman. He'd never stayed inside a woman long enough to share his seed. Not ever.

He surged forward, taking her down onto the mattress, wild to be fully sheathed inside her. Realizing the abrupt move, he froze.

Wide cinnamon eyes stared up at him, her hair swirled across the bed like waves of fire. "It's not hurting," she said.

"Only pleasure." He kissed her lips. "I promise."

Her eyes bright with desire and *trust,* she shifted, the cradle of her thighs caressing him as she adjusted to the new position. The sensual movement drew him deeper into her body, causing them both to tremble.

He pushed into the tight satin heat, filling her completely. Desire exploded into shared cries of ecstasy.

"Cora Mae?"

Awash in sensation, Cora locked her legs around his hips, wanting to keep him deep inside her. His body shifted against her, the friction a hot rush of pure, wild pleasure. He moved again and she lifted to meet his thrust.

Every powerful movement flooded her body with sensation, the pleasure building with each stroke. She called his name as he filled her again and again. Tension coiled harder, his tempo increasing with each wild surge.

"*Cora Mae.*"

She opened her eyes, meeting the heat of his gaze. Passion burst through her. She flexed against him, crying out as pleasure pulsed to every point of her body.

Chance shuddered with each sharp, shocking pulse of Cora's climax, her cries of completion pulling him over the edge into the blinding rush of his own release. She locked around him, all warmth and softness, caressing him clear to his soul. Her name was torn from him as he spent himself completely inside her.

A short while later Cora continued to hold the man lying on top of her. Warm, sated, deliriously *happy,* she didn't much care that she could hardly breathe beneath his relaxed weight.

He eased up, caressing her even as he withdrew from her body. She moaned, shivering as he rolled onto his side, taking her with him, keeping their bodies close. The involuntary sound echoed in the quiet room, and Cora suddenly realized just how vocal she'd been during their lovemaking.

Her breath stalled.

"What's wrong?" Chance asked.

"Nothing," she said, attempting to tuck her face against him, but he propped up on his elbow to look down at her.

"Tell me."

"I just…" She groped for the sheet, suddenly aware of her nudity.

"Cora?" He pulled her close, seeming to understand her modesty.

"Was I terribly loud?" she said in a whisper.

His chest vibrated against her and she realized he was

laughing. "No, darlin'." He kissed her blushing cheek. "Sweet, brave Cora Mae. You were perfect."

Before she could bask in the glow of those words, he rolled away from her. Cora instantly felt the loss of his warmth. She sat up and realized they'd been lying at the foot of the bed. Careful to keep herself covered, she scooted back to where she'd started.

Chance reached toward the floor and picked up a blanket. All the covers but the sheet she held against her breasts had been kicked off the bed. He smiled at her, setting off a flutter of sensation as his strong arms flapped the blanket out and across the big bed. He reached for the second blanket, and she couldn't look away from the sculpted lines of his body, skin gilded in the lamplight, every ounce of him molded to perfection.

He walked around to his side, stacked her pillow with his at the center and climbed in.

"You gonna share that sheet?" he asked, his big body dominating the middle of the bed, the two blankets pulled up to his waist.

Cora slid toward him. He held up the blankets and reached for the sheet, pulling it over him as he gathered her against his skin. She rested her head in the hollow beneath his shoulder as he lay back. His warmth and the soothing glide of his hand across her back drew her closer. She sighed and settled more firmly against him, her hand stroking across the thatch of golden hair on his chest. She felt strangely relaxed, yet wide-awake.

"Should I turn out the lamp?"

She liked being able to see him. "Could you leave it on?" she asked. "For a little while?"

"I'll leave it on all night if you like."

"You wouldn't mind?"

He shifted, turning her onto the pillow beside him. "Sweetheart, I'm just happy to be holding you."

Staring into his warm, smiling eyes, her body began to hum…and ache. "Will you kiss me some more?"

His lips brushed hers in a light kiss, stirring the wild wonderful tendrils of sensation that began to thrum through her.

"All over," he promised.

Chapter Nineteen

"A Miss Tindale is here to see you."

Salina glanced up from her desk at her housekeeper standing in the doorway. Shock stole her voice. She'd assumed that little tramp would be long gone by now. Grissom had seemed a determined and capable sort of fellow. She had planned to pay a visit to Chance this very evening.

She pushed back from her desk. If Cora Tindale thought she'd seek refuge here, she was mistaken. Her mind was still plagued by the image of Chance's arms wrapped around that woman, kissing her the way he had in the middle of the boardwalk.

Her stomach rolled on her way to the door. "Carmen, make some sweet tea, would you?" she said, pressing against the flat of her stomach.

The woman's gray eyebrows pinched inward. "Feeling ill again?"

Nothing that couldn't be helped by Miss Tindale's speedy departure. "I'm fine. I'd just like some tea."

"Yes, ma'am," she said, turning away.

Drawing a deep breath, trying to ease her morning nausea, she made her way to the parlor. Her eyes widened at the sight of Mr. Grissom. He stood beside an older woman sitting on the settee, her elegant black gown quite similar to the one she wore herself. A young girl, appearing no older than fifteen and dressed in white, sat to her left. Her gaze was fixed on her folded hands—clearly the lady's attendant.

"*Mrs.* Tindale?" she asked.

The woman smiled pleasantly.

Salina glanced at Mr. Grissom, perplexed as to why they would be paying her a visit.

"Mrs. Jameson," he said, "might I introduce my mistress? Winifred Tindale."

"A pleasure," Salina said, not about to forgo her manners. Lord knew she'd waited long enough to have a real reason to use them.

"I apologize for the intrusion," said Mrs. Tindale. "Mr. Grissom tells me you were helpful to us yesterday."

"As much as I could be. I gave him directions to the Morgan Ranch. I trust you found it."

"Yes. Unfortunately my daughter is not thinking clearly. I only wish to return her to her rightful husband."

"*Husband?*" said Salina.

"Yes," said Mrs. Tindale, "her intended husband. This entire business is quite disgraceful."

"What is it you wish to ask of me?"

"We only need access to the ranch," said Mr. Grissom. "I'm told your property borders the Morgans'."

"Yes, by quite a distance, a good fifteen miles."

"Is it possible to approach their ranch undetected?"

Salina sensed a plan brewing and smiled. They wanted Cora Tindale. She wanted Chance. "Yes. My men have, on occasion."

"Would one of your men be willing to guide me in?"

The only man on the ranch at the moment was Nigel. He'd have to do. The way Wyatt had been sulking lately, his absence was likely a blessing.

"Your tea, Mrs. Jameson," said Carmen, entering the room with a large silver tray. The sweet-scented tea added to the delighted stir welling inside her.

"Serve our guests first," she instructed, "and then send in Nigel. I have a task for him."

From the moment Chance had stepped in the back door for their noontime meal, a permanent blush had stained Cora Mae's cheeks. He hadn't awakened her this morning, allowing her to sleep in past breakfast. As she fluttered around the kitchen, not once meeting his gaze, he began to think not waking her had been a mistake.

Tucker and Skylar sat across from him, waiting patiently for his wife to join them at the small table. Baked chicken and fresh biscuits steamed on their plates, the aroma making his mouth water.

He should have woken her up. He nearly had. The moment he'd awakened and felt her warmth beside him, saw her face tucked so sweetly against his chest, his body had burned with the urge to wake her with kisses, to reawaken the passion they'd shared several times the night before. But if he'd done that, he'd likely have stayed in bed with her until noon.

He imagined she had surprised herself last night. She'd certainly shocked the hell out of *him*. He hadn't dreamed his bride would be so passionate. Okay, he might have dreamed it, but he truly hadn't expected her to come apart in his arms last night, to give herself so completely. Her openness, her honesty, it had burned him to the quick.

I love you.

Her breathless proclamation had been sounding in his mind all morning.

You give me so much.

He wondered if it all seemed different to her in the morning light. If she'd realized the words he'd withheld.

His brother's warning had nagged at him all morning, as well, and now seemed to shout through his mind. *I do believe proclamations of love are words most women want to hear on their wedding night. I was too damn scared to tell Skylar I loved her when I should have.*

He glanced at his sister-in-law. Judging by all the times he'd caught them lip-locked over the past few years, she must have forgiven him.

Skylar shifted in her chair. "Cora, come and sit down," she said. "The pans can wait."

Cora Mae turned from the stove. She eyed him up with the wariness of a green-broke filly looking to avoid a lasso.

Hell. She was definitely seeing things differently in the clear light of day. He'd rushed her; he knew he had. But damn it, the way she'd responded to his touch, his kisses—

"I made fresh butter," she said, turning away from him again.

"Cora, we don't—" Skylar snapped her mouth shut as Cora Mae disappeared into the pantry.

A low chuckle rumbled from his brother. Tucker grinned at him from across the table as he finished buttering his biscuit. "Morning-after jitters?" he asked in a low whisper.

Chance glared at him.

Skylar jabbed him with her elbow. "Why don't you and I eat in the front room," she whispered, picking up her plate and glass of tea as she stood. "It's not often the kids are all napping at once."

"Fine idea," Tucker said, picking up his plate to join her retreat.

"You don't have to," Chance said.

Skylar smiled. "You've always given us our privacy. We can do the same." She stepped beside him. "She's been nervous all morning," she whispered for his ears alone, then hurried through to the dining room with Tucker.

He appreciated the warning. He just wasn't sure what to do about it. Cora Mae came back to the table holding a small crock, her eyes widening at the sight of the two empty chairs.

"Where'd they go?"

"Wanted some time alone, I guess."

Her slow approach ate at his nerves. Maybe she just needed to be reminded that she liked being in his arms.

The moment she was in reach, he grabbed ahold of her apron and tugged until she plopped down onto his lap.

"Chance!"

He forced a lazy grin as he took the crock from her hands and set it on the table.

"What are you—"

"Kissing you good-morning," he said, "like I should have hours ago."

Her expression softened and Chance felt an ache in his chest, which only tightened as she leaned into his kiss, her hands sliding over his shoulders with familiar ease. Chance took care not to rush, teasing her lips with light caresses, followed by a deep tasting. The next thing he knew, she was clinging to him, kissing him back with equal intensity. As gradually as the kiss escalated, Chance backed off, easing his hold, the pressure of his mouth, until he was nibbling gently on her lush lower lip before releasing her.

"Much better," he said, quite satisfied with her rosy cheeks and complacent expression. "I should have done that before I went out to work this morning. Tomorrow I'll know better."

"I wish you had. I slept far too late."

"You needed the rest," he said, holding her on his lap when she would have stood.

She glanced warily toward the dining room.

"Skylar's likely on Tucker's lap in the front room," he said with a grin. A smile eased her tense expression as she relaxed in his arms.

"Tell me what's wrong, why you're so nervous."

Her brow creased with a frown. "I don't know. I didn't, I've never…*I just am*. We're *married*." She said it as though the news came as a shock to her.

"We are. You're having second thoughts?"

"No."

He drew a silent breath of relief.

"We've just not spent much time with each other."

"My fault," he said. "I'll take care to be home in the evenings."

"Skylar suggested I move my things into your room—"

"Our room," he amended. "And you should."

"I know," she said, her frown deepening.

"But you don't want to?"

"I started to," she said, her expression miserable. "My trunk is in your room. But when I opened your bureau and saw everything lined up so neat, the clothes folded so nicely in the drawers, I didn't want to mess it up."

She was upset because she didn't want to mess up his neat drawers? Laughter shook his chest, even as he tried to fight it. "Honey, you could put my clothes on the back porch for all I care. What matters to me is *you*."

"I couldn't move your things to make room for mine."

"Then we'll do it together. When I come in tonight."

Her smile touched her lips, though it didn't take the sadness from her eyes. "Okay."

"Honey, we're not talking about clothes, are we?"

"I just…I don't want to make a mess of things. You've seen Mother when she's in a dither, she can leave behind the destruction of a hurricane."

"I won't let her. She'll likely have to travel for a week to find the nearest judge."

"I hate knowing I've brought such a burden to this house. Did you talk to Garret?"

Chance doubted the news that he'd spent his morning working with Duce instead of Garret would ease her concern. Judging by the frigid glare he'd given him before riding out with Tucker, the kid was mad as hell. He'd taken for granted how well they'd worked together over the past few years.

"He just needs some time to cool off," Chance said, hoping that was indeed the case.

"Seems no matter what I do, I'm uprooting someone."

"At sixteen, he has plenty of time to find a place to spread his roots."

Her lips twitched with the start of a grin. "Unlike you, who's firmly rooted?"

He smiled. "Exactly."

The warmth in her gaze filled him with a sense of satisfaction. Strange, how soothing her doubts helped to ease his own. Her eyes seemed to search his.

Tell her you love her.

"I love the feel of you in my arms," he said, hugging her close. *Coward.*

"You really mean that, don't you?"

He smiled into her hair. "After last night, I can't believe you'd have any doubt." He felt the heat of her blush and laughed.

Had he ever laughed so much? He didn't think so. He kissed her smiling lips.

"Your dinner's getting cold," she said between kisses.

"I'd rather kiss you and go back to work hungry," he said, muffling her laughter with his mouth.

By the time Tucker and Skylar came back into the kitchen, Chance was leaning against the counter as Cora put away their clean plates. They had managed to eat, though he had kept Cora Mae on his lap the whole time.

"Ready?" asked Tucker.

"As ever," he said, starting for the back door. He glanced back at Cora Mae, returning her warm smile before stepping outside.

"Did you two work things out?" Tucker asked as they set off across the yard.

"I think so." They enjoyed being with each other. Hell, he could hardly stand being away from her. He was damn certain he loved her—an affliction he'd sworn he would never suffer. A few weeks ago he hadn't believed any woman could be worth such risk. He'd been wrong.

As they neared the first barn, Chance paused, detecting the faint scent of smoke. "Hey, Tuck?"

Tucker was already searching the clear blue sky for signs of a plume. "Where's it coming from?"

Hoofbeats pounded toward them as Garret rode into view. "Fire on the north pasture!" he shouted. He reined to a hard stop, the horse turning in a full circle. "Duce and I cut the fences. I'm rounding up the others. We need shovels!"

"We'll bring 'em," Chance shouted back, already running into the stable with Tucker.

Cora Mae couldn't stop smiling.

She pressed a rolling pin into a mound of piecrust and began flattening out a circle.

Thirty minutes inside the house, and Chance had slaked all her fears. Chance Morgan, her *husband.*

The very notion still amazed her. Everything had happened so fast, Mother's arrival, the wedding, *last night.* Her stomach dipped at the memory of the intimacy she and Chance had shared.

This morning, it had all seemed so overwhelming. She'd begun to worry she had guilted him into something he'd regret, but she couldn't doubt the truth she saw in Chance's eyes.

He loves me.

He didn't have to say the words for her to feel his affection. The man had just sat in this kitchen and hand fed her just to keep her on his lap. She never dreamed a man could be so endearing, not even Chance.

He'd soothed her doubts—his tender touch making her feel *cherished.*

Cora released a slow sigh and pressed out the edges of the piecrust. Breathing in an unexpected scent of smoke, she glanced at the stove. Nothing seeped from the oven door or the stovepipe. Realizing the smell was coming from outside, she leaned toward the kitchen window, searching the sky until she spotted thick gray clouds billowing up from the north, beyond the stables.

Good gracious! She set the rolling pin aside and hurried out the back door. Keeping her eyes on the massive plume, she ran toward the corrals. Only horses milled about in the various stalls. Not a single man was in sight.

"Chance? Tucker!"

The ranch seemed deserted.

Of course they'd have already spotted the smoke, she reasoned. To her relief, the fire appeared to be far off.

She crossed her arms as she stared across the pasture toward the rising plumes. Skylar was nursing her daughters. Cora wasn't sure if she should worry her. The wind was blowing northwest, away from the house. Surely the men would have alerted them if they were in any danger.

Assuring herself they likely had everything under control, she turned back to the house.

Movement to her left caught her eye. She turned as someone grabbed her from behind. A man's bruising grip strapped around her arms. His other hand clamped over her mouth as he lifted her off the ground.

Cora twisted and tried to scream. Each strained breath sucked in the foul scent of a cloth he held over her nose and mouth.

Her vision blurred.

Oh no.

Wyatt rode toward the Lazy J, anxious to see Salina's reaction to the news he'd just heard about Chance Morgan.

Having spotted what looked to be a brush fire on Morgan land, they'd gone to investigate and found a blaze moving through trees and pasture. A fire was every rancher's worst fear. He'd sent his crew to help contain it, and would have gone himself but he didn't put it past Morgan to shoot him on sight.

Not that he'd blame him. Blinded by jealousy, he'd been ready to kill the man. As it turned out, Morgan had married Miss Tindale after all.

A smile pushed high into his cheeks as Wyatt rode into the yard, but his good cheer was cut short.

A tall, sharply dressed stranger stood beside a fancy black coach, talking to Salina. Another woman dressed in black stood beside them.

What the hell is she up to now?

Wyatt spurred his horse. Salina turned, seeming startled to see him barreling into the yard. He leaped from his saddle, noting the tense expression of all three, as though he'd just intruded on a meeting of some importance.

"This is my foreman," Salina said, introducing him like some common cowpuncher as he stomped toward her. "Wy—"

"Wyatt McNealy," he said, extending his hand toward the fancy-dressed stranger. He slid his arm around Salina's waist and pulled her against his side, ignoring her pinched expression.

"Grissom," the man said, shaking his hand. "My mistress, Winifred Tindale." He motioned to the woman.

Mrs. Tindale's smile was more smirk than grin, her slender arching eyebrow suggesting amusement. She gave a regal nod, and Wyatt couldn't help but think how she reminded him of a much-older version of Salina.

"Tindale? You're kin to Miss Cora Tindale, or rather *Mrs. Morgan*, going by the news I heard this afternoon."

Salina stiffened beside him. *"What?"*

"According to one of their ranch hands, they were wed last night."

"Utter nonsense," said Mrs. Tindale. "She's been promised to another. Now that we have what I came for," she said brightly, "we'll be on our way."

A loud shriek drew their gazes to the tall black carriage.

"Miz Tindale!" shouted a girl's voice. The small carriage door burst open and a young girl dressed in white leaned out, her eyes wide with fear. "She's waking up!"

The girl yelped as she was forced forward and landed face-first in the dirt.

Cora fell to her knees in the open doorway, her hands bound in front of her. She blinked as though fighting to keep her eyes open. *"Chance!"*

Grissom was over her in a flash, pushing her back into the carriage as he pulled a brown bottle from his pocket.

"You can't do this!" she screamed, twisting as he struggled to hold a white cloth over her mouth. "Chance," she called, her voice reduced to a whisper.

Wyatt stared in horror as Grissom stepped up into the coach and tossed Cora's limp body onto the padded bench, none too gently. He glanced at the woman before him watching the scene with blue eyes that could have been cut from a glacier.

"You kidnapped her?" he asked, hardly able to believe what he'd just witnessed.

"I'm merely taking what's mine," said Mrs. Tindale.

"Madam," said Grissom, holding his hand out to help

the widow lady into the carriage. "We should go if we're to make the riverboat."

"Thank you for your assistance," she said to Salina, a pleasant smile transforming the woman's expression to one of sheer elegance.

The burning in Wyatt's gut intensified.

"My warm regards to her new husband," Salina said.

The look of satisfaction on her face sickened him.

Who the hell were they to take Cora from the man she'd chosen?

Grissom snapped a whip, and the coach rocked forward, pulling out of the yard.

"Salina, what have you done?"

"I fixed my problem," she said in a huff, "and helped a mother reclaim her daughter."

"*Reclaim?* Seems to me Cora Tindale is old enough to think for herself. She married Chance Morgan last night."

"You heard her mother," Salina protested. "She's been promised to another."

"Promises don't change the fact that Reverend Keats was at Morgan's place last night! I heard it straight from one of Morgan's men when we went to see about a fire on their—"

"Wait a minute," he said, the pieces clashing together in his mind the way thunder breaks through storm clouds. "Tell me you didn't have one of our men set that fire."

Salina pursed her lips, her usually pretty face set in a stubborn scowl. "Grissom did what he had to. There was no chance of it spreading here."

Wyatt could hardly believe the lengths she'd gone to in order to catch a Morgan. Then he reminded himself he'd lynched the man to ensure he'd have Salina all to himself.

My God. We're two of a kind. Ruthless, blind and dumb as ax handles.

"It's not going to work, Salina," he said, sounding as defeated as he felt. "How do you think Morgan is going to react to the news that *you* had a hand in kidnapping his wife?"

"How will he know?"

"Hell, woman! You took his wife! You think he won't be looking for answers? I'd be shooting down any man who took you from me! I hanged the last man who hinted at trying!"

Salina's mouth dropped open. "You did?"

"He doesn't want you, but *I do*. I've played along with all your schemes, knowing Mr. Almighty and Righteous wouldn't want a tramp for a wife."

Salina gasped.

"I don't even mind that, Salina. I know how it was with the old man, you needed time to test your freedom. And you kept coming back to *me*. I keep waiting for you to see, to realize—"

"Realize *what?*"

"That I love you!"

Salina jerked back, his words hitting her like a slap in the face. How dare he use something like that against her!

"Do you think I'd have stuck around this past year, putting up with other men in your bed, if I didn't love you? I know you have feelings for me, Salina."

No. Wyatt had his place. She enjoyed his company, but he couldn't give her the security she required.

"We've been through too much," he said.

She wouldn't be swayed. "Love won't save this ranch."

"To hell with this ranch! All I want is *you*."

She shook her head, refusing to give up her plans. She didn't need love—she wanted her house, her space, her comfort. "The Morgans have the land we need to expand our ranging. You can't manage this ranch well enough to support me, much less a child. How am I supposed—"

"A *child?*" Wyatt interrupted.

Salina tensed. Wyatt's wide eyes slid to her stomach and she wanted to whip the carelessly spoken words back into her mouth. "It was merely a figure of speech."

"A figure you've never used before." His eyes narrowed accusingly. "You told me you couldn't conceive."

"The facts are the same, Wyatt. If I lose this ranch, you won't ever see me again, child or not."

"Salina—"

"We are so close to having it all."

"You have lost your mind! You must have if you think I'll sit by and let Morgan move in while you're carrying my child!"

"You are not the only man I've been with!"

"You've had no one but me for months! I've spent more time in your bed these past few weeks than I have in my own saddle! If you'd stop being so goddamned pigheaded, you'd realize I'm the only man you really want!"

She stood stiff as a rooted tree, her jaw clamped tight, her arms wrapped around her middle.

"How long have you known?"

She averted her gaze.

"How long, Salina?"

"A few days," she murmured.

He'd take that to mean a week or better. She'd been feeling ill for more than a week…*because of pregnancy*. Having spent hours listening to her rant about her mamma's endless string of pregnancies, he figured Salina knew the signs well enough to recognize them.

She'd known. And she'd doubled her efforts to capture Morgan.

"My God," he breathed, his breath coming out as though he'd been kicked in the gut. She would have used their child to trap another man.

He stared at her and had to wonder if he was just seeing her clearly for the first time or if she truly was a stranger to him. How could he love her?

He turned away, unable to even look at her.

"Wyatt?" she called after him.

He kept walking, damned if he'd allow her to devastate another man as she'd just done him. Morgan had suffered enough on account of them.

"Wyatt, we can still make this work!"

He spun around. "That's where you're wrong, Salina. Do you think we're just pawns? Me, Cora, *our baby!* That we're so insignificant we can be picked up and moved to wherever you'd have us placed?"

"Wyatt—"

"And to think I nearly killed a man over you. Fine time to realize you were never worth it."

Her eyes popped wide.

"Hell." He shook his head in disgust. "Then again, I suppose you're no better than I deserve."

"Wyatt."

The tremble in her voice didn't do a damn thing to stir his sympathy. He turned away and mounted his horse.

"Where are you going?"

"To do what's right. *For once*." He rode toward her, the moisture in her eyes giving him a sliver of hope she wasn't completely heartless. "You wanted a ramrod, lady, you got one. If you're carrying my baby, I'm the only one you'll have for as long as it takes you to deliver my child."

Her eyes widened with fear.

"When I get back, if Morgan don't kill me first, you and I are going to have a long talk about this ranch and whether or not I still want you."

Chapter Twenty

Smelling nothing but smoke, tasting the soot coating his teeth, Chance couldn't shake his unease as he watched three men from the Lazy J walk back over the blackened field with Duce and the others. They dug their shovels into patches of ground still smoking, searching for hot spots. Thankfully they'd only lost a solid fifty acres of grass and trees, and none of the horses had been harmed.

"Awfully neighborly of Wyatt to send his men over to help," Tucker said as he wiped a bandanna over his soot-covered face.

"It doesn't make sense," said Chance. "If Wyatt didn't start this, who did?"

"That's what I was thinking," said Garret. The kid's face was fully blackened with ash but for the whites of his eyes. "Sun's not hot enough and there isn't a thundercloud in the sky."

Chance thumped him on the shoulder. "Nice job cutting the fences, getting the horses out when you did."

"Remember that when it's time to round them up." His teeth flashed behind his blackened face.

"I'm gonna head back," Chance said, anxious to see Cora Mae.

"Might want to hold up a minute," said Tucker, looking past him.

Chance turned to see Wyatt riding toward them over charred ground.

"Either he's in a hurry to hear our gratitude," said Tuck, "or something's on his mind."

The tension in Chance's spine doubled as Wyatt reined to a hard stop in front of them. To his surprise, Wyatt even stepped down from his saddle. Something was definitely weighing on his mind. His worried gaze moved between him and his brother.

"Chance?"

"Yeah?" Chance tugged lightly at the bandanna around his neck, revealing enough of his scar to widen Wyatt's eyes. His expression twisted with sheer misery as he met Chance's gaze.

"If this is about Salina, you can call off your lynch mob, firing squad or whatever the hell you're planning."

"I'm sorry for the hanging. I was—"

"The *hanging?*" Tucker shouted.

Wyatt took a wary step back. "You didn't tell him?"

"You're still breathing, aren't you?"

"What hanging?" Garret demanded.

"I've never had feelings for her," Chance said to Wyatt, ignoring the alarm in Garret's and Tucker's expressions.

"Wish I could say the same," Wyatt muttered. "She wants your land real bad. She won't stop. She won't listen. She planned to seduce you and convince you she's heavy with your child, even though she knows full well she's carrying *mine.*"

Holy hell. No wonder the man looked a breath away from eating a bullet.

"Wyatt, I married Cora Mae Tindale last night."

"That's why I'm here. They took her."

"What?" His gaze whipped in the direction of the house.

"That fella, Grissom, he took her from—"

"You little bastard!" Chance lunged. Tucker's grip on his shoulders was all that restrained him from tearing into Wyatt.

"What do you mean, *he took her?*" Garret shouted, closing in beside him.

Wyatt lurched back. "It wasn't me! I just found out. Salina and some lady claiming to be her mother set it up!"

"I swear to God, Wyatt," Chance said in a growl, "if they hurt her—"

"I don't think so," said Wyatt. "I got to the ranch as they were leaving. She woke up and kicked the lady's maid from the coach and called for you. Grissom doused a rag with liquid and held it over her mouth until she passed out again."

My God. His whole life he'd underestimated Winifred. And yet again, Cora Mae had paid the price.

"Which way?"

"Southeast. Her mama said something about making it to a riverboat. But I imagine they'd have to catch the rail first. Nearest rail town is a four-day trail ride."

"How long ago?" asked Tucker.

"Long enough for me to ride out here and find you."

A good hour. "If we take the stock trails—"

"We can make up the time," Garret said, already running toward their staked horses.

Chance closed in on Wyatt.

"You don't gotta worry none about Salina and me."

"I know." He slammed his fist into Wyatt's face, knocking him out cold.

Leaving him lying on the ground with his newfound conscience, he turned and mounted the horse Tucker had retrieved.

"They'll stick to the main trail, then follow the stage line," said Tucker.

"We'll head them off."

"The bridge before the miner's camp," said Garret.

Tucker looked skeptical. Chance tugged his hat low and spurred his horse, ready to ride as far as it took to get her back.

She hurt everywhere. The room rattled.

Cora tried to swallow, but her tongue felt as though it had turned to cotton.

What happened?

She'd been rolling out pie crusts. The scent of smoke had drawn her outside. She'd spotted the plume rising into the blue sky… She tried to open her heavy eyelids.

"I'm sorry, madam," said a girl's voice—a familiar voice. One of the maids, a lady attendant from the manor.

No.

It was a dream, *a bad dream*. She couldn't be back at the manor.

"I expect you to take greater care in the future."

At the sound of her mother's voice, Cora forced her heavy eyelids to open. She sat up and blinked, trying to make out two figures sitting across from her in the dim light. The dim light of a coach, she realized.

"Mother?" she said to the dark figure blending with the shadows.

"Cora Mae. I do hope you are ready to behave yourself."

She leaned back against the cushion, her head throbbing, the shift and jostle of the seat adding to her discomfort. She tried to move her arms and realized her wrists burned from the rope tied around them. Closing her eyes, she remembered waking once before and seeing them, her mother, Salina, and trying to fight off Mr. Grissom. He'd sneaked up on her in the yard, covering her mouth until the world had gone dark.

Distantly she wondered how long she'd been unconscious. As more of the haze lifted from her mind, her predicament began to sink in. Fear closed over her.

Mother had kidnapped her.

"They're going to come for me," she said, certain Chance wouldn't let her be taken this way.

"My man assures me we have quite a lead," her mother said mildly.

As Cora's eyes began to adjust to the dim lighting, she was able to make out her mother's relaxed expression. The curtains drawn over the small windows bounced with the movement of the coach, letting in flickers of light. Charity, one of her mother's maids, stared at her with wide, terrified eyes. A bloody scrape marred her chin.

"Should they find you worth the trouble of pursuing," her mother continued in a droll tone, "*you* will be in Scotland before they make it across the country."

"I won't go."

"You will."

The finality in her mother's voice infuriated her. "I'm happy here. I love Chance!"

"Do not speak to me of love! You are a Tindale."

"Does that make me incapable or unworthy of love?"

"Neither is relevant."

Cora slowly twisted her wrists and tried to ignore the sting as she tested the tightness of the rope. "Why couldn't you have left me in Massachusetts?"

"You have obligations to the family that raised you, Cora Mae."

"*Obligations?* The Tindales have never done anything for me!"

"How dare you!" Winifred shouted. "You were raised in the finest of luxuries, provided with the best tutors—though you could never apply yourself, preferring instead to blend in with common filth. When I'm finally able to give you the chance to repay me for the shame and disappointment you've put me through, you *disgrace* me."

Realizing her mother couldn't hurt her any further than she already had, her callous words rolled over Cora like water off a frog's back. Cora knew what it was to be loved. Nothing her mother said could take that from her.

"You will marry Laird Ambrose Campbell and you will be grateful!"

"No." She'd be with Chance or die trying. "I have a husband," Cora said, discretely slipping her hands from the coil of rope. "If that Scottish beast is so important to the Tindales, *you'll* have to marry him, Mother."

Cora lunged up and reached for the door. Her mother moved to block her.

Cora shoved her away.

"Grissom!" Her mother's ear-splitting shriek echoed through the carriage.

Cora pushed the door open to a flood of sunlight, and jumped.

She crashed against hard wood, the impact of her fall taking her breath. Pushing up, all she could see was rushing water. The hush of a river filtered through the ringing in her ears.

A bridge. Her gaze locked on the green hills, the mountains. *Home*. She pushed to her feet. Before she could take a step, a hand clamped onto her shoulder.

"I'm sick of chasing you down!" His fingers dug into her arms as he lifted her off her feet.

She strained against his hold and screamed as she collided with Mr. Grissom's thick chest.

A gunshot exploded.

"Unhand my wife!"

Cora's heart leaped. "Chance!"

Released from the vise of Grissom's grip, she fell to the bridge.

Grissom turned and dodged Chance's fist. Chance's next punch connected with Grissom's jaw, knocking him back.

Cora's mind spun as a blur of figures flashed before her. She struggled back to her feet and someone grabbed her arm. She saw black from the corner of her eye, and struggled against her mother's hold. Winifred tripped over the low railing and in a flutter of black fabric, fell to the water below, her scream cut short by a splash.

Cora gasped at the sight of her mother flailing in the swirling rush of water. "Mother's in the river!"

Chance turned toward the sound of Cora Mae's voice and stepped over an unconscious Grissom. "Cora Mae?"

"Chance!" She glanced up, her expression distraught. "Mother can't swim!"

Tucker stepped up to the edge beside them. "Now ain't that a cryin' shame?"

Chance looked from the cold rage in Tucker's eyes to

the sheer horror in Cora Mae's. He and Tuck could easily allow Winifred to sink straight to hell without feeling a twinge of guilt, but Cora Mae couldn't. He wouldn't allow Winifred to cause her more pain, not even in death.

Biting out a curse, he unlatched his gun belt, dropped it to the bridge and leaped over the railing.

"Chance!" Tucker shouted after him.

Cora's heart stopped at the sight of Chance diving into the water.

"Goddamn it!" shouted Tucker. "That's pure snowmelt! They're likely to freeze before they drown."

Cora held her breath as she watched Chance cutting through the water, risking his life to save a woman he loathed. Her mother went under. Chance dove beneath the surface. Forever seemed to pass as she searched the rippling swirls for signs of him.

It's taking too long. Tears fogged her vision.

Chance's blond hair broke the surface. He surged up, gasping for breath, hauling a dark figure up beside him.

Air rushed from Cora's lungs with a sob of relief. She'd have collapsed to the bridge had a strong arm not caught her.

"It's all right," Garret soothed. "Chance is climbing up the bank and dragging that lady through the mud with him."

"Garret," said Tucker. "Take Cora to Mrs. Stone. Have her tend the rope burns on her wrists."

Anxious to see Chance, she didn't object as Garret led her toward the dirt road. Cora was shocked to discover the bridge was indeed just outside of Slippery Gulch, the stretch of buildings not far off the river. People had gathered at the edge of town, obviously coming to see what all the ruckus was about. Heat burned in her cheeks.

Oh, my goodness.

"Hey, kid?" shouted Tucker.

She and Garret glanced back. Tucker motioned to her mother's young attendant, trembling and crying beside him. "Take this girl with you."

Garret looked questioningly at Cora.

"She's just a maid."

"Come on!" Garret ordered, glancing back at the girl.

Cora tried to take a step and swayed. Garret's arm locked around her shoulders. "I'm quite dizzy," she said, surprised by the fact.

Garret held her steady. "We'll get you inside Mrs. Stone's kitchen. After a cup of warm tea, you'll feel better."

She glanced past the bridge as they reached the end, but couldn't see beyond the bend in the river.

"Tucker will tell him where you're at," Garret assured her, gently urging her toward town. "He'll come for you."

"Thank you."

"Heck, you don't have to thank me. That's what family's for."

Not always. She wondered if Garret knew just how fortunate he was to belong to such a family.

Winifred coughed and sputtered as Chance dragged her to the top of the embankment. He dropped to his knees on the grass beside her. A crowd of folks rushed toward them from the edge of town. He spotted Tucker driving the carriage up to the livery. He didn't wait for Winifred to catch her breath. Ignoring the chill of his own wet skin, he lifted her slight, trembling form into his arms and stood.

Spud broke away from the gathering spectators and rushed toward him. "What the hell happened?" he shouted.

"I heard gunshots and saw you diving off the bridge. Is that Mrs. Tindale?"

"Sure is," Chance said, walking past him, watching his brother haul Grissom's unconscious hide from the carriage. "She tried to kidnap my wife."

"Skylar?" Spud said, rushing along beside him.

"*Cora Mae.*"

"*Chance?*" said Spud, his eyes wide.

"That's right."

"I'll be damned."

Winifred struggled against his hold. "Put me down!"

Chance did just that.

Winifred hit the dirt with a shriek. "How dare you!" She struggled to her feet, fighting the weight of her wet dress.

"How dare I what?" he said, leaning over her. "Save your worthless life?"

She blanched. Her mouth snapped shut.

"Don't bother thanking me. If it wasn't for Cora Mae, I'd have let you sink straight to the fires of hell. *Walk*," he said, pointing to her carriage waiting beside the livery.

Shivering, Winifred turned and did as she was told.

"That's one way to handle a mother-in-law," Spud said, staying in step beside him.

Chance grunted. "Mrs. Tindale needs a ride to the nearest rail town. I'll pay you or one of your stable hands a hundred dollars to drive her. *Right now.*"

Spud tugged on the rim of his battered hat and grinned. "I been needin' a trip into Cheyenne. Whenever the lady's ready—"

"She's ready now." Chance stepped in front of Winifred and reached for the carriage door.

"I'm wet!" Winifred snapped.

"Change on the way," said Chance, opening the door and motioning for her to climb in.

"I'll catch my death."

"If you don't get out of my sight, you won't have to catch death. I'll bring it to you."

Tucker stepped up beside him. Chance sensed him rather than saw him, for he never took his gaze off Winifred. Her frightened blue eyes moved between them.

"I never meant harm to either of you," she said. "I wouldn't have come if Cora Mae wasn't important to me. I've invested everything into her future. She's my only daughter."

"And we're all choked up about that. Aren't we, Tuck?"

"It does tug at the heart strings." Tucker thumped his chest, his mournful tone nearly convincing.

"I've paid her dowry. She's all I've got left."

"Seems to me you've still got the only thing you ever cared about. Yourself. Now, are you going to climb into the carriage, or do I need to put you in?"

Her face pinched into a frown, Winifred gathered her skirts and reached for the handle beside the open door.

"You about ready, Spud?"

"Yessiree," Spud said, coming out of the stable with a pack over his shoulder and a bundle under his arm. "Here's a blanket for the lady."

Chance took the thick wool from him and tossed it into the carriage.

"Where are my attendants?" she asked before he could shut the door. She pulled the blanket around her trembling shoulders and held his gaze as though he owed her an answer.

The lady had more nerve than sense.

"Grissom won't be far behind you," said Tucker. "Right now he's shackled in a stable."

"Shackled?" said Spud, looking down from his high perch. "Those rusted things I had hanging on the barn wall?"

"Yep."

"I ain't got no keys for 'em."

"That'll be the marshal's problem, not ours."

Chance found some satisfaction in the fear darkening Winifred's eyes as the gravity of the situation began to sink in.

"Your fancy man kidnapped my wife and set fire to my land," he said, making sure she absorbed the full meaning. "He'll be charged with such."

"What of my maid?"

"She's decided to stick around," Garret said from behind him.

Chance glanced back at Garret leaning against a hitching rail.

"Mrs. Stone talked her into attending the town social on Friday," he said. "Ten dollars says she's married off within the week."

"You're sending me into the wilderness *alone?*"

Winifred's voice wasn't quite so high and mighty.

"Spud will get you to the nearest railway and put you on the first eastbound train. What you do from there is your business. My advice—*keep heading east.*"

"You cannot keep me from Cora Mae. I'm the only family she's got!"

"Lady, I wouldn't let you near my dog, much less my wife. Cora Mae is no longer a Tindale. You try to come near her again, and you'll wish I'd let you drown."

She shrank back against the velvet seat.

"That's a promise, and the only warning you'll ever get

from me." He slammed the door shut. "Get her out of here," he said to Spud.

"Will do."

Chance stood in the road, watching the coach until it drove out of view. The crowd of townsfolk who'd been watching from a distance began to disperse.

"You must be half-frozen," Tucker said, his hand closing over his brother's shoulder.

"I'm all right."

"Well, she's gone for good. Feel better?"

As usual, he didn't feel much of anything. "No," he said truthfully. "Not really."

"Chance!"

He turned to see Cora Mae charging across the street at a full run. The concern in her eyes warmed every cold place on his body, inside and out.

"Now I feel better," he said, smiling as he strode toward her. She leaped into his arms. He held her against him, despite his wet clothes. She didn't seem to mind, clinging to him with just as much force. He kissed her lightly on the lips before he set her away from him, mindful of all the onlookers. She'd surely suffered enough social trauma.

"I was worried about you," she said.

He smiled and tugged on a loose curl. "Didn't think I could handle your mother?"

"Where is she?"

"Gone."

"Gone where?"

"Damned if I care, as long as she's not meddling in our lives. I think it's safe to say you won't have to worry about her any longer. You're free of her. We both are."

Relief showed in her expression as tears hazed her eyes.

She reached for him, and nothing could have kept him from pulling her close, lifting her against his body again as she hugged him.

"You're cold," she said after a moment.

"Not anymore."

She tilted her head back to gaze up at him, and Chance felt a rush of emotion like no other—stronger than desire, deeper than passion.

The intensity in Chance's gaze took Cora's breath away.

"*I love you,*" he said, the words bursting from his lips.

To actually hear him say the words was a marvel.

"I must," he said, his voice filled with wonder. "Nothing else could make me feel this good."

"It's a good thing," she whispered, even as she kissed him. She wished they were back at the house, in the privacy of their room, beneath the sheets of their bed. "I fear you've made me rather wanton."

Chance laughed as he hugged her tight. "I must be blessed that way. *Let's go home.*"

Surrounded by his strength and a land as wild as it was beautiful, Cora knew she was already there.

Epilogue

"The California coast was nice, but I don't miss traveling through those deserts. Have you ever seen so much flat yellow ground? I was afraid we'd melt before reaching the Sierra Mountains. My favorite place was the hotel on the ocean cliffs. San Francisco was fun to visit, but I really preferred the smaller coastal towns."

Keeping the horses at an easy pace, Chance grinned down at his wife chattering away beside him. She wore one of her fluttering apricot dresses, despite the new clothes packed in her trunks. A thick auburn braid trailed down her back. He'd rented a covered wagon to keep the sun off her fair skin.

"Isn't it nice to be back in our own hills?"

"It is," he agreed.

"It really was a wonderful trip."

His arm curled around her. "It was."

"I've missed everyone," she said, leaning into him as she reached up to hold the hand resting over her shoulder. "I bet we'll hardly recognize the girls, and Joshua will have grown a full inch."

"I bet you're right," he said, watching their ranch come into view as the wagon crested a nearby rise.

"Oh, Chance. *Look*."

He smiled, glad to see she was just as happy to be back. He'd kept her away a little too long. The past few days she'd been plain exhausted. "Feels good to be home, huh?"

"It does." Cora Mae hadn't minded being away, but they'd both been anxious to return. When Chance first suggested they use his meeting with a California rancher as a honeymoon, she'd been hesitant to take such a long trip, having no desire to be away from the ranch. She was glad he'd talked her into going along and even happier about the two extra weeks they'd taken to visit the coast.

The entire trip had been wonderfully romantic, and they'd certainly made the most of their honeymoon. But once they'd stepped off the train in Wyoming three days ago, she couldn't wait to get home. The month-long journey had taken its toll on her. The past three nights she'd been asleep within minutes of hitting the pillow in their hotel room. She was looking forward to climbing into her own bed, with her husband.

As they rode into the yard and stopped near the porch, a man with a woman in a light-pink dress stepped out the front door. As they turned, Cora Mae was stunned by the faces of Wyatt and Salina Jameson.

She met Chance's wide gaze. "What do you suppose?" she whispered.

Chance stepped down then turned, placing his hands on her waist. "No telling," he said, lifting her with easy strength and setting her beside him. His fingers laced with hers as they ascended the steps.

"Mrs. Jameson," Cora Mae said in greeting.

"Actually," said Wyatt, "it's Mrs. McNealy."

"Oh," said Cora, her eyes popping wide.

Wyatt slid his arm around his wife. "We were married a few weeks ago."

Salina seemed to be studying the grain of the wood porch.

"Congratulations." Chance held his hand out to Wyatt. Wyatt was slow to return the friendly gesture. Cora Mae figured he needed all the good wishes he could get.

"Thank you. Now that Garret owns the Lazy J, things ought to run real smooth for you."

"Garret?" said Cora Mae.

"Well, I'll be damned," said Chance.

"While helping to string the new fencing to make up for Grissom starting the fire, I mentioned we were going to sell. Garret said he had the money to buy. He and Duce met us in Cheyenne last week." He glanced at Salina. "Sweetheart, is there something you wanted to say to the Morgans?"

He nudged her shoulder before Salina glanced up. Her gaze moved briefly between Cora Mae and Chance. "I'm sorry for all the trouble I've caused."

"We both are," said Wyatt, hugging his wife close. "Hope it works out for Garret. His sister sure wasn't pleased by the news. But it's a done deal. Salina and I leave for New Orleans first thing in the morning."

"New Orleans?" said Chance.

"My hometown. Salina's never lived in a city. I do believe she's rather excited, aren't you, sweetheart?"

"Yes," she said, her lips tipping with a smile as she looked up at him.

"I have four older sisters. With the baby coming, I know they'll be a big help for her."

Cora Mae glanced down and noticed the rise of Salina's belly. *A baby.*

A tingling rush raced across Cora Mae's skin as she pressed her hands to her own stomach. *Oh, my goodness.* In all their weeks of traveling she'd been wholly preoccupied with Chance, the sights and shops, long walks along ocean sands...she hadn't missed the monthly inconvenience that hadn't come since before they'd married.

"We wish you all the best," Wyatt called back as he guided his wife down the porch steps.

"I'm old enough!" Garret's voice rang clear from inside the house.

"Uh-oh," said Chance, feeling a sense of dread as he pushed open the front door.

"No, you're not!" Skylar's voice rattled through the walls of the study.

"I wouldn't want to be on the receiving end of Skylar's fury," Chance murmured.

Tucker stood outside the closed door of the study and smiled at the sight of him. "Welcome home, big brother," he said, meeting him halfway across the room, greeting him with a one-armed hug and a back slap. "And little sister," he said, winking at Cora Mae. "You two finish buying up the state of California?"

"Not quite," Chance said with a laugh, spotting the pile of crates and parcels stacked in the corner of the parlor.

"Chance!" Cora said, obviously following his gaze.

He grinned down at her shocked expression. She wouldn't let him spoil her the way he'd wanted to, so he'd had a few items shipped home. "I did some early Christmas shopping."

"In July?"

Chance hugged her against his side. "Figured I'd make up for all the ones I missed."

The escalating voices inside the study drew their attention.

"You've always said that money was mine!" shouted Garret.

"To use when you're *grown*. You're sixteen!"

Chance exchanged a wary glance with his brother.

"My woman's having a hard time letting go," Tucker said beneath his breath.

"How'd the kid do with the buyout?" Chance asked, wondering if Garret had invested too much in the cattle ranch.

"I'm old enough to seize a good opportunity," Garret raged. "Dammit, Sky! You raised me to be a cattleman!"

"He made out like a bandit," Tucker said with a grin. "Unfortunately, he was as sneaky as one, too, not bothering to tell his sister his plans. First sight of her reaction to the news and Margarete scooped up the girls and Josh and headed to her house."

The door of the study opened. A red-faced Garret stepped into the parlor, slamming the door shut behind him. His eyes widened at the sight of them.

"You're back."

"Apparently just in time to see you off," said Chance.

His frown deepened. "It's not like I'll be moving across the country. How can I gain any independence with her hovering over me all the time?"

"Cool your fire," said Tucker. "She knows she's being unreasonable—love does that to a person."

"I knew she'd be mad," Garret said, his expression miserable, "but I didn't think she'd use tears against me. I didn't mean to make her cry. She pregnant again?" he said to Tucker.

Tuck shook his head. "I don't think you're giving yourself enough credit, kid. She might not be your mother, but she did raise you. Springing this on her the way you did may not have been the best plan."

"I didn't want to fight with her," Garret said, crumpling his hat in his hands.

"I'll talk to her, see if I can help you snip some of those apron strings," Tucker said softly.

Garret grinned. "Thanks, Tuck." He glanced over at Chance and Cora as Tucker stepped into the study. "Sorry to muck up your homecoming," he said, dropping into a parlor chair.

"I think you made a smart move." Chance clapped him on the shoulder.

"Thanks," he said, regarding him with a cautious look. "Duce signed on as my partner. He's going with me."

"Stealing my crew as well, huh?"

"Only fair," he said with a slight grin.

Chance wasn't about to argue. Cora Mae was still a sore spot between them. The kid was polite to her, and Chance had worked with him a few times before he'd left, but things hadn't been the same.

"Least you won't have to worry about your cattle and horses."

"You know I'll help out any way I can."

"I can do this," he all but shouted. "Does *everyone* expect me to fail?"

"Kid, you've got to knock that chip off your shoulder. I have no doubt you'll be a hell of a cattle rancher."

The study door opened and Tucker poked his head out. "Come on in here," he said to Garret.

Heaving a great sigh, Garret hauled himself from the chair. As the door shut behind them, Chance glanced down at the woman standing quietly at his side and found her gazing up at him, her eyes gleaming with tears. He wasn't sure what he'd done to deserve such a bright smile.

"What?"

"I think I'm pregnant."

Chance felt his mouth drop open. He glanced at her hands pressed to her dress. "Pregnant?"

"I don't feel ill," she said, "but…we've been married for at least…"

"Six weeks, four days and eighteen hours," he said as he pressed his hand over hers. *A baby*.

His own smile stretched wide as he met her searching gaze. *Their baby*.

"I've been so preoccupied," she said, looking dazed. "I never even thought—"

"Hot damn!" he shouted, lifting her off her feet before scooping her into his arms as he headed for the stairway.

"Chance!"

"I know just how to celebrate."

"It's midafternoon and I'm covered with four days of trail dust!"

He laughed and kissed her nose. "Which is why we're headed for the tub."

Her eyes sparkled with interest. The slow curve of her lips put a kick in his pulse. Lord, he loved this woman.

"Shouldn't we unpack first, and—"

"I've got all I need right here," he said, holding her tight as he ascended the stairs. *"The whole world."*

Her expression softened in a way that melted his heart. "I love you so much."

"I love you, too," he said with an ease that came from the freedom she'd given him, the freedom to love.

On sale 6th February 2009

A DARING PASSION
by Rosemary Rogers

Legacy of danger…

Headstrong, sheltered Raine Wimbourne longs for
adventure – and when her ailing father reveals a closely
guarded secret, she seizes her chance. Disguised as England's
most notorious highwayman, Raine vows to uphold her father's
legacy as champion of the poor. Then a midnight encounter
with the powerful Philippe Gautier reveals the price of
protecting her family's honour…

A hostage heart

Philippe Gautier has a mission of his own…and his beautiful
captive could help save his brother's life. But travelling from the
town houses of London to the streets of France, can he convince
his untamed captive to risk it all on the promise of passion?

MILLS & BOON
Historical

On sale 6th February 2009

Regency

LORD LIBERTINE
by Gail Ranstrom

Whispers are spreading through the *ton*…notorious rake
Andrew Hunter is becoming fascinated by the enigmatic
Lady Lace. Bewitched by her mixture of practised flirtation
and heartrendingly innocent kisses, he is desperate to
seduce her and learn the truth…

KNIGHT OF GRACE
by Sophia James

Grace knows the safety of her home depends on her betrothal
to Laird Lachlan Kerr. She does not expect his kindness or
strength. The cynical Laird himself is increasingly intrigued by
Grace's quiet bravery. Used to betrayal at every turn, her
faith in him is somehow curiously seductive…

KLONDIKE DOCTOR
by Kate Bridges

A troubling secret sends defiant Dr Elizabeth Langley north in
search of answers. But she's forced to travel under the protection
of Mountie Sergeant Colt Hunter, who firmly believes the
wilderness is no place for a lady. Together they tread a path
fraught with duty, danger – and inescapable passion…

Available at WHSmith, Tesco, ASDA, and all good bookshops
www.millsandboon.co.uk

Wanted: Wife

Must be of good family, attractive but not too beautiful, but calm, reasonable and mature... for marriage of convenience

Suddenly

New York Times Bestselling Author

CANDACE CAMP

Spirited Charity Emerson is certain she can meet Simon "Devil" Dure's wifely expectations. With her crazy schemes, warm laughter and loving heart, Charity tempts Simon. However, the treacherous trap that lies ahead, and the vicious act of murder, will put their courage – and their love – to the ultimate test.

Available 19th December 2008

2 FREE

BOOKS AND A SURPRISE GIFT!

We would like to take this opportunity to thank you for reading this Mills & Boon® book by offering you the chance to take TWO more specially selected titles from the Historical series absolutely FREE! We're also making this offer to introduce you to the benefits of the Mills & Boon® Book Club™—

- ★ FREE home delivery
- ★ FREE gifts and competitions
- ★ FREE monthly Newsletter
- ★ Exclusive Mills & Boon Book Club offers
- ★ Books available before they're in the shops

Accepting these FREE books and gift places you under no obligation to buy, you may cancel at any time, even after receiving your free shipment. Simply complete your details below and return the entire page to the address below. You don't even need a stamp!

YES! Please send me 2 free Historical books and a surprise gift. I understand that unless you hear from me, I will receive 4 superb new titles every month for just £3.69 each, postage and packing free. I am under no obligation to purchase any books and may cancel my subscription at any time. The free books and gift will be mine to keep in any case.

H9ZED

Ms/Mrs/Miss/Mr ....Initials ....
                                                              BLOCK CAPITALS PLEASE

Surname ....

Address ....

....

....Postcode...

Send this whole page to:
UK: FREEPOST CN81, Croydon, CR9 3WZ